I0666712

Heartline Roll

A Novel by Luke Joseph Jackson

Cover Art by Luke Joseph Jackson

Illustrations by Luke Joseph Jackson

For Mom and Dad, my family, students, and two cats, Lucy and Chelsea,

whom I love equally.

. . .

Especially Chelsea.

AUGUST

BREAKFAST

THE DAWN SUN PIERCED through the window. Its warm rays landed upon Tristan's face in an early-morning light show, disturbing his slumber. Ordinarily, the 17-year-old high school student would have drawn up the covers and rolled on his side to face the wall; but today, he pulled himself up with a smile. Tristan preemptively disabled the digital alarm on his bedside before standing to stretch. It was that time of year again: time to forcibly wake himself up at 6 am and chug unreasonable amounts of caffeine to make it through the commute to yet another year at Roosevelt Charter Academy.

Striding over to his wooden cabinet, he gathered the clothes he had set out for himself the night before and headed to the bathroom. Viewing himself in the mirror, he laughed at the aggressive cowlicks that had formed the night before. Shocks of bright red hair stood up at awkward angles all around his head. A shower was always the proper solution for bad hair days. Tristan was grateful the sun had roused him early enough to make time for one that day. After drying himself off and changing into his hoodie, he followed his nose to the kitchen.

A sumptuous aroma of decadent delights rose from a series of frying pans on the stovetop. Clare Collins was pouring fried peppers and onions into the heart of what was to be an omelet as her son entered the room.

"Hi, honey." Clare smiled. "Breakfast is almost ready."

"Wow, that smells great!" said Tristan. "Peppers and onions?"

"And four cheeses," she added coyly as she unwrapped a slice of American cheese. "Just the way you like it."

"You're really going all out today, huh?" Tristan chuckled as he circled to the coffee maker. He gestured to it with a raised eyebrow.

"Go grab a cup," said Clare. Tristan nodded and obliged, helping himself to the beverage in his favorite red mug. As he seated himself at the island countertop, the front door opened.

"Morning, Dad." Tristan smiled.

"Morning, Tristan." Marc Collins locked the door before striding over to the counter. He set down the morning paper he had retrieved from the mailroom and hugged his son. Still wearing the bright smile he entered the room with, he circled the counter and wrapped his arms around his wife.

"Morning, beautiful." He smiled before sealing the compliment with a kiss.

While he had some reservations regarding his appearance, which he found somewhat lanky, Tristan had always thought his parents could have been models. His father was tall and muscled, wearing his short brown hair in an elegant fashion with his business attire. Clare's bright orange hair fell down over her shoulder in a soft, fishtail braid, as was her penchant. They emigrated from Ireland the year before Tristan was born, making him and his brother first-generation Americans. While he didn't share their accents, he was grateful to have inherited his mother's hair and his father's pale blue eyes.

"So," Marc began, pouring himself a cup of coffee, "are the adoption papers all ready?"

"Uh-huh." Tristan nodded. "I'll call to confirm after school, but everything should be in order." At the stovetop, Clare was folding the omelets onto a trio of glass plates. Marc smiled at his wife's cooking in approval.

"Good." Marc nodded. "I've never been much of a cat person."

"That's what you say now." Clare snorted, serving her boys at the counter with a pair of prepared plates. She set out a separate plate of toast and a butter dish. "But give it a few days. I'll make a cat dad out of you, yet!"

"You and your cats." Marc shook his head before looking back at his son. "Your mother had three of them back in Cork."

"Four," she corrected with a curt look. "My sisters took them in when we moved. Grace?"

The trio bowed their heads and said the blessing. After making the sign of the cross, they dug in.

"Delicious Mom, thank you." Tristan nodded with a mouthful of egg.

"Yes honey, wonderful," said Marc.

"You're welcome. Take some bread." Clare gestured toward the toast. "Today's a big day. I want to make sure we're all prepared."

Tristan took a bite of his omelet. The parmesan, cheddar, American, and mozzarella cheeses melted together into a symphony of flavor that gave him a shudder of contentment.

"Ah, that's good." He sighed. "Thanks, Mom."

"Yes, thank you, darling," Marc said.

"Of course." Clare smiled before turning back to the sink to scrub out the pans.

"Oh honey, that can wait till later," Marc said with a wave of his hand. "Sit and eat first." She was obstinate at first, but she relented at the sadness in Tristan's eyes. She walked to the counter and pulled over a stool. Forcing a wry smile on her lips, she joined her family for breakfast.

Clare Collins hadn't made a decent breakfast for herself in years. She spent most of her days at her youngest son's bedside in

St. Luke's Hospital on Starlight Hill. Tristan and Marc had finally managed to convince her to take a day off and let her sister babysit Will for a while.

This revelation was not lost on the Collins family, who finished their breakfast in relative silence. This reticence wasn't somber, though. Secretly, they all knew that after today the fourth bar stool at the island countertop wouldn't be empty anymore.

The cancer was in remission and William Collins was coming home.

COMMUTERS

ISOLDE WHITE DESCENDED the concrete steps of Starlight Station.

"Crowded as usual," the girl thought to herself. She clutched the strap of her shoulder bag with both hands, trying to make herself as small as possible in the sea of people. Quite a difficult thing to do when you're nearly six feet tall.

At the base of the stairs, she swiped her MetroCard and navigated through the gossamer skein of the pathway that proceeded from the turnstiles. Standing in front of one of the station's red iron support columns, she pulled her phone out of her satchel. She opened the camera and began to ruminate on her appearance.

Regrettably, there was only so much damage her deuteranopic eyes could detect. It had only been about a year since her colorblindness had been uncovered. Her inability to distinguish red and green pigments meant that she saw the world in what others would consider to be shades of yellow and blue. Thick golden locks streamed down her back, framing a pair of bright blue irises. These were the only two features of her physical appearance that she loved, as the deuteranopia made them pop. Wetting her index finger with her tongue, she wiped away a bit of mascara that had begun to smear. Satisfied with the adjustment, she put the phone away and waited for the train.

The deafening screech of the subway gave her a chill. Unconsciously, Izzy wrapped her beige cardigan tighter around herself. A descending major third played as the train stopped and flung its steel doors open. She entered. Walking past the densely populated orange seats of the car, she was convinced she'd have to stand for the remainder of the journey.

"Izzy?"

The unexpected greeting gave her a start. She yelped and threw her hands in front of her face. After her mind caught up with her actions, she opened her eyes, only to see a familiar face grinning at her from the seat below.

Makiko peered up at her through her mid-length black hair. She could hardly suppress a chuckle when she asked," You uh... wanna sit down?"

Izzy felt her face flush, though she happily accepted her offer.

"Jumpy today, aren't we?" Maki laughed as she lifted her bag from the seat beside her and placed it on her lap, making room for her friend. Izzy thanked her.

"Just nervous I guess." Izzy laughed. "New year, new classes, new faces..." she shrugged. "Lots to think about."

"I know what you mean," Maki replied. "I'm certainly not too keen on sitting through another AP science class. But hey, someday it'll help pay the bills." She forced a smile. "What about you? Planning on auditioning for any shows this year?"

At this, Izzy broke into a beaming smile. "Um, yes!" She laughed. "I spoke to Ms. Debbie on the phone the other day. She told me that the theatre department is putting on a recital this December. She wants me to prepare a song."

"Well, well, look at you go, Miss White!" Maki smiled, punching her friend on the arm.

"Thanks. Dr. Nightingale, my voice teacher, said she's got some big plans for me. Whatever that means." Izzy shook her head. "And *you've* got to help us with the set design this year!" She punched her friend back. Maki rubbed her arm with a wince. Standing at five-foot-eleven, Izzy often didn't realize her strength. In contrast to the feminine gentle giant, the five-foot-one Okinawan immigrant was petite and lithe. What neither of them knew was that each of the girls was envious of the traits of the other.

"Yeah…" Maki said quietly before drifting into an awkward silence. The only voice that could be heard was the previously comforting clattering of the train's wheels. Izzy bided the time by focusing on the lights flitting by in the darkness of the tunnel. Her fingers unconsciously drummed a 7/8 pattern on her shoulder bag.

"Listen, Izzy," Maki finally continued. "I really wish I could. I just…"

"I know." Izzy nodded with a frown. She cursed herself for being so forgetful and inconsiderate. Growing up together, Izzy had met Makiko's father many times. A kind marketing manager at an electronics company, Mr. Nakamura had high hopes for his daughter. Perhaps too high. Any extracurriculars aside from those that made money were out of the question. While she had never explicitly asked her, Izzy suspected that her friend's decision to apply for Roosevelt University's medical program had not been entirely her own, either.

There had to be something she could do to lift her friend's spirits. She pondered this for a minute. Suddenly, an idea came to her.

"I gotcha covered!" Izzy cried with a wink and a smile. Maki watched with a befuddled expression as her friend excitedly rummaged through the contents of her bag. At last, she found what she was looking for.

"Here!" she proudly exclaimed, genuinely excited after the successful hunt for Maki's gift. She took the card and scrutinized the verbiage. "It's a gift card for The Turquoise Fox!" Izzy explained. "It was from when I sang the National Anthem last year. It should still be good!"

"Oh wow, uh… thanks, Iz. You sure?" Maki inquired.

"Mm-hmm!" Izzy nodded. "Positive! It's not like I need it anyways…" Worried that she may have sounded rude, she rephrased, "I mean, since I can get stuff for free whenever…" she stammered. "Because you know… my dad…"

Maki raised her shoulders and chuckled. "Heh, yeah very true. Though let's be honest, retail coffee isn't nearly as good as Brandy's. You and your dad make a great team!"

"Well, that's 'cause we have the greatest little helper on our side!" Izzy smiled.

They felt the train slow as the brakes shrieked out their deafening song. The lights of the tunnel flittered by at a reduced rate. A descending major third preceded the announcer's words.

"Now arriving at University Station."

"Looks like it's that time already," Izzy said. Her companion checked her phone and nodded.

"Yeah, I've gotta run. Class is on the far side of campus." Maki rose from her seat and threw on her black and violet backpack. "Catch you later?"

"Absolutely." Izzy nodded. "Call me tonight!"

Makiko nodded and gripped her esophagus between her fingers. "Don't bust a vocal cord!" she laughed. Turning around, she pushed through the crowd and hustled out the doors with Izzy following shortly after.

THE TURQUOISE FOX

"A 'LIMIT' IS THE VALUE the function is approaching as it goes to an x value," the teacher droned. "It is useful for integrals and derivatives."

Day one of AP Calculus, and already half the class was asleep. At least that's how it felt to Tristan, who was seated near the back of the 30-person classroom which was broken up into several rows of long, slender tables at which multiple students were stationed. Having already solved the problems on the board, he bided the remainder of his time with his sketchbook.

To the casual observer, the small, leather-bound book appeared as insignificant as any other journal. But to his little brother, Tristan's sketchbook acted as a portal to infinite worlds of adventure. The pages were filled with wacky creations from stories they'd come up with together from over the years. From tales of heroes in suits of armor to the zany misadventures of Nada Shark (a Hispanic shark on a hoverboard who constantly protested that he was indeed, "not a shark"), Tristan knew that this book was the key to making his little brother smile.

It also served as a source of comfort to him on his darkest days. Tristan had long since developed a nasty habit of zoning out when things got rough, as they so often did throughout his life. He couldn't think about Will's cancer if he was riding a dragon across the sea and he couldn't hear his parents shouting over the wind that was rushing past his ears. This strategy served him well until around his junior year, where new thoughts began to creep in:

"You'll never be good enough."

"Your parents only love Will."

"He's going to die and there's nothing you can do about it."

These torturous thoughts would often keep him up at night. Unable to vocalize these thoughts to his parents, Tristan managed them in the only way he knew how: with the creation of a new character. He called him Kieran, his Other: a doppelgänger that poked and prodded at every one of his fears. No matter what he did or where he went, he could feel him watching—waiting for the perfect opportunity to strike. But he *wouldn't* strike today. Tristan wouldn't let him. He trained his every thought on what he was going to do when Will came home, cancer-free.

The lecture finally ended with the chiming of the school's digital bell and the prisoners of the room wasted no time in making their escape. Not interested in getting caught up in the tempest of students rushing out the door, Tristan took his time packing up his belongings.

"Finally done for the day," he thought to himself with a smile. He put away his red spiral ring calculus notebook before reaching for his black sketchbook. He flipped through the pages once more, gaining a sense of self-satisfaction for the progress he had made thus far. Out of his peripheral vision, he could feel a pair of eyes looking down at his work. Tristan turned his head.

The girl's shoulder-length black hair danced in the air as she rapidly averted her gaze from the book and broke into the crowd. She had already disappeared by the time Tristan had raised his hand to wave.

"Wow," Tristan thought to himself. "She's got pretty eyes."

Even in the poor lighting of the old classroom—which boasted no fewer than three busted florescent lights—Tristan had been able to make out her unmistakably bright green irises. He replayed the image in his head. Her piercing gaze. The way her thick, short hair had danced so playfully in the air.

"No," Tristan thought; snapping himself back into reality with a shake of his head and a smile. "Down boy." He rose amidst the sea of people and shuffled his way out of the room.

Tristan and his parents had been preparing for this day for nearly a month. After countless hours of praying, they were going to bring his brother home. If there ever was a time to celebrate, it was then. He simply didn't have the emotional energy to spend doting on a pretty girl at school.

Exiting the brick building, Tristan was greeted by a world of color. The effects of the bright sunlight, blue sky, and cool breeze were all the more powerful after deciphering the mumbles of a unenthusiastic, tenured teacher in a dim room for an hour. His route took him past a large lake overlooking the city's skyline—a welcome break from the uninspired, brutalist structures that fenced in the school's campus. Roosevelt Charter Academy resided on a city block adjacent to its affiliate college, Roosevelt University. Already being familiar with the commute to his tuition-free charter school, RU quickly became Tristan's top choice in his college hunt, and it was views like the adjacent skyline that gave Tristan much-needed reassurance that he had picked the right major in mechanical engineering.

On the way, he pulled out his phone and dialed.

"Hello, Starlight Adoptions. This is Brian. How may I assist you today?"

"Hi Brian, this is Tristan Collins. I just wanted to confirm that everything is settled to pick up Phoenix tonight."

"Sure thing. Let me just see here…" Through the phone, Tristan heard the distinctive rummaging of papers. "It looks like all the paperwork is ready to go. You can stop by any time before 7 pm tonight."

"Fantastic, thank you so much!" Tristan cheered.

"No problem, sir. You have a great day."

"You too, thanks!"

All he could think about was how excited Will was going to be. Nothing else mattered to him that day. His brother was coming home and the celebratory plans were in motion. Putting his phone away, he looked up at the sign that marked the end of his hike. Positioned above a set of double glass doors and beneath a set of three, square windows rested the sign to the famous Turquoise Fox.

"Correction," Tristan thought, "famous to the overtired, sleepless, and caffeine-addicted students that called this place home." The cartoonist in him always got a smile from the oversaturated cartoon fox with a pipe and blue scarf on the sign's circular logo.

The cafe was crowded, as usual. The burgundy walls were difficult to make out beneath the tacky paintings and filigree that were the status quo in modern design. All of the Fox's homey design choices were in a vain effort to overcompensate for the facility's copy-and-paste nature. If it weren't for the decorations cluttering the walls, this shop would be a facsimile of the ones throughout the rest of the world—a fact that Tristan found to be quite irksome.

Since his father wouldn't be off work for another hour, Clare Collins had insisted that Tristan take some time to caffeinate himself before his subway ride over to the hospital.

"The line is pretty long," he text his mother. "I could be there in 20 if you'd like."

"Please sweetheart," Clare replied. "It's a special day. Treat yourself."

Tristan joined the line and began to study the oversized menu. When it came to coffee at home, he took it black. Out on the town? He'd order a Café Americano or a cappuccino. What were those? He had no idea, but they sounded normal and tasted all right.

To Tristan, the more foreign something sounded, the more pretentious it seemed, at least when it came to cafes. Curiosity getting the better of him, he reached into his pocket for his phone to Google whatever a "Strawberry Açaí" was. While doing so, he caught sight of something out of the corner of his eye.

Someone.

The Asian girl from class was standing directly behind him.

Glancing back for a beat, they made eye contact. The girl's eyes quickly flitted away. Did she recognize him? Tristan couldn't be sure. The line was moving at a snail's pace. This left Tristan alone in his own mind—a situation that often served to amplify his anxieties.

"Maybe I should say something," he thought to himself. He turned back to the faux blackboard sign above the cafe, twisting his body 90 degrees. This put the girl squarely in his peripheral vision. All he had to do was wave. Smile. Introduce himself. Talk about how boring the class was. Unfortunately for Tristan, he wasn't very experienced when it came to talking to women. He had a date or two that that led to a less than spectacular junior prom, but beyond that, he was clueless.

At a loss for words, he was grateful when the bearded barista cried out, "Next in line!"

Tristan approached the counter and placed his order. As the bearded Indian man rang him up, there was very little to distract him from the black-haired girl standing just behind him. His cheeks began to flush as he nervously placed his hands into the pockets of his black and cerulean-lined hoodie.

"Is she intentionally avoiding eye contact?" Tristan thought. He shoved the thought aside once more. "Just get the drink and go to St. Luke's. Will's waiting on you."

Thankfully, it wasn't long before the coffee had been prepped. Tristan had long since discovered that cafe visits were quick if you kept your orders simple. Not many people go into the Turquoise Fox asking for a black coffee, but the truth is that it saves time. He knew that it would pull him away from his inability to chat up a beautiful girl that much sooner.

Grabbing the burgundy paper cup from the counter, he made his way to the store's rear exit. His hand had nearly fully depressed the door's panic bar before he completely froze. He shut his eyes, cursed himself, turned around, and shuffled over to a nearby cocktail table.

"This is such a stupid idea," he thought, shaking his head.

After burning his tongue, he removed the lid from his coffee and set it atop a square white napkin.

"Good," he thought once more. "Now you've got an excuse to be lingering."

If Tristan had chosen to be perfectly honest with himself, he'd have admitted that the girl wasn't the only reason he had changed his mind about leaving the cafe. On the days following his darkest moments, he'd discovered that a change of routine had the power to lift his spirits. Going to new places, talking to old friends, and trying out new hobbies would fill him with peace.

While he was certainly excited to be bringing Will home, having a little brother with leukemia was no picnic. Though they tried hard to stay positive, there were many days when darkness would descend on the Collins household. Tristan would slip into a funk, his parents would argue, and all of them would seriously wonder whether they would soon be reduced to a family of three.

Tristan often thought of his life as a rollercoaster. Sometimes he'd be at the bottom of an ascent with the G-forces pinning him to his seat. But he knew that if he survived that, he'd get to the apex of the top hat and feel lighter than air. Of course, the top hat was always followed by another drop...

The Turquoise Fox was an excellent change of pace from his usual daily routine, especially after having just come off summer break. Spending so long cooped up at home frequently left Tristan fraught with worry about the health of his brother. He found that when he was surrounded by the same four walls day in and day out, there was very little he could do to escape his inner demons. An inert life made him a slave to his thoughts.

Tristan closed his eyes. The warm, bitter odor of his uncovered beverage danced lusciously up his nostrils. Inhaling through his mouth, he could taste the sumptuous grounds. He noted the playful difference in temperature between the sleeved and unsleeved portions of the paper cup beneath his hands. Opening his eyes, he gazed into the tiny bubbles of his coffee. He smirked in curious amusement, having never noticed them before. Listening, the cacophony of the room transformed into individual students discussing parties and homework, the soothing melodies of jazz piano over the speakers, the raised voices of the baristas, and the steaming sounds of the espresso machines.

This was certainly a good place to take his mind off things for a while, Tristan thought to himself. Gazing around the room, he acknowledged the diverse cast of characters he saw before him. The patrons were a conglomeration of high school and university students: a sight that made for some fascinating people-watching. There were students in groups, students alone, some studying, some laughing. Some crazily dressed radicals, some cliques, some athletes, some Hasidic Jews… all so different and yet all part of Roosevelt. Such variety—yet try as he might, he still couldn't fit in. He took a sip of his coffee.

"What do you mean, 'it's no longer valid?!'"

The sudden outburst made Tristan jump, leaving his hands scalded with uncomfortably hot liquid. After groping for a napkin to wipe himself down, he looked for the source of the commotion. The green-eyed girl was holding up a turquoise gift card, shouting at the cashier. Her face was contorted into a rage that Tristan felt to be comically disproportionate to the situation.

The girl slammed her fists onto the counter. "There's no expiration date on it. It should be fine!"

"I'm sorry, that's just what the computer is telling me," the barista replied defensively. "Do you have another card you'd like to try?"

The girl's gloved knuckles bore into the countertop as she leaned over in a suppressed rage.

Her head was turned to the floor. The girl's eyes were closed with her jawline held tensely shut. She was grinding her teeth and monitoring her breathing. She was trying to calm herself down.

"The poor girl needs help," Tristan thought.

"No. Just—just forget it," she said tersely with a dismissive wave.

The girl did an about-face and made her way toward the exit, pausing at the halfway point. Her voluminous hair dangled playfully from her forehead as she studied her shoelaces through shut eyelids. Suddenly, she wasn't looking at the floor anymore.

She was looking at Tristan.

Her piercing, green, glassy eyes locked with his as he held his drink. He wanted to shout, "No, here! Take mine! Hey, I'll buy you one—just wait one more second!" But no words ever came out. The girl's cold stare broke away to the floor as she rushed past him and out the door.

Standing both disappointed and slack-jawed at the departure of a stranger in the Turquoise Fox, he felt like an idiot.

In Tristan's overactive imagination, *he* appeared.

Kieran: his Other.

He and Kieran looked identical, save for the latter's colorless features. Though to be fair, Tristan was pretty pale to begin with; especially so when compared to the dark honey complexion of the girl who got away. His Other berated him with a sardonic grin.

"Aw, what's the matter?" he said, gripping Tristan's shoulders from behind in a mock gesture of reassurance. With a quick, cartoonish spin, Kieran was engulfed by the smoke of a miniature dark tornado. When the smoke dissipated, Tristan's black and white friend had transformed himself. Save for the bright cerulean cat-eared headband and matching tail, he had become a perfect double of the girl he had been eyeing. She bent her elbows and let her wrists go limp as she flirtatiously pressed her head into his arm. "Cat got your tongue?" she chided, peering up at him with eyes bluer than his own.

Tristan felt the blood quickly flood his face as he rushed out the door. The girl was still cackling behind him, her giant fangs on full display to everyone in his imaginary world.

THE HOSPITAL

PULLING OFF HIS HEADPHONES, Tristan stared up at his favorite building. St. Luke's Medical Center stood tall and proud against the backdrop of Starlight Hill at the western outskirts of the city. Away from the cacophony of Roosevelt, the hospital offered onlookers a breath of serenity. Just past the hills laid the Sound, and past that, the rest of the country. Tristan often daydreamed of scampering over the hills and exploring the mainland. Will's illness had always kept his family tethered to Copperfield, but all that was about to change.

He received a visitor's pass sticker from the receptionist and made his way into the South Tower's elevator. The complex was an eastern-facing masterpiece designed by architect Bertrand Nomura in the late seventies. When viewed from the front, it resembled a castle with its strong foundation and three distinct towers. The lower floors were of a brutalist design and stretched beneath the towers, connecting the entire facility.

The towers themselves were constructed predominantly of concrete and increased in height from right to left. To the right lay the parking garage, which was typical save for its unusually large size. Clare Collins found navigating it to be incredibly stressful, which Tristan and his father found to be incredibly funny.

The central and southern towers were some of the most remarkable structures Tristan had ever seen. The OR was housed in the central tower—commonly referred to as The Cube for its uniquely geometric shape. To the left of the concrete and glass cube was the tall concrete clocktower. A majority of the hospital's patients resided in this southern structure, including William Collins.

After exiting the elevator Tristan was greeted by a nurse's station adjoined to a grid of slender hallways. What the clock tower had in height, it lacked in girth, making navigation simple. It wasn't long before he found what he was looking for: "1303, W. Collins," the placard read. Tristan felt himself bursting with excitement. He reached for the metal door handle when, much to his surprise, it turned by itself. The heavy wooden door flew into the room at a dangerous speed, revealing the aggressor within.

His mother stood before him with an expression that was equal parts devastated and furious. While the former was concerning, he was ashamed to say that he feared the latter more.

"Where have you been?!" she began in an agitated *sotto voce*. "Why didn't you answer your phone?!"

"I'm sorry, Mom," Tristan said, rubbing the back of his neck with his palm. "I didn't have any signal on the subway." He knew it was a lame excuse. In retrospect, he could have gone above ground for a moment to text about the train delay; but he was too lost in his own reverie about that night to have been thinking clearly. It was then that he noticed the pain in his mother's eyes. Clearly, she wasn't just angry about his arriving late. Something was off.

"What's wrong?" Tristan asked cautiously. "...Is Will okay?"

That instant, the fury on Clare's face dissipated, leaving only shock. She maintained eye contact as her lip began to pout. A moment later, the tears began.

"What... what's wrong, Mom?"

Clare tried to derive comfort from tightly clutching onto her own, thin arms as she wept. Marc appeared from within the room to provide comfort with his own. His severe expression was all but concealed by his wife's flaming red hair. After a few moments, he turned his attention to Tristan. His next two words changed his life forever.

"It's back."

"What?!" Tristan stepped back in complete disbelief. Marc let go of Clare and tried to explain. He reached out his hand to place it on his son's shoulder.

"Your brother's had a relapse and…"

"No!" Shoving his arm away, Tristan began to shout. "The doctor said he was getting better. That's not fair!"

Marc imitated his wife's previous combative whisper. "Keep your voice down! He still doesn't know." Again, like Clare, Marc's temper mollified to sadness. "He's been looking forward to seeing you. It's all he's been talking about."

Not knowing how to respond, Tristan found himself looking at the floor, lost in his own head.

"Was this how the girl at The Turquoise Fox was feeling when she left?" he wondered. He was shaken from the thought by the pressure of a hand on his shoulder. His mother had regained the ability to speak.

"Tristan, honey," she began, "I need to get some air. Please just… spend some time with him for a while. Do your story-thing you two like to do together. Just don't tell him yet." She started to choke up as tears welled in her eyes. "Tonight, we have to…" She couldn't go on. Marc placed a comforting hand on her shoulder and turned to Tristan.

"We'll be back in a little while," he said before guiding her to the elevators at the start of the hall. Tristan couldn't remember ever having seen his father look so hurt. Growing up, he had often thought the man to be invincible, but that night shook him.

Standing alone Tristan took a moment to compose himself. The situation certainly was bleak, but they'd find a way forward. Right? They had to. They always have.

Like the green-eyed girl, he shut his eyes, took a deep breath, and opened the door.

The slender hallway within was bare save for another heavy wooden door to his right, leading to the bathroom. The hallway was a bottleneck leading to the patient's room proper, just a few feet away. From this hallway, he could just barely see the bed's baseboard. His mind was racing.

"How am I supposed to keep a smile on my face knowing that any day, he might—?"

"Tristan?"

The voice within broke his train of thought. He entered the room. As if to spite the growing darkness culminating out the window, the fluorescent bulbs and rising moon flooded the room with light. Rising in the bed was the sallow figure of his ten-year-old brother. He shot upright, his motion causing his bright red hair to bounce and shimmer in the room's florescent lighting.

"Tristan!" he exclaimed with his arms outstretched. Tristan couldn't help but smile. Will's elation had always been contagious—one of his gifts. Throwing his bag down on the floor, Tristan bolted across the room and embraced his little brother with a bear hug.

"Will, so good to see you!" he said before kneeling at his bedside. "How are you feeling, buddy?"

"Not so well. I'm really tired." Will began with a frown that quickly turned the other way around. "But I'm really happy that you're here!" In his excitement, he motioned to sit on the edge of the bed. His brother stopped him with a gentle touch on the shoulder. Beneath the gossamer white and blue speckled patient gown, his skin was eerily cool to the touch. This shocked Tristan; he tried not to let it show.

"Well, you need to lean back and get some rest!" said Tristan. Standing, he began to fluff and arrange pillows to help his little brother sit upright. It was clear to him that Will was struggling, though he appeared to be masking it involuntarily.

"Yeah but, tonight is going to be awesome, right?" Will pushed back the covers and sat completely upright on the side of the bed. "Are we still going out to eat at that fancy pizza place? I was thinking that afterward, we could play Jenga together, and then we could hook up the old N64 and play some *Goldeneye*—just you and me!"

Tristan felt his stomach drop.

"I think maybe we should just wait to see what the doctor has to say first before we get all excited," he said as he got his brother settled back into the bed. Will looked panicked.

"What do you mean?" he asked, his eyes wavering in newfound trepidation. "I'm going home today, right?"

Shaken, Tristan's gaze broke from Will's. He turned around, letting the decal of a cartoon penguin playing ice hockey become his focal point as he composed himself. Settling on the right words, he turned back to his little brother; putting on the best smile he could muster given the circumstances.

"Well, that was the plan, right?" he said. Tristan reached into his backpack and slipped out his sketchbook and pencil. "Tell me, do you want to hear another story?" Will was elated.

"Of course! Tell me! Tell me!" Flipping open the book, Tristan seated himself on the side of the medical bed. Will's favorite tales often came from spontaneous bursts of inspiration: a fact to which the dozens of illustrations pinned up around the room's walls could attest. Tristan peered out the large sliding window adjacent to the bed. The thirteenth floor (Bertrand Nomura didn't suffer from triskaidekaphobia) of the clock tower offered some fantastic views of the sound that surrounded Starlight Hill. The moon was gently reflected in a silvery glow upon the calm waves of the Copperfield Sound. For just a moment, Tristan felt a sense of peace. His reverie was soon broken by a herring gull that rushed past the window.

"Whoa!" he exclaimed, startled out of his seat. Will was bellowing with laughter. "Alright, alright," he said, returning to the bed. That heart attack of his had given him an idea. "Tell me," he said, raising an eyebrow, "have you ever heard of Lawrence of Australia?"

"Do you mean that scary war movie you had to watch for a film class?" Will asked, turning somewhat away with squinted eyes. Tristan chuckled and began to draw.

"No, no, that was *Arabia*. I'm talking about a bird. The most adventurous seagull of them all!" Turning around his book, Tristan revealed his first-ever drawing of Lawrence of Australia: a cartoon seagull with a backpack and a yearning for adventure. When the character's goofy expression got another hardy laugh from his little brother, he knew that he had struck gold.

"Tell me the story!" Will exclaimed, tugging at the sleeve of his jacket. Tristan smiled.

"Well, if you insist…"

"Lawrence is an adventurous seagull who likes to travel the world." A proud herring gull with violet eyes stood atop the spire of a great skyscraper. Wearing

a blue backpack topped with a green sleeping bag, he was well-equipped for wherever the call of adventure may bring him.

The ride back from the hospital was quiet and uneventful. Tristan offered to stay the night, but his parents insisted that he go to the adoption center. There were a few families interested in the litter, so Clare was worried that they'd give the cat away to someone else if her son didn't pick him up that day. Tristan knew it was ridiculous since the paperwork was already completed, but then again, whole situation was ridiculous. Given the circumstances, he couldn't fault his mother for her incoherent judgment. He smiled and obliged.

"He's a silly guy, who loves to make friends everywhere he goes."

Tristan carried the diminutive cardboard box into the living room. He opened it, sat across the room on the floor, and waited. A few moments later, a small, black kitten poked his head out of the box and locked eyes with his new owner. Tristan kicked off his shoes and hung up his jacket. He got the cat's food and water dish set up in the kitchen and poured litter into the pan in the bathroom. He picked up Phoenix and dragged its little paws across the litter, showing it where to go. Later, he found the little black cat trotting alongside him into his brother's darkened room.

"A seasoned traveler, this little seagull is an expert at packing!"

Turning on the light, Tristan walked toward the snack table placed in the center of the room. He repackaged the sheet cake in its box. The words, "Welcome Home" bore into his skull.

"But no matter how far away he explores—"

Solemnly, he sat on his brother's small mattress. Phoenix climbed up to join him, purring softly on his lap.

"He always takes care of his family and friends."

Petting the small animal, Tristan felt his phone vibrate.

"So, no matter what happens, you can always be sure:"

He checked the message. It was a photo.

Will looked so strange without his red hair.

"He'll be there for you till the very end."

FAMILY DINNER

CLACK!

CLACK!

CLACK!

THE RICE BOARD SNAPPED BACK with each strike with a satisfying clack. Dressed in a gray tank top and jeans, Makiko stood before the makiwara in a forward stance. Her right hand was positioned in a down block that hovered above her right thigh. Her left fist was drawn up to her hip, palm facing the ceiling. Still as a statue, focusing her aim at a place a few inches behind the rice board.

CLACK!

Drawing momentum from her waist, she'd pull back her right hand and strike the board with her left, pausing at the spot before resetting. Every ten strikes, she'd swap sides. All the while, she'd focus on her breathing, trying to stay centered. Trying to stay grounded. Allow the aggression within her to dissipate into nothingness.

CLACK!

There was a knock at the door. It broke her concentration.

"Be right out!" Maki called.

"Help me set the table when you're ready," her father's muffled voice answered.

Stepping away from the rice board, Maki sighed and took a sip of water. She disguised the stench of her sweat with a squirt of perfume before tossing on a knit brown sweater. Opening her nightstand, she looked down at her hands with a frown. The backs of her hands had adapted to her many years of training on the rice board. Thick chunks of white flesh rose disconcertingly above otherwise healthy skin. While she was grateful they no longer bled during training, she hated the way they looked. They reminded her of the bloated cadavers she'd have to study in pre-med next year.

After a bit of consideration, she decided on a black pair of crocheted gloves to pair with this evening's attire. She smiled as she pulled them on. They covered her hands quite nicely.

Makiko exited her room and followed her nose down the hall. Masashi was at the stovetop of their diminutive eat-in kitchen, stirring a steaming pot of udon.

"Set the plates," he ordered in Japanese. Masashi frequently spoke in his native language when it was just him and his daughter at home. Maki obliged. Navigating the tiny kitchen while someone was cooking was akin to playing a dangerous game of Twister. Hot grease bubbled up from the steak in Masashi's frying pan as his daughter twisted, turned, leaned, and stretched all around him to get the dishes and cutlery from the nearby drawers. After a few minutes of awkward shuffling about the room, the places were set.

Curious as to when the guests would arrive, Maki looked over the island countertop at the clock in the living room. The clock was positioned directly above a series of paintings: her mother's.

While photographs of the sea would fill her with dread, she had spent enough time around her mother's artwork to be comfortable with just the slight twinge in the stomach she felt upon gazing into the painted waves. An Okinawan native, the beach was a favorite subject of hers. Tonight, Makiko found herself lost in the waves of the ocean before the setting sun. In the foreground, a cherry blossom tree bloomed. Its leaves were being carried off toward the sunset by the wind, drifting delicately into the ocean. There was a deep sadness here. One she hadn't the capacity to explain.

The doorbell made her jump.

"Can you get that?" Masashi asked. "Sorry, my hands are kind of full." He was straining the noodles into a colander. In a few moments, he'd be plating the food into an old ceramic serving dish he had set aside on the counter. Maki nodded and proceeded toward the door.

"Hi!" Mama Yoko and her husband cheered. They entered the apartment wearing light jackets and bright smiles. Mama Yoko hugged and kissed her niece. After Masashi had finished preparing the dish, he limped around the counter to greet his sister with a hug and his brother-in-law with a quick handshake.

"Noodles?" asked Uncle John with a polite smile. "Smells delicious."

"Old family recipe," Masashi replied in English. He gestured to the round dining table. "Please, have a seat."

"Can I take your coats?" Maki asked.

"Of course, dear. Thank you," said Mama Yoko with a smile. She passed her and Uncle John's coats to her niece who carried them to the hall closet for hanging. Mama Yoko removed her shoes at the front door and placed them atop a nearby shoe rack. Masashi grimaced as his white guest crossed the threshold.

"John!" Yoko cried, sternly.

"Yes dear?" Her husband turned around, concerned. A quick glance at his feet was all it took for him to realize his error. He apologized for his discourteousness and placed his shoes beside his wife's. Masashi and Johnathan weren't exactly on good terms. Never had been. A veteran of the US Navy, Johnathan Daniels met his wife when stationed at a base in Okinawa. Nearly a decade later, Masashi still had a hard time seeing eye-to-eye with the man who stole his sister from their homeland.

John and Yoko seated themselves at the eat-in kitchen table. Maki sat at their side.

"Glasses," Masashi commanded. His daughter frowned as she stood up from the table. She felt like she was already back at work. She was just one tall opera singer away from serving at Brandy's.

"What can I get you to drink?" she asked her guests as she opened the refrigerator.

"Water please," said Mama Yoko.

"Got any Coke?" John asked, casually. Masashi's hairs shot up on the back of his neck, seething with displeasure.

"We do. Diet okay?"

"That's perfect, thanks."

Maki nodded and prepared the drinks at the table, pouring an extra glass of cola for herself. Finally able to rest, she joined her aunt and uncle at the table. Her father carried over the ceramic serving dish to the center and instructed his guests to help themselves. He eyed his daughter curiously as she joined her aunt and uncle in making the sign of the cross. John was the first to break the silence after grace.

"So," he began, "I hear you started school this week. How are classes going?"

"Not bad." Maki nodded, somewhat truthfully. "They keep me busy."

"My daughter is going to be an amazing doctor someday." Masashi boasted with pride. "Already accepted into RU. 4.0 GPA since freshman year,"

Maki said nothing. She stared off into the sakura painting.

John whistled and looked at his wife.

"Impressive. I'll be looking forward to your valedictorian speech," he said with a smile. "So, what made you want to be a doctor?"

An awkward silence fell over the table. Makiko continued staring at the painting, lost in thought.

"Maki," her father said, refocusing her attention.

"Sorry," she said. "Doctor. Hmm." She took a sip of soda to give herself more time to think of a proper answer. She could feel Masashi's judgmental stare all the while.

"I guess, well, after what happened with Mom… I don't know. I wouldn't want anyone else to go through that. I figured that I could try to help others." She shrugged. Her father seemed pleased at this answer. He put his hand on hers.

"Your mother would have been very proud of you," he said sincerely.

"Thanks, Dad," Maki replied. She flashed a sad smile.

"Asako was an amazing woman," Mama Yoko said, studying the paintings in the other room. "A great artist, too." She turned back to her niece. "You're an excellent painter, Makiwara. Have you made anything new recently?"

Sensing her father's eyes on her, Maki frowned once more.

"No," she replied a little too sternly. "I mean, I'd love to, but school has kept me pretty busy. Between that and the cafe, I have a pretty full schedule."

"I see," Mama Yoko said in a tone that Maki couldn't decipher. "Well, there's a time and a place for everything." She took another bite of udon. "Masashi, this really is delicious."

"Thank you, Yoko." Her brother smiled.

"Really, great stuff Masashi," said John. "Thanks."

They finished the rest of their meal with idle chatter. John and Yoko's ice cream parlor, politics, wars, inflation… boring stuff that held little interest for Makiko. She was relieved when the opportunity to bus the table had finally presented itself.

Makiko had just changed into pajamas and set her phone on the charger when she received a text. It was from her aunt.

"Some late-night reading for you: Matthew 25:14-30. Always lovely to see you. Sweet dreams, Makiwara."

At this, she raised an eyebrow. Her aunt had converted to Catholicism shortly after immigrating to America. When Maki fell in love with the religion after meeting Izzy, Mama Yoko acted as her godmother. Despite their strong faith, her aunt sending her a bible verse out of the blue was certainly unusual. Nevertheless, Maki retrieved her *New American Bible* from her bookshelf, propped herself up, and read.

SEPTEMBER

BRANDY'S CAFÉ

ELECTRONIC BEEPING TORE ITS WAY across the darkened bedroom. Part of him wanted to ignore the alarm; let it become a malignant white noise. Tristan was in a half-conscious stupor: unable to sleep and equally unable to face the day. Phoenix sat up, drawn by the noise. Her bright green eyes locked with his for a moment before curling back up on his chest. Taking the hint, he snoozed the alarm and shut his eyes as well.

A half-hour later, Tristan had managed to dress and stumble his way to the kitchen. His mother had already poured him a mug of coffee and was folding an omelet onto a plate. She put the plate on the table and instructed him to sit.

Despite nearing middle age, Clare Collins had managed to stay in shape thanks to a combination of healthy cooking, exercise, and a plethora of unhealthy stress brought on by the myriad of issues that plagued her two boys. While Tristan may not have shared her eyes or accent, he had his mother to thank for his flaming red hair. That day, hers was pulled into a side braid, as was her penchant.

"Toast will be up in a minute," she said as she refilled her ceramic mug.

"You made this for me?" Tristan asked as he seated himself at the wooden dining table. She smiled.

"I'm not allowed to care about *both* of my sons?" Clare replied as she took a seat across from him. It had been a week since Will's relapse and the family was still adjusting to the news.

"Thanks, Mom. You really didn't have to."

"I know. I wanted to." His mother's response was followed by an awkward stretch of silence that was interrupted by the popping of the toaster. She started to rise but her son was faster.

"This is hurting everyone, Tristan." Clare's eyes were locked onto his toast as he applied the cream cheese at the table.

"I know, Mom," he replied, flatly. His expression remained neutral.

"Honey, are you alright?" his mother asked, leaning in with a sincere expression of concern. He set the knife down.

"I'm fine, Mom."

Clare looked down before sliding over to the seat on Tristan's left side. She put her hand in her son's. Her piercing green eyes met his.

"Listen," she began, "I know you're hurting. Believe me, we *all* are. But you need to do something to get yourself out of this funk." His bangs fell in front of his eyes as his head slunk down toward the table.

"I'm not in a funk." Tristan sighed. He hated that expression. He didn't understand how his parents could understand how he was feeling when even he couldn't. Although, he knew they were probably right. The three of them were all facing the same terror.

"You're not acting like yourself, Tristan." Clare brushed the hair out of her son's face. "You're smart, funny… kind. You should be spending more time with people your own age. Not us old farts."

"I see people in my classes," Tristan responded, sitting upright.

"Right," his mother said in such a disbelieving way that even Tristan couldn't help but chuckle. "Do you know any of them by name?" she asked again. At this, his brief smile dissipated.

"Fair point,"   he said. "That doesn't change my situation, though. I still don't know anyone." His mother tapped him on the forehead with an open palm. Tristan looked up to see Clare laughing with incredulity. She held her face in her hands.

"Oh, God bless him, he's a melter," she lamented in prayer before raising her head. "How on earth could someone so smart be so stupid?" She cackled. "You say *hello*, Tristan. Smile!" He was grateful that Phoenix had walked into the room. He picked her up and gave her a few good scratches on the cheek.

"It's not that simple," he responded, remembering his failure at the Turquoise Fox. This school year had started on a Tuesday. That meant three consecutive days of deliberately avoiding eye contact with the girl assigned only a few seats away from him. At least she was seated behind him, Tristan thought. A few minutes into solving equations and crafting new characters for Will usually helped to keep her out of his head.

"Oh, won't you cut that out?" Clare snapped, her patience wearing thin. "If you don't believe me, I guess you'll just have to try it for yourself."

"I've *been* trying."

"Really?" She leaned in and raised an eyebrow. "When?"

"Uh oh," Tristan thought to himself. He gulped nervously. His imagination getting the better of him once more, he saw Kieran—his Other—appear in the chair beside his mother.

"Go on..." he taunted. "What's the matter?" From under the table, he picked up an abominable clone of Phoenix... the green-eyed girl's human head dwarfed the cat body it was attached to.

"Cat got your tongue?" the cat-girl cooed with a wink.

Tristan didn't know how to react to this new character. Perhaps he could use it in one of Will's stories. He pushed the thoughts aside for now. His imagination had always been a haven for him in times of distress. Now that he was an adult, he knew that he had to be more responsible with the moments when he chose to escape from reality. Now was simply not the time.

Also, the cat-girl kind of creeped him out.

"Uh, lots of times," Tristan responded to his mother at last.

"Uh-huh," Clare said with no change in her demeanor. A light smile formed on her lips as she leaned back in her chair. "Well, I think you just need a little involvement, Charlie Brown," Tristan smirked and continued scratching behind Phoenix's ears.

Kieran followed suit, scratching behind the furry ears of the cat girl. It purred and smiled with half-shut eyes.

"*Uwu!*" the monstrosity squeaked satisfactorily.

"Involvement how?" Tristan asked, genuinely trying to figure out what his mother was getting at. "Like joining a club? I suppose I could, but with Will in the hospital, I don't think I'm going to have that kind of—"

"I don't mean like that," Clare cut him off. "Just start by trying something new. Something small." She gestured with her hand. "Go see a movie or something. Visit a coffee shop. Walk over to GameStop and pick something out for yourself or Will. Buy a puzzle at Walmart. Get a new sketchbook. Just do *something* that doesn't involve lying in bed or staring at the ceiling. Okay?" Lethargically, Tristan managed to meet her eyes and nod.

Taking his mother's advice, Tristan decided to spend his Saturday morning at the local cafe near Starlight Station. Brandy's Cafe sat in the heart of Lenox: the last major slice of suburbia before the bridge to Roosevelt Island. As Starlight was the first stop on his usual line to University Station, he had never given the place much thought. You don't think much of what's above you when you're trapped underground.

The walk from Bedford to Lenox wasn't terribly taxing. On the contrary, Tristan found it refreshing. Crossing the border between the two towns felt like stepping between two worlds. The cracked, potholed-filled streets of the residencies of Bedford were replaced with the bright, cream-colored sidewalks of Lenox. Dreary brown apartment complexes became colonial homes that had been converted into nautically-themed storefronts, each selling their collections of overpriced crafts and antiques. The westward cityscape of Roosevelt Island loomed as a mythic mountain range from a fantasy novel—dominating the skyline. Starlight Avenue was a rapidly descending slope. Coupled with the view, the descent gave the feeling of falling—no… being sucked into the city. Sometimes, Tristan felt that Roosevelt Isle was a black hole that tore the color out of everything. Out of his studies, his parents' marriage, his life, his brother's…

He sighed and shook his head. Thoughts like that never solved anything. Continuing his descent, he turned his mind to the positives. Tristan had this game he liked to play with himself whenever he felt caught in a rut. He would force himself to see something positive in every situation.

Yes, his brother was sick. That just meant that he could write more stories with him in the hospital. Yes, his parents would argue. Their relationship was solid as a rock. Each time they'd fight, they'd bounce back even stronger. Yes, classes were boring and difficult. Next year, he'd be a freshman at Roosevelt University. Four years after that, he'd have his degree and could start applying for manufacturers.

Bolliger & Mabillard, Intamin, Mack Rides—he'd send his resume to them all. Ever since he was little, Tristan had an obsession with roller coasters that was almost fanatical. All it took was one trip to a local amusement park to start his addiction. The Rattlesnake. A simple, diminutive steel coaster he rode with his father. He begged the operator to let him ride again. After the third consecutive go on the ride, his parents finally dragged him home. In middle school, he'd impatiently tap his foot through his classes, eager to get home and test out new designs in *Rollercoaster Tycoon*. Summer vacations were spent adding notches to his roller-coaster riding list at some of the greatest parks in the United States.

Yes, school sucked; but Tristan knew it was a necessary evil. Someday, he'd be a roller coaster designer.

At the entrance to the subway station, he turned right and walked toward the door to Brandy's Cafe. The building's interior was humble, with yellow-orange walls and average wooden floors gave it a homey atmosphere. He approached the counter and surveyed the menu, scrawled elegantly in chalk by someone with a feminine hand. The prices were surprisingly reasonable for this side of town.

Hanging below the blackboards were sets of framed photos featuring a family of three—presumably the owners. One feature in particular caught his eye: a fire ax mounted above the "Employee's Only" door with an engraved inscription beneath. He was just about to make out the words when the door beneath it flung open and out stepped an employee equipped with a bright orange polo and green apron. When she lifted her head, the brim of her cap only emphasized the intensity of her piercing green eyes.

Tristan could almost hear the air being vacuumed out of the cafe as time seemed to stop. In his terror, he saw an intense glare of unrelenting anger flash across her irises. The outer edges of her angular eyes twitched in a microscopic scherzo of rage. After a period that felt like hours, the girl shut her eyes and turned away, busying herself with a small notepad and pen which she pulled from her apron pocket.

"What can I get you?" she asked, quickly. Tristan was still bewildered, trying to piece it all together.

"Hey, you're the girl from—"

"Are you going to order or what?" she snapped, glancing up for a moment. He felt himself start to blush. He rubbed at the back of his neck.

"Oh, I—uh," Tristan stammered, "I was just going to s—" Without looking up, she pinched her fingers closed in his face.

"Shut it," she pithily snapped. "What do you want?"

"Sorry," he conceded. "I'll take a cappuccino, please." The girl scribbled his order onto the pad.

"Cash or credit?"

"Uh, card," Tristan said, stupidly. Still without looking at him, she briskly pointed at the point-of-sale terminal on the counter.

"Insert." She spun around and rapidly began preparing his drink. The violence with which she operated had some of the nearby patrons stealing glances her way. It was obvious that she was attempting to complete this interaction as quickly as possible. Tristan couldn't blame her. He was feeling the same way.

He reached into his wallet and pulled out his debit card. He swiped it only to be met with an error message accompanied by an aggressive series of beeps. The girl whipped around, knocking over and shattering the mug she was filling in the process.

"I said *INSERT!*" she bellowed, "It has a *chip reader, moron!*" The entire cafe was silent as the patrons' heads turned toward the source of the commotion. The intensity of her glare was horrifying.

Thankfully, the guardian angel sent to rescue Tristan from this moment came in the form of a middle-aged man bursting through the employee door. He wore a look of pity on his face. He approached the girl slowly.

"Maki, why don't you sit down in the back for a second?" he said, sweetly. "I can finish here." The girl was about to protest, but the man held up a hand with a stoic expression. She turned to glare at Tristan once more before turning back to the man. After a beat, she looked down at the floor, sighed, and stormed off to the back room.

"Sorry about that," he said, half to the cafe and half to Tristan. "She just needs a minute to cool off." He grabbed a broom and swept up the shards of the ceramic mug off the wooden floor.

"I'm sorry, I didn't mean to upset her," Tristan said, genuinely remorseful.

"Ah, don't take it personally," the man responded, dumping the dustpan into the trash before sanitizing his hands. "She's a sweet kid, she just has some trouble controlling her anger. It's not her fault." Tristan went to insert his card into the terminal but the man stopped him.

"Please," the man said, "it's on the house."

"Oh, alright. Thanks," Tristan said, putting his card away. The man gestured to a set of booths adjacent to a series of wall-sized windows.

"Why don't you go take a seat? We'll have this ready for you in a minute."

Tristan obliged.

Maki leaned over the basin, shut her eyes, and started the faucet. The cool water filled her cupped hands before she raised them to her face. She steadied her breathing, feeling the cord of her apron tighten around her abdomen as she focused on activating her diaphragm. She splashed her face once more.

Sensing something, she opened her eyes to see Mr. White standing in the doorframe behind her. She couldn't look him in the eye.

"I'm really sorry, Mr. White," she managed to say, dolefully. To her surprise, he looked equally upset.

"It's alright," he said. "Do you need to go home?"

"No, I can finish my shift. Thanks."

"Okay," he replied unconvincingly. "Just let me know if you change your mind. I can have Izzy take over for now." Makiko straightened up and adjusted a few strands of hair that had fallen out of place.

"No, that's alright," she said, trying to muster up the facade of resolve. Unfortunately, she'd never been a very good actress. "I can come back out now."

Mr. White's dubious expression told her that he was still doubtful of her stability. He glanced down at the floor for a moment, then at something in the breakroom before locking eyes with her reflection. He became brusque.

"I still think Izzy should keep you company." He turned his head back to that spot in the breakroom. "Iz, can you come off break a little early?" A moment later, a blonde head cartoonishly popped into view from the other side of the doorframe.

"Of course, Dad. C'mon Maki, it'll be fun!" she said with a smile.

"She's always been the bubbly one," Maki thought. Smiles from those bright red lips were contagious. She chuckled once without humor.

"Alright, let's go," Maki conceded, pulling on her black, fingerless gloves as she went out the door.

Back behind the counter, it was time to resume the order for…*him*. Maki found it tough to even look in that boy's direction. She passed the buck to Izzy.

"It was a cappuccino." Without looking up from the counter, Maki nodded to the booth across the room. "For the redhead over there." When Izzy didn't move, Maki looked up to see a guise of apprehension painted on her face. Suddenly embarrassed, she remembered.

"The one in the booth by himself," Maki said, amending her previous statement.

"I just can't stop screwing up today, can I?" Maki thought, deprecatingly.

"Oh, *him*. I see," Izzy said with understanding.

"Sorry, I forgot."

"That's alright, don't worry about me," she said, reassuringly; though, Maki wasn't entirely sure how sincere her friend's attitude really was. Izzy easily could have been upset and was just playing it off for her friend's sake. She only just found out about her colorblindness a little while ago and was likely still adjusting to the shock.

"I can tell that it's red. I just second-guess myself a little now, that's all…"

Izzy let Maki continue her breathing exercises while she went off to prepare the boy's order. Was his hair really red? She never would have guessed. Then again, she wasn't paying that much attention. Her mind was still ruminating about the upcoming recital. This boy offered a nice distraction from her own head.

"Do you know him?" Izzy asked, genuinely curious. Maki busied herself by scrubbing down the countertop with a disposable wet cloth.

"He goes to our school," she began. "We're in AP Calc together. He caught me on a bad day this week and I guess seeing him here just brought all those feelings back." Maki didn't tell her that those same feelings of revulsion had sprung up every time she was forced to look past his stupid ginger head whenever she needed to see the board. Though admittedly, she knew this was just projection on her part. At least he couldn't see her wearing her derpy distance glasses from behind.

"I'm sorry, Maki." Izzy frowned.

"It's fine, thanks." Maki shrugged. "It'll pass."

They shared an awkward silence. Business was slow. With no new customers walking in, Izzy took some time to look around the room. At one table, a businessman was working on his laptop, at another, a sweet elderly couple sharing a pastry, and at still another, a young mother with her daughter who couldn't have been older than four.

"That's a shame about that boy," Izzy said. "I thought he was kind of cute."

Maki let out another one of her signature humorless chuckles.

"Really? Of all people, *HIM?* You're kidding, right? *That* idiot?"

Izzy caught sight of a few customers tossing dirty looks at Maki over their shoulders. An anxious gaze from Izzy appeared to calm her down. After a moment, a mischievous grin overtook Maki's face. Somehow, this expression only made Izzy more nervous.

"Maki..." she said, worryingly, *"I don't like that look..."*

"Why don't you go say hi?" Maki said, quickly.

"What? No! I can't do that!" As usual, while Izzy was aghast, Maki was smiling. A common occurrence in their friendship.

"Yes, you can," Makiko continued. "You bring the order over to him and introduce yourself." Evidently having snapped out of her funk, Maki took over in prepping the boy's order.

"I can't just do that!" Izzy protested; her maturity suddenly demoted to that of a whiny twelve-year-old. "It would be so *awkward.* I don't know how to talk to boys. You saw that at Elaine's party!"

At the start of the year, Makiko's neighbor had invited her to a Lunar New Year celebration at her family's Chinese teahouse.

Izzy had tagged along as her plus-one. Not only did Izzy fail to impress, but she nearly downed a cup of milk tea in the process (a potentially deadly error for someone allergic to dairy). Her inability to distinguish between the red and green cups on the table was what first alerted her to her deuteranopia.

"Well, that was a party, and this is your job: you're the one in control now. You'll be fine!" Maki concluded. She finished preparing the order.

"Um... are you sure about this?" Izzy said, hesitantly.

"Not really." She shrugged. "But what do you have to lose?"

"My dignity," Izzy replied, morosely. Her stupor was shattered when her friend thrust the serving tray into her hands with a smile.

"You're nineteen years old and have a 'Chocobo crossing' sign on your bedroom door, Iz. You lost whatever dignity you had a *long* time ago."

"Hey!" Izzy protested.

"I'm messing with you." With one swift motion, Maki grabbed her friend by the arms and pushed her into the dining area. *"Now go bring the doofus his coffee!"* Izzy started to turn and make a silent protest but was answered by a dismissive wave of Maki's hand. She was already assisting a new customer—her mood suddenly elevated to an all-time high.

"Hi! What can I get for ya?" she chirped. Izzy cussed her friend under her breath.

"Okay," she sighed to herself. "Keep it together."

She approached the boy's booth with a cheery smile.

"Hey, uh… cappuccino for…?" The boy looked up from his notes. Something sciency, from the looks of it.

"Oh, Tristan. Thanks," he said with a smile. Izzy removed the cup and saucer from the tray and placed them on the table.

"*Tristan,*" she recapitulated. "No problem. Hey, um, I'm sorry about before," she continued, referencing the incident with Makiko. He showed off a solemn smile; not at all unattractive.

"It's fine, really. I'm the one who feels bad, actually." He looked past her to see Maki bantering with some customers at the counter. She gave Izzy a smile and Tristan a death stare before turning back to laugh with the newcomers.

"Don't worry about it," Izzy assuaged. "Maki and I have been best friends for years, trust me, she's alright." Though her words were sincere, his pitiable expression showed they had little effect.

"If you say so," he replied. "Thanks."

"No problem," Izzy said, beginning to return to the counter. "Just let us know if you need anything else."

"Um, yes actually. I thought the cappuccino was supposed to come with milk."

A chill ran down Izzy's spine.

"She didn't," she thought to herself.

Izzy returned to the table to examine Tristan's mug. Evidently, *somebody* had deliberately neglected to add milk to the drink. She glanced back at her "friend" behind the counter. Maki wore a sickening smile across her face.

"Are you serious?" Izzy mouthed from across the room. Unfortunately, her words had the effect of a feather gun: resulting in Maki collapsing onto the counter, snorting with suppressed laughter. She returned her attention to Tristan.

"You're right, it is," she said, anxiously. "I'll be right back." Tristan checked the time on his phone.

"Yeah, sure. Take your time. Thanks," he replied, convivially.

After returning to her workstation, Izzy retrieved the milk jug from the fridge. Wordlessly, she locked eyes with Maki. She looked like she was about to explode and Izzy felt as though she'd be the first one in line to see it happen.

"What's wrong?" Maki began through stifled chuckles. "You forget something?"

"You forget something?" Izzy mocked. Her face was burning as she returned to the table. Though she couldn't see it, Izzy was certain that her scarlet face was visible to any non-deuteranopic eyes within 100 miles of the Isle.

"Alright, here you go. I am so sorry about this," she said, setting Tristan's drink on the center of the table.

"Please, it's no trouble," he said with a raised hand. With frayed nerves, Izzy attempted to lighten the drink with the shape of a leaf. Unfortunately, her anxieties got the better of her. A shaky hand caused her to miss the cup entirely, spilling milk onto the table.

"Oh my gosh, I am so, so sorry!" Izzy gasped as she snatched a cloth from her apron. Raising her hand as she leaned in, she banged her knuckle on the underside of the table, spilling even more of the mixture onto the table. The steaming cappuccino poured over the sides of the cup and right into Tristan's lap. He winced in discomfort.

"Gosh, I'm so, so, so sorry!!" Izzy shouted in a panic. Fortunately for the sake of her sanity, the boy let out a laugh as he patted himself dry with a napkin.

"It's okay, don't worry about it," he said with a smile. "It happens."

"I should really be more careful. Sorry, I'm such a klutz."

"Please, it's fine... uh... Izzy." Her head shot back up, suddenly too overwhelmed with panic to process reason.

"How do you know my name?" Izzy spat out. Tristan looked as though he was nervously withholding laughter as he gesticulated towards the pin on her apron.

"Um, it's on your nametag," he said, nonchalantly. Glancing down, she tapped it with two fingers in acknowledgment.

"Oh." Izzy chuckled, embarrassed. "Of course it is." Her thoughts were racing in a spiraling Fibonacci series of self-admonitions. In retrospect, she supposed that this introspection must have felt like an eternity to the poor boy who just wanted to drink his drink in peace. Not knowing what to say, she found herself rocking on her heels, completely unaware of the time that had passed.

"Um..." Tristan cleared his throat. "Thanks for the milk," he said, breaking the silence.

"Oh, yes of course!" Izzy said a bit too loudly, snapping out of her reverie. "You're welcome. Uh, enjoy, okay?"

Starting backward, she found herself stumbling over the chair of a patron sitting with his wife.

"Hey, watch it!" he cried as his tea splashed over the sides of his cup and spread across the table in a pink deluge. Mortified, Izzy's hands flew to her mouth in embarrassment.

"Gosh, you're right as rain. I am so sorry!" she exclaimed as she began scrubbing down the table. "I'll get you a fresh one, okay?"

She returned to the counter under the gaze of her dark-haired friend. Makiko was leaning forward on one hand and holding back her shoulder-length hair with the other. Her expression was a mixture of many emotions. Izzy gathered some cleaning supplies together from the backroom and reentered.

"Can you prep another Açaí?" she asked.

"That physically hurt to watch," her colleague responded flatly whilst maintaining her thousand-yard stare.

"Just shut up and prep the drink, please." Izzy snorted before returning to right the mess she had made on the floor.

To Tristan, Izzy certainly had made quite an impression. She was pretty. Bright blonde hair and blue eyes. Perhaps a little plump, but in a way that was somehow endearing. If he wasn't so distracted by the devastating news regarding his brother—not to mention what happened with the other girl behind the counter—he might have even asked for her number.

Izzy was mopping up a mess she had made at the table adjacent to him, much to the chagrin of the elderly couple endeavoring to enjoy a peaceful meal there. Rising to leave, Tristan found himself baffled. A quick bounce on his toes proved that the girl stood a good two inches taller than he. Tristan smiled to himself. He was by no means tall himself, but this girl with her larger-than-life personality and features was pretty cute. He placed a five-dollar bill next to his saucer.

"Thanks again, Izzy. Have a good day," he said with a smile. Glancing up quickly, she noticed the amount on the table.

Flustered and slightly out of breath, she exclaimed, "Oh, wow, thanks. You too!"

What a bright smile. A smile to melt away worry and fear. Terrified of what awaited him at the hospital, Tristan relished in the warmth of it. He tried to return the expression; though, something about it just didn't feel quite right. Exiting the cafe, he gave a polite smile and nodded to the girl behind the counter as the doors shut behind him. Her green eyes pierced right through him the entire time.

The creak of the swinging door to the bar broke her from her malevolent reverie. Maki shook herself back into the present and forced a light smile.

"Wow, five bucks. Not bad," she said, gesturing to the leather check presenter poking out the top of Izzy's apron. Her friend smiled with humility.

"Well, he did get a free drink," she said with a shrug.

"Uh-huh," Maki chided. "Or maybe he just felt bad for you." As usual, her mean-spirited humor fell on a set of giant, deaf ears.

"Yeah." Izzy sighed. "You're probably right."

Maki attempted to rectify this with a good punch to the bicep.

"Ow! Hey!" Izzy hollered, massaging her arm.

"I'm kidding!" Maki cried. "He probably liked you."

"You really think so?" she replied, in a manner that was more an exclamation than a question.

"Who knows?" Maki shrugged. "He left a tip as big as the tab, so it's anybody's guess. Maybe he'll come back." She turned to face her. "Did you at least catch his name?"

"Tristan," Izzy said.

"Hm." Maki nodded. She wasn't sure what it was, but something about hearing the names "Tristan" and "Izzy" together sounded so familiar to her. She set the thought aside.

After thanking an elderly couple as they departed the cafe, Izzy and Maki set out to bus the table. They continued their conversation over half-eaten biscuits and soiled napkins.

"Well, I can tell you one thing for sure," Maki began, smirking with the anticipation of her friend's reaction to what she was about to say. "Tristan totally checked you out." As she expected, Izzy's face turned redder than Rudolph's nose.

"What? No, he didn't!" she whispered in a failed attempt to remain professional in front of a house full of customers.

"Uh, yeah, he did." Maki nodded. "A few times, actually."

"Nuh uhh!" Izzy pouted with the demeanor of a child. "When?"

"He sized you up as he was leaving."

Izzy's hand shot to her mouth.

"Oh my gosh. No. He didn't. Please tell me he didn't."

"Yep," Maki said with a chuckle. "Stood on his toes and everything."

Izzy looked down at the ground, humiliated and defeated.

"Probably thinks I'm some giant fat weirdo," she lamented with a sigh.

Maki circled around the table to her, smirking with folded arms.

"Izzy, he was *smiling,*" she said, quietly. Izzy looked back, a little confused.

"Smiling how? Like I was some sort of freak?"

"No, no, no—" Maki began, placing a comforting hand on Izzy's arm. "It was more like he just saw a puppy."

It took a moment for this statement to register, but when it did, Izzy leaned in.

"*...Really?*" she responded in amazement. Removing the filled bus tub from the now-sparkling table, Maki smirked back at her friend.

"I have a feeling he'll be back," she said as they made their way back behind the counter. Izzy looked back down at the floor, picking at a strand of her hair: a nasty habit that began in February.

"Gosh, I... I really hope so," she said quietly—almost to herself. Maki stopped preparing the next drink order for a moment to pull her hand away from her head. She met her eyes with a start.

"So, are you finally going to start believing me when I tell you you're pretty?" she asked. Returning to the drink station, Maki finished preparing the latest order. Out of the corner of her eye, she saw that her friend's smile had finally returned.

THE WINELAND ROOM

FROM THE DOORWAY, TRISTAN could hear the faint sound of cartoon antics emitting from a small television. He knocked and entered.

With the aid of a few pillows his mother had set up, Will was sitting somewhat upright watching Nickelodeon. The screen's illumination only served to emphasize the thing Tristan most dreaded seeing that day. The light bounced effortlessly off Will's shaved scalp. Tristan felt a hole in the pit of his stomach. He regained his composure with a sigh and proceeded.

Clare Collins was seated beside her youngest son in a wooden visitor's chair, holding his hand. She was exhausted. Her head turned in slow motion to greet Tristan with a slight smile which only served to exacerbate the multitude of bags under her eyes.

"Tristan!" Will shouted, snapping his head toward his brother. In contrast to Clare's, Will's eyes, though fatigued from sickness, were brightened by the joy of his brother's arrival. Tristan smiled despite himself.

"Hey buddy!" he exclaimed, "It's good to see you!" He sat on the side of Will's bed and embraced him—careful to avoid tugging at his IV. He stood for a moment to hug his mom before returning to his position on the bed. He looked at Clare.

"You too," Tristan said, more severely. "Are you feeling alright?"

"Oh, fine, fine," Clare said with as much joyfulness as she could muster with a wave of her hand. "Just... *yaaaahhhh*..." She yawned. "Just a little tired."

More than a little, it seemed. Tristan offered to let Clare catch up on some much-needed rest while he took his brother down to the playroom. She was obstinate at first, but she eventually agreed. By the time he had led Will out the door, he could already hear her snoring.

The playroom of St. Luke's pediatric department was easily Will's favorite place in the entire hospital. Recently renovated, the room was filled with bright colors, dangling paper butterflies, children's artwork, and more toys than you could possibly count. For the sick and the downcast, the Wineland Room shined as a bright haven.

Tristan seated his brother at a round, off-white plastic table. Once he made sure that his IV stand didn't interfere with any of his movements, he rapidly circled to his front. Tristan removed his jacket and draped it over his arm as a pseudo-serviette.

"What'll it be today, old chum?" he said in his best cockney accent.

"Lego!" Will exclaimed with a laugh. Tristan brought a bin over to the table.

"Lego! Righty-o my good chap!" he cried, continuing his butchery of the English accent. "And what will the young master be making today?" His brother thought for a moment.

"A fort!"

"A fort you say?!" Tristan shouted out. "My dear boy, from what will we be defending ourselves from?" Will looked around the room. He picked up a toy velociraptor lying next to him.

"Didn't you hear?!" Will chimed excitedly, playing along. "The raptors are coming!"

"My word! We must construct our defenses post-haste!"

They spent half an hour building their fortress and another taking turns attacking and defending it: dinosaurs versus spring-activated cannons. Even some of the other kids joined in on the fun.

An hour later, the table was in shambles. Half-destroyed Lego buildings and vehicles lay in ruins across the tabletop and floor. Plastic minifigures and dinosaur toys were tossed about. The remnants of the beautiful chaos of play. The Collins brothers let out a mutual sigh.

"That was really fun," Will said softly. Despite his good humor, Tristan could see the fatigue in his brother's eyes.

"Come here," he said. Will walked toward his open arms, gently receiving the hug.

"Want to lie down?" Tristan asked. Wordlessly, Will nodded. Tristan lifted his brother onto his hip and grabbed the IV stand with his free hand. Knowing he couldn't put his brother to bed without a story, he looked around for inspiration. Near a toybox, a middle-aged mother was shaking her head in humorous disapproval of her daughter. Racing around the room without shoes had resulted in her tearing a hole in her new blue socks. Despite her mother's comical remonstration, the little girl continued to bounce around the room with her big toe protruding from her right sock. Tristan smiled and carried his brother down to his room.

Clare was still asleep when they entered. Tristan dragged the IV stand to the side of the bed and tucked in his brother.

"Tristan?" Will asked, weakly. "Can you tell me a story?"

"Of course," Tristan smiled gently. He extracted his sketchbook from his bag and seated himself at his brother's side.

"You know," he began, "those dinosaurs caused a lot of trouble today. The soldiers in the fort hardly stood a chance!"

"Yeah, they were pretty crazy!" Will laughed.

"Well, I know who could have helped save us from the dinosaurs," Tristan said with an obvious facsimile of severity in his voice. Catching his drift, Will played along with a gasp.

"Who? Who?!" he cried, quietly so as not to wake their mother. Tristan began sketching.

"Have you ever heard of the Holey Sockman?" he asked with a grin.

"Gentlemen, I'm afraid tonight may be our last."

Sergeant Faden frowned out the window of the brick fort. A pack of velociraptors howled at the gates. They rammed it repeatedly. Tearing at the wood with vicious teeth and claws.

"In a few moments," the Sergeant continued, "the gate will collapse. After which, we will put up our last stand. We will very likely be overrun."

"But sir!" cried Private Malcolm. "Surely there must be something we can do!"

"Your bravery is commendable, private." His superior smiled sadly, placing a kind hand on his shoulder. "But we must face facts. They have us outnumbered ten-to-one. We simply don't have the arms or the manpower to take on such overwhelming forces."

Private Malcolm frowned.

"But sir," he countered, "there *is* someone who might be able to help us."

A flash of recognition appeared in Faden's eyes. His smile remained for just a moment before dissipating.

"No," he said with a shake of his head, "he hasn't been seen in years."

"But sir, we *must* try!" the private cried. "Surely something is better than nothing!"

The raptors had torn a large enough hole in the gate that some had been able to stick their entire heads through; snapping at the men at the front of the bailey.

"You're right, son," the captain said. "We must have hope!"

Captain Faden ran to the top of the fort and shouted down at his men.

"Everyone! Remove your boots! Raise your socks to the air!"

The bailey was filled with a cacophony of desperate shouts. Boots were strewn about as the men plopped to the ground and removed their socks.

"Slit the socks and wave them high!"

The men obediently followed the command, piercing their socks with their hunting knives. They waved the garments high above their heads, large holes in each.

"Now cry! Cry for help!"

With   one   voice,   they   all   cried: *"HEEEEEEELLLLPPPP!!!!"*

The captain looked to the collapsing gate and then to the horizon line. His stalwart visage was belied by the desperation in his eyes.

"Again! Louder!!"

"HEEEELLLLPPPPP!!!"

More and more wooden planks were torn from the gate. The raptors were pouring through.

"Once more!!!"

"HEEEELLLLPPP!!!"

The raptors charged in. A young soldier on the front lines raised his rifle. A raptor charged straight for him. He smelt the stench of rotting meat on its teeth. Its eyes were as black as death. The raptor tossed the man's rifle to the dirt and pounced on him. It snarled and opened its jaws.

It didn't see the kick coming.

Seemingly out of nowhere, a man's bare foot came out of the night and landed a powerful blow to the side of the dinosaur's head. It hit the dirt and immediately fell unconscious. The soldier looked up in amazement at his savior.

"It... it... it's you!" he stammered.

The man looked down and smiled.

The Holey Sockman charged forward into the crowd of charging monsters. The giant sock he wore as his garment flapped in the evening wind. Holes for the eyes, mouth, and arms allowed for complete freedom of movement as he knocked out the creatures one by one. The cross around his neck glinted in the moonlight.

"Cross?" Will asked.

"Well, you see," Tristan explained, "when he was still little, Hubert Salazar and his parents went to see a movie. Still a child, he got scared of the film and asked to leave early." Lifting his sketchbook, Tristan sketched a trio of silhouettes entering a dank alleyway. "Then all of a sudden—"

"They were jumped by muggers?" Clare dryly interjected, having just awoken from her slumber. Tristan blinked slowly.

"Uh, yeah," he said perplexedly. "How'd you know I was going to say that?"

"That's Batman's origin story," she answered flatly.

"No. No I don't think so," Tristan reviewed his sketches with a frown.

"Yes honey, it really is."

"R-really?" he said again. "Are you sure?"

Clare shook her head and closed her eyes. "I'm going back to sleep," she said with a sigh, dismissing her son with a wave of her hand.

"Anyway…" Tristan cleared his throat. "Here's what happened."

One of the bandits had lost a shoe. When Hubert's father refused to hand over his wallet, he kicked him in the face with a socked foot—a sock tarnished and covered in holes!

That night, young Hubert Salazar ran away in terror. He ran and ran through the darkened streets of the city. Eventually, he found himself at the steps of a monastery. The monks took him in and he studied their ways. Through it all, he couldn't bear to look at the thing he feared the most. He couldn't wear socks at all! Thankfully, these monks weren't your everyday priests. They were masters of martial arts.

He trained with them for two decades before he went back into the world, vowing to never again run in fear. But he needed a disguise.

A symbol.

Going back to his linen closet, he faced his fears. He pulled out all of his childhood socks. He stitched them together and tore gaping holes in the pattern to create the ultimate visage of terror.

That night, he became justice incarnate.

Fighting for truth, justice, and Christian morality, Hubert Salazar became…

The Holey Sockman!

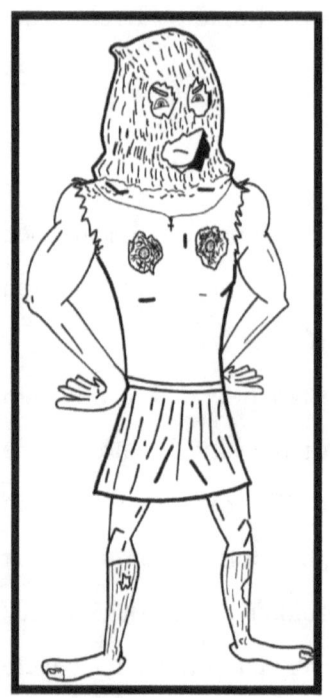

"Hold your fire!" Captain Faden commanded, not wanting to hit the Sockman. Within minutes, every raptor in the bailey was knocked unconscious. The men cheered and lifted the Sockman into the air.

"Holey Sockman, you've saved us!" cried the captain. "How can we ever repay you?"

The Sockman put a hand on his shoulder and said to the man, "You should take a page out of Private Malcolm's playbook. It was his faith that saved you all today. Not me," Captain Faden turned to smile at Malcolm. When he turned back to shake the Sockman's hand, he had already disappeared.

"What does that mean?" asked Will.

"What does what mean, buddy?" replied his brother.

"You said that the Sockman didn't save them. But he did! He stopped the dinosaurs from eating everyone."

Tristan thought for a moment before responding.

"Before the captain ordered the men to call out to the Sockman, did he think they were going to be alright?" he asked.

Will shook his head.

"No," he answered, "he thought the raptors were going to break down the gate."

"That's right," Tristan nodded. "And what did Private Malcolm want him to try?"

"He wanted him to try to reach out to the Holey Sockman anyway."

"Yes!" Tristan smiled. "You see, sometimes things can seem really scary. Life can seem like there's no way out. But it's in those times that your faith is really put to the test." He got off the bed and knelt at his brother's side. "So, what do you think you could do if you got really worried about something?"

Will furrowed his brows for a moment. His face lit up with revelatory glee.

"I could pray!" he said. Tristan smiled and nuzzled his nose between his fingers.

"I knew you were a smart one," he chided. "Let's get you tucked in." Tristan pulled up the covers before turning to his mother. He gently shook her knee. She stirred up with a start.

"Mom, want to say prayers?"

Clare smiled at her boys and joined them.

They drove home in silence. Tristan was behind the wheel; his mother was fast asleep beside him. Finally parked, he gently jostled his mother on the shoulder. He pulled her suitcase and handbag out of the car before locking it with the key fob. They circled the oversized brick box an architect convinced their landlord was an apartment complex and entered the lobby. A silent elevator ride later, they stood at the door to apartment 403.

Home.

While they were away, Marc had prepared a meatloaf for them to enjoy. Although none of them were in the mood for enjoyment, they ate it all the same. No one had much to say, save for Phoenix, who kept begging for Tristan's attention by bunting his shin with her head.

Still taciturn, he galumphed his way into his room and settled into bed. The cat followed him. Tristan pulled her up to his chest where she stayed for the several hours which it took for him to fall asleep.

HARD-WORKING MOLES ARE GOOD MOLES

AFTER HER HUMILIATION at the Turquoise Fox, Makiko avoided the local cafe and instead chose the Saint Anna Wang Center to be her new place to regain focus. The cultural center was a joint project between the Roosevelt Catholic Diocese and notable donors from Yellow Harbor, providing both Roosevelt University and Charter students with access to its meditative grounds. While the modern Asian cultural center boasted numerous art exhibits scattered throughout its minimalist interior, its principal draw was much more humble: it was quiet. She was seated on a low black marble wall with a long, shallow fountain to her right. Light streams of water were being vomited out the mouths of the Chinese zodiac signs bolted to the walls above, peacefully gurgling upon landing below. The acoustics of the Center caused these sounds to reverberate around the whole facility, creating a sense of serenity of which she was in desperate need.

Maki smiled to herself. She couldn't tell if praying the rosary beside the pagan symbols in a center dedicated to a martyr of the Boxer Rebellion was ironic or poetic. In many ways, she related to the saint. Though she certainly wasn't Chinese, she knew what it was like living between worlds.

Her father would never understand.

Taking one last breath, Maki checked her watch and decided that it was time to get moving.

While not her favorite subject, the young student was grateful that calculus posed little challenge. She sat in the back row of the classroom, taking the seat adjacent to the wall. Still recovering from her rough week, Makiko was glad to be tucked away behind a sea of people. The brim of an old baseball cap helped to confirm her anonymity. She hated being seen wearing her derpy distance glasses. Here, surrounded by blank faces and numbers, Maki could finally escape and relax—

"Oh no," she thought to herself.

A shock of flaming red hair entered the scene and he was heading straight for the back row. After her prayerful morning meditation by the fountains, Maki had almost managed to get through the entire school day without thinking about the boy she had humiliated herself in front of.

Wonderful.

Maki shoved her glasses into her bag and dragged her bangs in front of her face, hoping that would keep him from noticing her. After all, there were probably over thirty students in the classroom. The odds of this boy recognizing her would have to be relatively low—

"Good afternoon," he said. Tristan excused himself as he awkwardly pushed himself into the narrow skein of pathway between the long slender tables that acted as shared desks for students, sliding into the seat beside her.

"...Afternoon." Maki's eyes flitted to him and back again in a manner that matched her pithy response. The boy gestured to her jacket before pointing at his own.

"Hey, we almost match." He wore a black hoodie with cerulean cloth for the hood and cuffs. It was nearly an identical pattern to her purple-lined jacket. Disdainfully, she unzipped hers and leaned back.

"Yep. I guess so," Maki sighed. Tristan set up a notebook and pen on the table.

"Oh, I almost forgot," he said, suddenly turning to her with an outstretched hand.

"I'm Tristan. It's *Mackie*, right?" She paused and let out a subdued sigh before shaking his hand.

"*Mah-ki*," she enunciated. "It's short for *Makiko*." She quickly returned her gaze straight ahead. Tristan rubbed the back of his neck in embarrassment.

"Oh, right. Sorry," he sputtered.

"Don't worry about it."

After a period of awkward silence and squinting at the projector screen across the room, Makiko elected to remove the cap and shake out her hair. The last thing she'd want would be for the nascent teacher to call her out in front of the class for wearing a hat indoors. It took all Tristan had not to stare. He held his eyes straight ahead. First her perfume and now her citrusy shampoo were gliding flirtatiously through his nostrils and into his heart. No longer able to concentrate on the board, he pointed to the blue "D" emblazoned on the girl's cap`.

"Dodgers?" he asked.

"Dimmsdale. Small town near San Diego," she explained. "They've got a minor league team there."

"Interesting," Tristan lied, knowing nothing about baseball or sports in general for that matter. "Are you from California?"

"No. Roosevelt. I was visiting family." Tristan nodded in understanding. Another awkward period of silence passed. Makiko figured that he was either preparing his notes for the class or was waiting for her to say something else. Considering how he had forced his way to the seat beside her, she correctly assumed that it was the latter.

"My cousin used to live nearby but she goes to school out west," she continued. "I don't get to see her too often anymore—not since she started her ROTC program, anyway."

"Which branch?"

"Air Force."

Tristan smirked. "Air Force... nice."

"...Yeah."

"I had thought about doing that but, I don't know," he shrugged and looked away. "I guess it just wasn't for me," he said somewhat distantly.

Not long after this exchange, Mr. Chang began a barely comprehensible soliloquy on derivatives. Unfortunately, he was one of those teachers who insisted on reading directly from the textbook verbatim. Of course, it didn't help that English was likely his second or third language, either.

To make matters worse, Makiko found herself squinting to see the slides on the screen. Having already decided against humiliating herself further by becoming a four-eyes, she chose instead to copy off her new neighbor.

Tristan's handwriting was terrible. Knowing that she'd bear witness to some of the worst handwriting on earth as a doctor, she chose to steel herself—but that still didn't excuse his shoddy penmanship. Triangulating his toddler text, Chang's broken English, and the squiggly blurs on the board, Maki was able to get a decent grasp on the day's lesson. Although it wasn't the math that she was focused on just then. Lined around Tristan's notebook was a series of caricatures that could have come straight out of a comic book.

"You draw?" Maki asked. He seemed genuinely surprised by her question—perhaps even a bit embarrassed.

Had he never shown anyone his artwork before?

"Uh, yeah," he said with a cough. "I guess you could say that. Not much, but I try. I'm going to apply for the mechanical engineering program at RU, so it helps to know how to sketch."

"Oh," Makiko said. She pointed to a few of the sketches. There was a seagull wearing a backpack talking to what looked like a Hispanic shark holding maracas riding a hoverboard. "That's not bad."

"Thanks," Tristan smiled. "So, what about you?"

"What?" Maki asked.

"Are you planning on going to college?" he asked. She looked down at her notes and frowned. Her response came after a brief delay.

"—Pre-med," she said with an involuntary frown, "Also at RU."

Tristan raised his eyebrows and nodded with a pouted lower lip.

"That's pretty cool," he said. "So, you want to be a doctor?" Maki sighed and continued jotting down her notes.

"I guess so." She shrugged.

Another awkward silence passed. Tristan picked up the conversation this time.

"I've heard the program there's pretty competitive. You must be pretty smart."

Maki shrugged again. "I just study, that's all."

Her cell phone vibrated. She checked it under the table to see a text from Izzy.

"MAKIIIIIII!" it read. "I've got some AMAZING news!! I've gotta tell you the next time I see you! I'm so, so, SO excited!!!!!!"

"Well," Makiko thought, "she's acting like herself again." Suddenly it hit her.

"Of course; Izzy must have said something to him. I hate it when people act like I have some sort of *disability.*"

Frowning, she shoved her phone into her pocket.

"You really don't have to do this," Maki said flatly.

"Do what?" Tristan responded, quizzically. She spelled it out for him.

"Act all nice to me because of what happened the other day. It's fine."

His voice became firm. "I wasn't acting. I just thought I'd say hi, that's all." His eyes fell to his notebook, suddenly somber. "Sorry, I didn't mean to bother you."

"Don't worry about it," she said, more quietly than she had hoped.

After a long hour of incoherent mumbling and blurry equations, the bell rang. Tristan was the first to stand. He turned toward the girl.

"It was nice seeing you again, *Maki,*" he said with a smile. She did her best to return a faint one of her own.

"...See you later," she replied faintly. Tristan nodded and left the classroom. Makiko gathered her things and stood, watching the boy disappear into the crowd.

She sighed and exited the building.

Upon opening the house doors to the Roosevelt Charter theater, Makiko Nakamura was immediately greeted by a welcoming, acrid scent. Students dressed in paint-splattered overalls were applying primer to the theater's massive cyclorama at the rear of the stage. She had nearly approached the front of the house when Izzy appeared from behind the stage left tormentor. She was dressed for manual labor. Her golden hair was pulled back in a loose ponytail and was tucked under a pale blue cap that matched her denim overalls. She was holding a comically oversized paint roller that dwarfed her nearly six-foot frame—all of which was covered in white paint. She gave Maki a wave with a bright smile.

Izzy turned to the wing and shouted, *"She's heeeeeeeerrrrrreeeeeee!"* She returned her gaze to her friend and beckoned her to come onstage. Maki set her bag down on one of the first-row seats and vaulted onto the stage. They started to hug before realizing that would be an awful idea. They found a brief chuckle and nod to be preferable to Maki covering her favorite jacket in paint.

"What's going on?" she asked.

"You know Jenny? Jenny Salvador?" Izzy replied, her voice low.

"The one with the weird laugh?" Maki asked with a raised eyebrow. Izzy's face turned red as she shushed her. After throwing her head around the room to make sure no one had heard, Izzy breathed a sigh of relief and laughed.

"Yes, *her*," she continued. "She was our crew's lead painter. She was supposed to paint our back wall for our cabaret but she... uh..." she stammered.

"Little Miss Snort Snort?"" A flamboyant senior chimed in as he strutted past the girls with a paint bucket. "Her dad is sick. She's taking the semester off to help care for him."

"What he said," Izzy said, ruefully; jerking a thumb in the direction of her sassy friend. "David, this is Maki. Maki, David is one of our costumers."

David extended a tattooed arm in Maki's direction. She accepted the limp-fish handshake with a smile. "So, you're Maki," he began. "I've heard so much about you." He lifted her hand almost as if to kiss it. "Love your gloves. And with the jacket and the hair—Izzy, you never told me your best friend was such a femme fatale!"

Makiko wasn't sure whether she should blush or puke. She settled for a hesitant chuckle and a word of thanks. Maki never understood the eccentricities of theatre people. She was grateful that her friend was a musician. Entirely different breed of nerd.

"I'm sorry to hear about Jenny," Maki said.

"She's doing alright," said David. "The cast and crew put together a care package for her."

"Her dad's in rough shape, but he should pull through," Izzy said. "The doctor said that Jenny being there is really lifting his spirits, aiding his recovery. Does that really work?"

"That's wonderful news," Maki smiled before nodding. "Attitude is everything. Your body is a machine. All the parts need to be functioning for survival. That's why there have been so many studies done on holistic medicine—"

"Miss Nakamura?" a husky voice cut in from behind. Suddenly, Izzy stood up straighter, as if at attention. David in contrast remained relaxed and began to open another can of primer. Out from the wing came a short, stout, dark-skinned woman sporting prescription lenses and a purple bandana to hold back her dreadlocks. Her small stature was offset by the briskness and authority of her walk.

"Yes ma'am?" Maki said, hesitantly. Compared to David's greeting, this woman's handshake was an unexpected vice grip. She reminded Maki of an ant: small and mighty.

"I'm Dr. Kinley, but you can just call me Debbie."

"Nice to meet you Doct—Debbie." Maki could never wrap her head around arts teachers and their eccentricities. They all seemed so informal compared to the ones in STEM.

"Izzy told me that you're quite the painter. As you could probably tell, we're down our best Monet," Debbie explained.

"When I found out about what happened to Jenny," Izzy interjected, "I told Debbie about how you used to paint for our stage crew back in middle school." Debbie nodded in verification.

"I did," Maki said, flattered. "But I don't know. It was a pretty long time ago. I've been out of practice for a while."

"Nonsense!" Debbie shouted. "Art is like riding a bike. You never really forget. Besides, the cabaret is coming up in two months and we're desperate. Those landscapes you painted were simply breathtaking! You really should consider working for a commission." Maki shot Izzy with a surprised glare. Her head retreated into her shoulders like a frightened turtle.

"Thanks," she said, "I'm glad you liked them. I only ever post them on a *private account.*" Makiko punctuated the final two words by leaning closer to her friend. Izzy's jawbone was in her clavicle. Debbie was too hyper-focused on the topic at hand to acknowledge her indiscretion.

"The goal is to give the cyclorama the impression of Starlight Hill," Debbie explained, crossing stage right as she examined the priming process. Nearly all of the oceanic views of last year's pirate musical had already been covered. She spread her arms wide as she looked toward the heavens—or one of the busted overhead bulbs.

"A bit of local culture to accentuate the magic of the arts taking place here at RC." She dropped her arms. "Or at least that's what the program's going to say." Debbie returned her gaze to Makiko. "Think you can do it?"

Maki took a few steps back to take in the full view of the cyclorama. She envisioned a stream of primer coasting along the wall, streaking it stark white from stage right to left. A pencil sketch began to form on the oversized wall. Hills, valleys, grass, distant buildings, the moon—all rapidly scratched themselves into her mind's eye and onto the oversized canvas before her. Suddenly, the hills bloomed shades of green, highlighted by the purple overtones of the sky. The buildings were silhouetted by the light of the rising moon, whose brightness was comparable only to the lights of the thousands of blue stars that punctuated the night sky. She opened her eyes and smiled at the teacher.

"How soon can I get started?"

THE LOVER'S GHOST

ENTERING THE LOBBY of her apartment complex, Makiko checked the time.

"Gah!" she snarled. "Dad's gonna kill me."

Her cellphone was loaded with missed calls and texts from her father. She tried to explain that she would be back late, but she wasn't brave enough to admit why. An intelligent man, her father was easily able to poke holes in her explanations and clearly wasn't satisfied with her hiding behind a veil of gossamer excuses.

The truth was that Makiko had spent an additional three hours at the theater, drafting preliminary sketches for the various backdrops that could be used for the show. Her passion for art was akin to a woman suppressing an addiction. Just the tiniest taste of it had sent her into a full-blown relapse.

On instinct, she hit the button to call the elevator. She was so caught up in her worries that it took her a full minute to notice the "out-of-order" sign on the steel doors. She cussed and proceeded to the stairwell. Makiko prayed throughout her ascent, asking the Holy Spirit to guide her toward the proper words she needed to face her father. On the tenth floor, she thanked God for inspiring her to keep up long-distance running.

After a few minutes, she had finally ascended to the fifteenth-floor landing. She pushed open the heavy metal door with a grunt and entered the white and gray corridor that led to her apartment. Standing outside her unit, she steeled herself with a sigh before unlocking the door.

Her father was in the living room to her right, seated on a pale green couch in front of their television. He shut off the TV, grabbed his cane, and stood.

"Hello, Dad," Maki greeted sheepishly. Unable to meet his eyes, she was happy to spin around and bolt the door shut behind her. Her father remained silent, limping closer. When she turned back around, Masashi was glaring at her with folded arms.

"Do you have any idea what time it is?" he demanded. His daughter gulped.

"I'm sorry Dad—"

"Apologizing doesn't change the clock," he snapped. "You were supposed to be home two hours ago. I reached out to you over and over again and you kept dodging my questions. Each time I called, you rejected it and responded with a text."

"I'm sorry, Dad. I was busy."

"Busy?! You could have been dead!" Masashi shouted. His wooden cane clicked against the dark oak floors as he paced the apartment. His daughter stared at her feet with shoulders raised in humiliation.

"How could I have known if someone had you locked up in the boot of a car and was texting me on your behalf?"

"I know. I said I was sor—"

"Again, 'sorry' doesn't change reality, Makiko." Masashi sighed and walked past the island countertop to Maki's left. He seated himself in one of the wooden dining chairs.

"Listen," he began in a calmer tone. "I know you can take care of yourself. That's not why I was worried." He looked at his daughter with an expression that made her squirm. "I know you're lying to me."

"Dad, I—"

"I asked you a thousand times today, but I'll ask you again: where were you?" Maki's gaze fell on the sakura painting hanging in the living room. The cherry blossoms were still being swept away by the current. She gulped. Knowing she had no other options, she told her father the truth.

"Izzy's singing in a recital this winter," she began. "They lost their lead set painter and her theater teacher asked me to step in."

"No," Masashi said firmly.

"But Dad, I—"

"The answer is *no*. You're not at Roosevelt to paint, Maki. You're not going to make any money as some landscape artist."

"But Mom was always—"

"Your mother," Masashi cut her off, "was an amazing painter." He rose from the table and circled the living room, gesturing at the multitude of paintings created by his wife. "And I know you are, too."

Maki almost smiled at the compliment. Her father walked over and put his hands on her shoulders.

"But you're never going to make a living that way." He brushed aside her bangs. "You're smart. So, so, so smart. Too smart to let such a beautiful mind go to waste."

Feelings of paternal warmth rapidly shifted into unbridled rage. Maki gripped her father's arms and threw them down to his sides.

"No!" she shouted. "You never listen! You don't care about me! You just care about your image!"

"How dare you raise your voice to me, young lady!" Masashi shouted back.

"You just want to put me on a pedestal and say, 'Oh, look I have a doctor in the family!'"

"You know full well that that's not true! I'm setting you on a path to success!"

"You're ruining my life, that's what you're doing!"

"Go to your room!" he screamed, violently pointing his cane finger down the hall.

"Go to my room?" Makiko shook her head incredulously. "I'm almost eighteen. You can't just say—"

"I pay the rent, I made you, you do as I say!"

"But—"

"GO!" he bellowed. *"NOW!"*

Overcome by so many intense, conflicting emotions, Makiko felt herself beginning to shake. She bit her tongue and stormed down the hall into her bedroom. She slammed the door behind her and hopped onto her bed. A set of yellow eyes burned into the back of Maki's head. Her old Neko Nikki stuffed animal stared at her from the foot of the bed. She lifted the orange cat to her chest and rested her head on his. His blue bowtie tickled her neck as she buried her face into a pillow and wept.

There was a thunderstorm outside. A common occurrence in Okinawa during this part of the year. Normally, this weather blessed the residents of 33 Sakuraba Drive with comforting sounds to fall asleep to. Unfortunately for them, rest was hard to come by.

It was 1 am and most of the lights were off. Occasional lightning strikes would illuminate the low wooden furniture that made up a majority of the house's interior. Masashi Nakamura paced across the polished hinoki floors of his three-bedroom home. The right side of his hip was still in agony from the collision.

A small child wept in his arms.

It didn't matter that his body was on fire. He would walk on glass for his little girl.

At long last, a pair of headlights shone in from the front windows, providing a break in the monotony of nature's intermittent flashes. Drenched from the rain, Yoko Daniels entered the house. Masashi greeted his sister with a hug. The rainwater disguised her tears as her brother remained stoic in silence. Jonathan entered with his bags soon after, offering condolences of his own.

"Come here, sweetheart," Yoko said, taking the little girl into her arms. Makiko hugged her aunt as she continued to sob.

After several minutes of pacing and unpacking, the guests reclined at the kitchen table with evening coffees. Maki was still in the arms of her aunt—still upset, but quiet. Jonathan returned from the guest room with a bundle in his arms.

"Yoko?" he said, getting his wife's attention. She smiled at him and nodded in acknowledgment.

"Makiwara," Yoko began, "your uncle John and I got something for you. Do you want to see?" Maki hesitated before nodding. John gave the bundle to his niece-in-law who unwrapped it. Her frown instantly disappeared when she saw what was inside.

"Neko Nikki!" she cheered, pulling the bright orange cat to her in a tight hug.

"Your daddy told me you loved that show," Jonathan said in English. Yoko translated for her husband.

"We saw it in the city and knew you had to have it," Yoko added with a smile.

"Thank you," Maki said quietly.

"You're welcome Makiwara," Yoko said. "Now, it's late. Let's put you to bed."

"But I want to stay up with you and Uncle Johnny..." she protested sleepily. Makiko let out a big yawn and closed her eyes.

"I'll lay her down," Yoko announced before leaving the room. Her husband and brother sipped coffee in silence until her return.

"Yoko," Masashi began with an unmistakable solemnity in his voice. "The toy. It wasn't for Makiko, was it?"

Yoko gazed down at the coffee in her mug and silently shook her head. Masashi sniffled with a frown.

"Mamoru would have... would have..." he couldn't complete the sentence. "...Th—thank you."

Yoko sidled over to her brother and put her arm around him.

He was awakened by the ringing of his cell phone.

"He—hello?" Masashi answered. He looked at the alarm clock. "Yoko, it's 2 am? What's going on?"

Makiko jumped at the knock on her door. She was even more surprised by the somber tone of her father's muffled voice that came in from the other side.

"Honey, can I come in?"

Makiko returned her cell phone to her nightstand, walked to the door, and opened it. She returned to sit on the side of her bed as her father entered. Tension lingered in the air as Masashi struggled to find the right words.

"Makiko... do you *really* like painting?"

Maki looked away and hesitated before nodding. The familiarity of the gesture was not lost on her father. He shuddered.

"I do," Maki said softly.

Masashi walked around the room, examining the high school art and passion projects hanging on the walls. There were a few portraits of celebrities in stippled graphite and charcoal experimentations, but small canvas paintings dominated the scene. Everywhere, these acrylic, oil, and watercolor paintings depicted vistas from all over the world. Masashi had always been impressed that his daughter had inherited his wife's talent, but he had to be responsible. It was his duty to teach *her* to be responsible, too. But still…

"I'll make a deal with you," he said. He placed his hands in his pockets and looked at the floor. "If you can promise me that you'll keep a 4.0 this year, you can paint for the show."

Maki sprung up from the bed and answered her father with a bear hug. Masashi smiled and returned the gesture.

"Thank you, Daddy," she said, beaming.

TRISTAN UND ISOLDE

"HONEY, ARE YOU FEELING ALRIGHT?"

Izzy jumped at her father's sudden inquiry.

"Wha—?" she gasped stupidly.

It was early Saturday morning. Izzy had been lost in thought: ruminating on her preparations for the cabaret. She hadn't realized she had been tugging at a strand of hair above her left ear. A nervous habit of hers.

"Oh, yeah, I—I'm okay. Yeah," she said. Izzy took her hand away from her head and watched as a few strands landed on the cafe table she had been wiping down. Frantically, she scooped them up with a paper towel. "What makes you think I'm not okay?"

Her father ignored the biohazard she had just spawned and mended.

"You just seem a little anxious, that's all." Gilbert shrugged sympathetically. He proceeded to flip over the rest of the upturned dining chairs from their tables. "Is school getting you down?"

"Um... not really," Izzy said nervously. "I mean, I've got an AP English presentation coming up that I'd like to get the jump on soon, but I've got some time."

"And the recital?"

Izzy gulped.

"...Making progress." She winced.

"I think you're working too hard," Gilbert said, punctuating his statement with a utilitarian crumb-filled palm swipe of the table he had been setting. He speed-walked to the cafe's front door, unlatched the lock, and flip the sign to "Open" before going behind the counter to check if the cutlery was in order.

"I'm glad Maki joined the team," he continued. "She's a great friend."

At this, Izzy couldn't help but smile.

"Yeah," she said, "she is." Izzy was about to begin bussing the next few tables but her father waved for her to stop. She joined him on a barstool at the counter. They spent the next few minutes watching the morning commuters race their way to their shifts on the Isle. Izzy was the one to break the silence.

"She's such a good artist, Dad," she said morosely.

"She is, honey," he responded, just as downcast.

"I just," Izzy stammered, "I just wish that she could—"

"I know," Gilbert interrupted. "But it's not our place to say anything."

"I know," she whispered.

After another minute of car watching, the door opened and Izzy greeted their first customer of the day.

"*Tristan!*" Izzy cheered with an animated wave. "Hi! Welcome back!"

Startled, Tristan approached the counter.

"Oh, uh… hi Izzy!" he replied, smiling back. "Hello sir." He greeted Gilbert with a nod.

Izzy's father replied with a cordial "hello" as he and his daughter hopped off their stools and circled behind the counter. The man turned his back on the kids as he busied himself with some silverware that needed polishing. Facing Tristan, Izzy began running her hands up and down her hair as though she were operating a pulley system.

"So, what'll it be today?" she asked perhaps a bit too eagerly. "We've got cappuccinos, flat whites, cold brews—"

"Izzy! Just let him read the menu!" Gilbert interrupted with a laugh.

"Oops, sorry!" Izzy espoused with a flinch. "Take your time!"

Tristan couldn't help but chuckle.

"That's alright!" he said as he examined the menu. "Um... actually, I think I'll try the cold brew."

"Sure!" Izzy chirped. She hit a button on the touchscreen before gesturing to the flashing POS in front of him.

"*Chip*, I remember!" Tristan said with a smile. His self-deprecation drew a nervous laugh from the girl.

"And you want this *with* milk?" she countered.

"Yes."

Izzy tapped her temple with her pointer finger.

"*I* remember!" she stated firmly. As Izzy turned to prep the order, Tristan inserted his card into the machine and examined the filigree on the wall that had piqued his interest the last time he was here. There was the fireman's ax with a plaque beneath it. It was still difficult to make out, but it appeared to date back to the terror attack from when he was a kid. Presumably, the owner was retired RIFD. Alongside a series of photos was the family portrait Tristan didn't get a chance to examine so closely last time. It depicted the opening day of the cafe. A younger version of Gil stood next to a woman bearing a striking resemblance to Izzy. Between the couple was a little blonde girl smiling with her arms stretched high above her head.

"Oh, so you're um...?" Tristan said, gesturing to the photograph. Izzy looked at him from over her shoulder before following the direction of his gesture with her eyes. Her father cut in.

"Yeah, that's right!" he said, walking over to the counter with a smile. "Gil White. Pleased to meet you." After nearly breaking Tristan's hand with his vice grip, he continued. "We've been open for about 13 years now. That was from opening day."

Tristan nodded. "Very cute." He looked back at Izzy. "Nice weekend job, too."

She shrugged and smiled. "It has its moments."

At the sound of the dissonant beep, Tristan removed his debit card from the terminal. He returned it to its rightful home in his wallet and took a seat at the counter.

"You know," he began, "Maki and I share a class together. I sat with her yesterday."

"Oh, did you?" Izzy replied with raised eyebrows.

"She seemed to feel a little guilty about what happened last time. She seems really nice."

"Yeah, she is," Izzy said with a frown. She placed the concoction she had made in front of the boy and stared in silence— her eyes darting between the glass and his eyes. After a few volleys, Tristan let her score and took a sip. She stood with the posture of a nascent boxer: shoulders raised to her ears, elbows bent, and her fists eagerly tapping at the knuckles in front of her mouth. The drink had so much milk in it that he could barely taste the coffee.

"Mmm, that's delicious," Tristan said, forcing a smile. "Thanks."

"Yay! I mean, welcome. Haha!" she cried, bouncing up and down on her toes. Tristan thought he saw her father shake his head. He couldn't help but chuckle, himself.

After an awkward bit of silence that was occasionally perforated by the clinking of silverware, Izzy resumed.

"So, I take it you're more into the sciences?" she asked. Tristan rapidly swallowed what remained in his mouth and tapped his lips with a serviette.

"Yup. Applying for mechanical engineering next year." He placed his napkin down and looked up. "You?"

"Music!" she chimed with an involuntary pop of the shoulder and tilt of the head.

"Really? At RU?" Tristan asked in surprise. Izzy nodded. "That's so interesting! I didn't even know there was a music program at over there."

"Yeah." Izzy rubbed the back of her neck with her hand. "It's a really small department, but that just means you'd get to know all your professors on a first-name basis! Most classes have about twenty students maximum." She paused for a beat. "Golly, your math lectures would probably be *gigantic* in comparison!"

"Yeah, they're definitely going to be crowed for sure," Tristan agreed. "So, do you sing or play anything?" he asked as Izzy groped beneath the counter for something. She straightened up nodding with a bottle of hand sanitizer.

"Mm-hmm! I'm a singer!" The cheery girl beamed; generously coating her hands with the gel.

"Wow, that's awesome!" Tristan exclaimed. At this, Izzy looked at the floor and appeared to blush. For Tristan, that was a first for him. Her eyes flitted back in his direction. His face grew hot in turn.

"Thanks!" She exhaled. "I've always wanted to act, honestly," she admitted with another shoulder pop that was more of a half-shrug than a cartoonish flirt.

"Oh, like on Broadway, you mean?"

"Yeah!" Izzy smiled, her cheeriness returning. "But the more I train, the more I want to do *opera*. Classical singing is *WAY* different from what you hear on the radio or even in Times Square." Her eyes went to an indeterminable spot over his shoulder. Speaking mostly with her hands, her words increased to a rate that would rival an auctioneer.

"I've always had a kind of *full* sound to my voice, you know? I do the plays and musicals at RC, but the leads always go to the same people. Kind of a popularity contest, I guess. So, I decided to keep on studying, training, and singing in the advanced choirs and music theory classes. Pretty soon, when I had to decide on a school to go to, I knew there were a myriad of options available, but I didn't want to have to travel so far. Plus, Roosevelt University had a rather reputable choral department considering its ties to the theatrical district, so it seemed to be a good fit.

"Anyway, back to my voice. My tessitura is naturally quite high, but I've got a resonant timbre, so it never fit so well with traditional theatrical roles—I mean, let's face it, I'm no Disney princess. But it *does* seem to mesh pretty well with the role of a *dramatic soprano* as opposed to a *coloratura*—"

"Sorry, come again?" Tristan's head was spinning. Thankfully, this interruption snapped the girl out of her reverie.

"Oh, sorry!" Izzy exclaimed with a wince. Looking over her shoulder, she saw her father give her a knowing look before returning to his polishing with a grin. Izzy spread her hands wide and deliberately reduced her pace. "*Really big sound.* As opposed to being super agile and jumping around all over the place." Mr. White walked over a bin of polished cutlery and retreated into the back room. Izzy nodded and got to work on rolling them into the cloth napkins before placing them into a nearby translucent tub.

"Ah." Tristan nodded, genuinely impressed. "That's ...*incredible.* I've never met anyone who wanted to do that before!"

At this, the girl internally squealed—rocking back and forth on her toes and bobbing her head with an intoxicatingly bubbly smile that stretched from ear to ear.

"Thanks!" she chimed. "So, what got you into engineering?" she asked, gesturing a spoon in his direction. Knowing his answer, Tristan looked into his nearly empty glass and externally laughed as he internally cussed himself. He told her the truth.

"I want to be a coaster designer. You know, for theme parks."

"No way, that's so cool!" Izzy exclaimed. Tristan met her eyes and laughed.

"Not as cool as music, but it's not too bad!" he countered—just thankful that she didn't laugh. "I've loved them ever since I was a kid." The girl placed a knuckle on her flaring hip.

"Well, *I* like roller coasters," she said matter-of-factly. Without missing a beat, Mr. White slid his head out from behind the employee door behind the counter.

"Lying's a sin, Izzy," he said, disappearing as quickly as he came. Izzy dropped her confident visage.

"Okay, I'm *terrified* of roller coasters," she admitted. "You must be pretty brave."

"I'm glad you think so," Tristan said with a laugh. "They're actually really fun!"

"Growing up, my dad could *NEVER* get me on any of those things."

Tristan downed the last of his milk with a side of coffee before responding.

"Well, you could always start small and work your way up. Start with Disney, then Universal, then Six Flags." Izzy picked up his glass and lifted her eyes while keeping her head down.

"Well," she said, her volume noticeably reduced. "Maybe if you went on one with me, I'd try it." Her father returned behind the counter with a raised eyebrow. Tristan tugged at the collar of his shirt.

"Wha—what do you mean?" he asked apprehensively. Undoubtedly having detected his tone, Izzy winced. Her face grew bright red as her character reverted from hopeless romantic to hopelessly lost.

"Oh!" she gasped. "I—I meant if someone *like you* went on one with me—you know? Like a friend who knew a lot about the way the ride works to help me calm down, *then* I'd try it!" Her father was shaking his head, smirking.

"Oh... uh... of course!" Tristan said, stammering as well. "Yeah, I get that!" Looking for something to do with his hands now that his fidget toy in the form of a milky cold brew was gone, he checked the time on his phone. Izzy tilted her head like a concerned golden retriever, sending a pound of voluminous golden hair cascading toward the ground. The adorability of the sight was blighted only by the perturbed expression she had scrawled across her face.

"Oh, sorry. Am I bothering you?" she inquired with a frown. "I know I have a tendency to ramble." Rapidly, Tristan glanced up.

"What? Oh, no—not at all! It's just that I have to take the S train and I wasn't sure how long I had." He gestured toward the door behind him. "The station's right outside, so I've got another minute or two."

"Oh, I see!" Izzy smiled. She leaned forward, resting her elbows on the counter and resting her head on a closed fist. "So, where are you off to next?" Feeling as though she had stepped out of bounds, she straightened up and placed an apologetic hand on her heart. "If you don't mind my asking, of course."

Tristan smiled at her. "No, it's alright. I'm heading across the bridge to the hospital."

The girl wrapped one arm around her torso and placed the fingertips of the opposite hand on her oversaturated scarlet lips. She was just a few Ben-Day dots short of a Lichtenstein painting.

"Oh no, are you feeling alright?!" she exclaimed in shock.

"I'm fine, don't worry!" Tristan replied, raising his palms. "Thanks, though. I'm visiting my little brother. He's very sick."

Izzy pouted her ample lower lip. "Oh gosh, I'm so sorry. I hope he gets better!"

"I'm sure he will…" he responded unconvincingly. Unable to meet her eye, he looked away. Even less convincingly, he said, "he always pulls through."

"What's his name?" she asked.

"William. He's ten."

"*Aww…*" Izzy cooed, somberly. Just then, she reached into the oversized front pocket of her shamrock green apron and pulled out a small notebook and pen, presumably used for taking orders.

"We can add him to the prayer list at church if you want!" she cheered. Suddenly, her expression turned dour. "I mean, um… sorry, I probably should have asked before—"

"No, no—that's really sweet of you, actually," Tristan interjected. "It's William Collins." She copied the name down with a smile.

"Collins… Are you Irish?" she asked.

"Yeah, I am."

"Oh my gosh, *me too!!*" She gasped, slamming the notebook onto the countertop in front of her.

"Really?" Tristan asked. "I've got some family in England but most of them are in Cork. I'm a first-gen American. My parents were immigrants."

"Wow, that's so cool!" Izzy said, impressed. "I'm second gen—no… third, I think." She looked toward her father with a puzzled expression. "Yeah, because Grandpa and Grandma were first, right?" Mr. White walked over and put a hand on her shoulder.

"Yup," said Gilbert. "You'll have to forgive my daughter; math was never her strong suit."

"*DADDY!*" Izzy shouted with a stamp of her foot. Gilbert walked back to the other side of the counter in raucous laughter.

"I'm just saying!" he called out over his shoulder.

"Well," Tristan said, rising to leave, "I've got to go. But it was really nice getting to see you again, Izzy."

"Oh, already?" she said with a pout. "I'll be praying for you and your brother."

Tristan had fully planned on thanking her and walking out the door. All he had to do was get on the train and go to the hospital. Yet despite his convictions, he found himself unable to take his eyes off the notebook resting on the counter.

"Thanks," he said, before pointing to Izzy's notebook. "Can I see that for a second?" She raised an eyebrow in genuine confusion before sliding it over.

"Uh, yeah. Sure," she said in polite confoundment. Tristan jotted down his name and number before returning it to her. After the initial shock wore off, a gentle smile appeared. It wasn't quite as perceptible as her previous beams, but it was definitely there.

"We should grab lunch sometime," he said as he swung his gray and cerulean bag onto his back. "It'd be fun to chat with you some more."

It took her a moment to respond. "Yeah, definitely. That would be fun!" Izzy was silent for a little while longer as Tristan approached the door. "I'll text you later so you have my number, too!" she shouted so he could hear her. "See you later, Tristan!"

"See you at school!" he said with a smile and wave as he exited the cafe.

After the doors closed, Izzy felt the burn of her father's eyes on the back of her head. She turned to see Gilbert staring at her with a smirk that was more befitting of her coworker than her father.

"Don't look at me like that!" She turned away, laughing.

ADVICE FROM A SYNESTHETE

MAKIKO WAS FIFTEEN FEET off the ground, painting the cyclorama a bright blue. Izzy was pacing beneath her, reviewing her music. Dr. Nightengale, her private vocal coach, had really been pushing her hard lately. This was too much, but she had to rehearse. No other choice. Every day was consumed by a mixture of homework, vocal exercises, rehearsals, and stress baking. And worst of all, she couldn't stop pulling her hair.

Makiko looked down at her friend, watching as strands of her luminous yellow hair glinted in the light as they glided to the floor behind her like a trail of pixie dust. She sighed and looked at her wooden painter's palate. Colors had always soothed her in a way that she couldn't explain. She figured she didn't need to, since she was sure everyone else felt the same. Right?

No.

Makiko frowned, remembering Izzy's problem. While she was no longer sensitive about the topic, Maki made a point to avoid bringing up her friend's colorblindness too often. She sighed, knowing that her friend would likely never understand the way painting made her feel. Though perhaps talking about it would help distract her from her thoughts.

Couldn't hurt to try.

"You know, I've always really enjoyed the color aqua," Maki called out to Izzy below. "It tastes delicious, like refreshing toothpaste or a cold glass of ice water with just the hint of a milky texture to it... like when you drink it after a good workout."

Izzy stopped dead in her tracks. It took a few moments for her brain to transition from internal anxiety to general confusion.

"Wait, what?" she asked, looking up.

"What?" Maki glanced down.

"Did you just say you can taste a color?" Izzy asked perplexedly.

"Yeah." Maki continued painting. A moment later she stopped and furrowed her brows. She looked back down at her friend. "Wait, are you saying that's not—?"

Izzy shook her head, her mouth agape. Maki put her hands on her hips.

"You *don't* know what aqua tastes like?"

Izzy paused then shook her head.

"...*No!*" she shouted.

Maki descended the ladder. She contorted her expression in concentration.

"What about days of the week?" Maki asked. "Like how Tuesdays and Thursdays are yellow like the letter *C*, and Fridays are red like *F*?"

Izzy's expression remained horrified.

"That's... not normal either, Maki," she said slowly, shaking her head.

Maki paused to think again. "*G* isn't purple?"

"...No Maki..." Izzy responded slowly as if trying hard to explain a basic concept to a child. "Colors don't mean things... or have flavors..."

Maki considered this notion before dismissing it with a wave of her hand. "...Well, you're colorblind, you wouldn't know." Spotting David in the wing, she got his attention with a wave.

"Hey, David! The color scarlet tastes like a Big Mac, right?"

"Did you hit your head or something?" he shouted back.

Maki looked back at Izzy with a shrug.

"Well, as far as I'm concerned, you're *both* nuts."

Maki reloaded her brush with paint before hopping back on the ladder. It was clear to her that Izzy was getting herself worked up about the big show. Naturally, as her best friend in the whole wide world, it was Maki's duty to get under her skin as much as possible.

"Don't even get me started about colors and subjects," Maki began with a smirk.

"Yes, please don't," Izzy replied with a frown, looking back down at her vocal score.

"Math as a *subject* is red, yeah, but not all kinds. Calculus and geometry are red, but trig is green, algebra is blue—"

"Okay, you're really starting to freak me out!" Izzy exclaimed, lowering her music.

"You're a musician, though!" Maki said, pointing at her friend with her brush. "You don't feel colors when you listen to music?

"NO!" Izzy shouted.

"Well, that's why I go along with your Shimomura and Debussy nonsense. They're both super colorful."

"THAT was what you meant?" Izzy cried, utterly stupefied. "I thought you were being metaphorical!"

Maki tilted her head. "That's used as a metaphor?"

"YES!"

"No!" Maki began to gesticulate with her hands, painting an invisible picture in the air:

"Okay hear me out: to me, the music *literally* feels like biting into a dense deli sandwich. The kind with the really thick, golden-toasted bread, packed with all sorts of different flavors and condiments. As the flavors pirouette on your tastebuds, you look up and peer into a starfield lit by a kaleidoscope of beams of neon light—only you feel the beams dance inside your chest and across your shoulder blades instead of seeing them. It's filling and delicious—not to mention beautiful. The cool night breeze feels super refreshing, too: like aqua or robin egg blue. Sometimes I listen to it when I'm feeling a craving so I don't stress-eat. Other times it backfires and just makes me really hungry.

"Do you ever feel that way sometimes?" Maki asked, looking back down at her friend. Izzy's arms hung at her sides as her left eye began to twitch. She proceeded to scream as she repeatedly slammed her music into her face. David stuck his head out from the wing.

"Is she alright?" he asked.

"I don't know, she's weird." Maki shrugged.

"*I'm* weird?" Izzy shouted. "Look who's talking! You're crazy!" she exclaimed with a laugh.

"Oh, *I'm* crazy?" Maki called back. Quickly, she descended the ladder and pointed the paintbrush at her friend. "What about you? Huh?"

"Uh, what about me?" Izzy scoffed as she playfully pushed the brush aside. Maki smirked one of those scary smirks that Izzy knew always spelt mischief.

"How long have you had that boy's number in your phone?"

"Oh my gosh, not this again," Izzy blushed as she stepped away. Maki cut in front of her path.

"Like, a day or two…" Izzy posited.

"Try THREE!" Maki held up her fingers in front of her friend's face. "Three days, Izzy."

Izzy shook her head. "Yeah, so?"

"So, you've had it for three days but haven't made plans to meet up?" Maki asked.

"Isn't that his job?"

"Well yeah, but if he doesn't have the guts to ask, you're going to have to be the one to extend the invitation." Maki asserted in her usual forthright manner.

"I don't know, Maki… You know how terrible I am with these things."

"Keep it simple. Invite him to the park tomorrow."

Izzy looked horrified. "No! I barely even know him!"

"That's the whole point! How else are you going to get to know him?"

"I don't know…" She looked down at her script. Her mind was obviously preoccupied with other matters. She thought for a moment and sighed. "I'll invite him if you promise to come with me."

"Me?" Maki blurted out in surprise. "Are you serious? Izzy, this could be a date."

"I don't know if I want it to be or not," Izzy said, anxiously.

"Well, how will you know if you don't go?"

"I won't go unless you come with me," she countered firmly, crossing her arms.

Maki paused and tried to read her friend's expression. It wasn't the visage she'd expected.

"I thought you said you liked him?" she asked. Izzy shook her head and shrugged.

"I said I thought that he was 'cute,' not that I was in love with him, Maki." She sighed and approached the edge of the stage. She and her friend sat and dangled their legs off the side.

"He seems really nice," Izzy admitted. "But I don't want to go crazy. I shouldn't be so impulsive."

"Izzy, you're literally just eating together in the park. Couldn't possibly be more casual. Plus, I'll be there."

"Why does part of me now think that'll just make me more nervous?" She laughed.

"Would you rather do this alone?" Maki cocked her head to the side.

Izzy smiled and raised her eyebrows. "Definitely not."

Maki punched her friend on the arm.

"Then tomorrow it is," she cheered.

"Yes. Tomorrow." Izzy nodded.

LUNCHTIME

AFTER SCANNING THE PARK with a series of twirls, Izzy finally spotted her target. She frantically adjusted her cardigan and belongings—eager to look her best for the newcomers. Fifty feet away, Maki and Tristan were navigating the serpentine path concrete path. It was just after three, and Teddy Park was bustling with activity. Located just a block away from University Station, the modest park served as a reprieve for many beleaguered students looking for a bit of fresh air. Students at the local high school would often forgo their lunches during their designated period in favor of an afterschool outdoor picnic. By laying her belongings across a few seats, Izzy had managed to snag a wooden adjacent to a quaint stone fountain.

Finally, her guests approached.

"Izzy!" Tristan said with a smile, "It's great to see you again." Izzy rose to greet him. She eyed Maki over his shoulder—easy enough to do considering she was a good three inches taller than he was—pleading for help. Unsure of how to break the tension, they stood in a prolonged awkward silence. Makiko, finding the situation hilarious, offered no comment. The obvious confusion of whether or not to go for a hug settled on an awkward handshake.

Izzy removed her things from the seats and beckoned her guests to sit down. After exchanging pleasantries, the teens took out their bagged lunches and dug in. What had begun as a tense rendezvous with romantic undertones quickly transitioned into a cordial exchange among equally yoked friends. The trio bonded over their mutual dislike of math and began reviewing their notes.

Though Izzy was too insecure to say it, school came easy for her. Blessed with intelligence that made Maki envious—though she would never dare to say it—Izzy blasted through each school year without a second thought. Unfortunately for her, brains would make it difficult to relate to those around her. Finding the pop culture of her contemporaries to be nothing more than frivolous banalities, she would often try to introduce her own niche hyper fixations on others. Naturally, these attempts were often met with derision. Comments about her height. Her weight. Her nose. "What's *Final Fantasy?*" "*Zelda's* a kid's game." She'd heard it all.

But Maki was an outcast, too. An amazing friend who had always stuck with her from the beginning. She was glad to have her by her side today.

Intelligent as she was, math just wouldn't click for Izzy. She twirled her hair and tapped her pencil on the table in ever-mounting anxiety. Finally, she gave up.

"Maki, do you know how to solve this?" she asked. Makiko slammed her hands on the table and leaned forward.

"Why—because I'm *ASIAN?*" she sarcastically sneered. Izzy slammed her own hands onto the table and matched her pose.

"*YES,*" she said firmly. There was an awkward pause before Maki spun Izzy's notebook towards her with the fingertips of one hand. She scanned it for about two seconds before returning it to Izzy with another quick turn of her wrist.

"Negative cosecant theta," she said flatly. At this, Tristan couldn't help but snort with laughter. Maki held a finger up to Izzy's face.

"But that's not because I'm Asian," she said before jerking a thumb in his direction. "It's that Tristan's too much of an idiot to be of any help."

"Hey, why are you getting me involved?!" he protested.

Without looking, Maki held a flat palm in front of his face.

"Irish need not apply to this conversation!" she said, eyes fixed skyward before glancing at Izzy. "Except you. You can stay."

"Okay, wow," Tristan said. "That actually *was* offensive."

"Yeah, like I care." Maki shrugged as she bit into her tuna fish sandwich.

Tristan looked over at Izzy and asked, *"How are you friends with her?"* Izzy nearly spat out her drink from laughing.

"Thanks," Izzy said, coughing as her soda went down the wrong pipe. "I needed that."

"What's wrong?" Tristan asked.

"Oh, that's right." Maki cut in. "Don't you have to give some sort of presentation tomorrow?"

"Presentation?" Tristan asked.

"Music theory." Izzy nodded, screwing the cap back on her cola. She cleared her throat. "Yeah. I'm analyzing some music by Yoko Shimomura."

"Of course you are." Maki sighed and held her head, resting her elbow on the table.

"I've heard of her." Tristan joined in. "She's that video game composer, right?"

"Yep," said Maki, "Izzy's *obsessed* with her."

"Okay, I am *NOT* obsessed!" Izzy snapped defensively, raising her pointer finger.

"Sure, you aren't. Remember that day in the library?"

It was spring. In the silence of the Roosevelt Charter library, dozens of students were pouring over their notes and reference materials in preparation for finals. Izzy and Maki were seated at a table, side-by-side. Maki's nose was in a book while Izzy was joyfully bouncing up and down in her seat. Suddenly, she pulled off her headphones and shook her friend by the shoulders.

"Oh my gosh, I just realized 'Night of Tragedy' is in 5/4!" Izzy shouted. "How did I not know that until right now?! I feel so *stupid!*"

"*Shush!*" Maki retorted in sotto voce. Students at nearby tables were giving Izzy the stink eye. "What are you talking about, anyway?"

"The Realm of Darkness battle theme from *Birth by Sleep,* Maki! C'mon, keep up!" Izzy explained, nearly as loudly as before.

"What? Is that *Kingdom Hearts?*" she asked. Izzy nodded. "How on earth am I supposed to know that? I'm not a weeb like you!"

"But it's *so cool!*" Izzy continued, ignoring the derisive comment. "The only other ones I can think of off the top of my head are probably 'Night of Fate' and 'Hollow Bastion,' but since 'Scherzo' is in ¾, this is one of the only battle themes she did in an asymmetric meter for the entire series! Considering the titles and subject matter of the two 'Night' pieces, the more I think about it, the more sense it makes!" She slammed her fists on the table. "Ugh! How did I not realize this before?!"

Maki tried regaining her friend's attention with a tap on the shoulder, but Izzy shrugged her away. Regardless, Izzy went on faster than an auctioneer, completely lost in thought.

"Well, I mean, there *is* 'Omnis Lacrima' which uses *hemiola*— even though it was conducted in a straight ¾ when they performed it live in London which makes absolutely *no sense* to me *and* they slowed it down, but as Leon says, 'beggars can't be choosers.' What I mean is, I guess, you *could say* that *Final Fantasy* really is the same—"

Mrs. Jensen—an older librarian who was well-acquainted with Izzy's peculiarities—tapped her hand on the table, snapping Izzy out of her reverie for a moment.

"Izzy?" she said. "You're doing it again."

"Oh, yeah." Izzy blushed and pulled her hair back. "Sorry. I'll quiet down."

Makiko, meanwhile, was simultaneously fuming and trying not to burst at the seams from laughter.

As soon as the librarian rounded the corner, Izzy continued—this time, in a loud whisper directly in Maki's ear.

"But if you *were* to count *Final Fantasy* as part of *Kingdom Hearts*, you'd have to count *Assassin's Creed,* too, because they had that crossover event where you could get a chocobo in *Origins* and Noctis could dress like Altair. But Yoko Shimomura never composed music for *Assassin's Creed,* so it depends if you're going by degrees of separation or just by the games she scored because it could really go either way—"

"IZZY, SHUT UP!" Maki shouted back.

Izzy bit her lip and blushed.

"Okay, maybe a *little,"* she admitted.

"Has she *always* been like this?" Tristan asked with a laugh.

"Yeah." Maki nodded.

"Hey!" shouted Izzy.

Maki turned to Tristan. "Back when that *Kingdom Hearts* game was getting rereleased exclusively in Japan or something—"

"That was *Kingdom Hearts 2: Final Mix,* Maki!" Izzy hollered, banging her fists on the table to accent each syllable.

"Yeah, whatever." Maki rolled her eyes. "Back when that game came out, *her* dad reached out to *my* dad who reached out to some family back home to mail her a copy."

"That was really nice of your family." Tristan nodded.

"Yeah, it was the best birthday *ever!*" Izzy clasped her hands together and cooed.

"Until it didn't work because you didn't have a Japanese console." Maki pointed out.

"I cried." Izzy nodded.

"Yeah... *a lot.*"

"*Shut up!*" Izzy slammed her fists on her lap before turning back to Tristan. "Anyway, I was blessed enough to find out that our local Mom and Pop electronics shop had a supply of *Swap Magics* on hand—basically a disc containing software you could use to trick your console into thinking it can play things it otherwise couldn't—" She made a circle with her fingers the size of a PlayStation 2 disc. "—and it was up and running by that night!"

"And *I* was her translator." Maki pointed to herself.

"Hey, it wasn't *THAT* bad! The dialogue was in English! *...Mostly.*"

Maki turned back to Tristan.

"I got non-stop phone calls for the next *month.*" Makiko pantomimed a phone in one hand and pitched her voice up a few intervals. *"Hey Makiiiiiiiii? Which one's Combo Plus?? Hey Makiiiiiii? Which one's Second Chance?"*

"Okay, that's true, you did help me out a *ton* with the abilities."

Maki sighed. "Tristan, keep in mind, this was before smartphones so she couldn't just send me a picture. She'd blow up our landline *every night* and describe the text to me with ludicrous descriptions that I'd have to somehow decipher."

"Well, how else are you supposed to read Japanese?!" Izzy shrugged with upturned palms.

Maki pantomimed the phone again.

"'What does it look like?' *'Oh, it's one horizontal line, next to two parallel horizontal lines, next to three parallel horizontal lines.'* 'That's one, two, three, Izzy. Those are numbers.' *'Why do numbers look like shapes?'* 'Because words and letters *are* shapes.' *'Huh?'*"

"In my defense, I was like, *ten!* How was I supposed to know how kanji worked?! I wasn't born in Okinawa like you!"

"English words and letters are shapes, too!"

"I know that *now!* I was just a kid!"

"You *still* act like a kid."

"Nu-uh! Do not!" Izzy retorted as she gingerly took a bite of her Uncrustables sandwich. Maki raised an eyebrow at Tristan.

"Hey, don't look at me!" he protested with raised palms. "I was told I couldn't speak!"

"Psh, fine." Irish are allowed back in."

"Yay!" Izzy clapped with joy. Maki rolled her eyes and scoffed.

"Speaking of kids," Izzy began—her tone much more somber than before, "how's your brother holding up?" Maki glanced back and forth between Izzy and her new acquaintance with confusion.

"He's doing alright, thanks." Tristan nodded with a frown.

"Brother?" Maki asked. "You have a brother?"

"I do," said Tristan. "He's um, he's pretty sick right now."

"What does he have?" Maki asked. Izzy glanced at her friend with surprise, unsure if this sort of question constituted as crossing a line.

"Leukemia."

A silence overtook the table.

"Yikes," Maki said.

"Yeah." Tristan nodded.

Izzy remained silent and stared at the table.

"It's alright," Tristan said. "I just try to be there for him whenever I can. He knows I like to draw, so he always asks me to write these stories for him whenever I visit."

"Is that what those drawings were of?" Maki asked. Tristan glanced over in surprise.

"What are you talking about?" he asked.

"I mean, in calc." she explained. "Your notebook's got a lot of sketches in it."

"Oh, those." Tristan chuckled and rubbed at the back of his neck, somewhat embarrassed. "Yeah, those are some of my characters. When I get bored in class, I brainstorm. That way I'll always have an idea ready to go when asked."

Looking over, Maki noticed that Izzy had been staring into space. She kicked her shin. Hard.

"Ouch!" she cried.

"Izzy," said Maki, "isn't that interesting? What he does for his brother?"

"What does he—oh, the drawings! Yes, that's very sweet of you, Tristan!" She smiled. "Sorry, I've just got a lot on my mind right now."

Tristan frowned. "Sorry, am I boring you?"

"What? Oh no, not in the slightest! I just... I have a lot going on right now with the presentation and the recital and…"

"Recital?" Tristan asked.

"Oh yes!" Izzy nodded. "My voice teacher has me preparing this big solo number for it. This semester is going to be crazy nonstop work for me. Speaking of—" she glanced down at her rose-gold watch. "I've gotta run. My dad needs me to help close the café tonight."

Izzy started pulling on her cardigan. Glancing at Maki, she remembered something.

"Say, Tristan. Would you like to meet me after rehearsal sometime next week?"

Tristan was pleasantly surprised by this invitation. After some deliberation, he nodded.

"I mean, um, yeah sure," he said. "I'd love to. I'm busy most nights because I'm at St. Luke's, but I'm free on Wednesday."

"Wednesday," Izzy repeated with a smile. She tapped the side of her head with her pointer finger. "Can't wait. See you then!"

"See you!" Tristan smiled and waved as she departed.

"That was… weird," Maki said mostly to herself.

"What was?" Tristan asked, still amazed by his good fortune. Maki paused then shook her head.

"That somebody would want to go out with a dork like you!" She smiled.

"Hey!" Tristan laughed.

There was a sudden change in Maki's countenance, although Tristan was unable to determine what it was.

"Listen, I uh," she stammered as she rose from the picnic table, "I've gotta go, too." She put the last of her belongings into her purple bookbag and zipped it closed. "Good luck with your brother." Tristan looked at the table and nodded sadly.

"Thanks," he said. Maki slung her bag over her shoulder.

"See you in calc?"

"As always." Tristan smiled at her.

"See you then." Maki nodded before she walked away, leaving Tristan at the table alone.

MASQUERADE

STEPPING OUT OF HIS ROOM, Tristan was greeted by a smile from his mother.

"My, you look quite dashing," Clare complimented. He thanked her. Tristan wore an old black button-up tucked into green pants with a lime-colored tie. It wasn't often that he got dressed up, so he had to make do with what he had.

Clare approached her son and dragged her fingers through his thick orange hair.

"Come to the bathroom," she said, jerking her head in that direction.

"Mom—"

"Come," she commanded.

Following her like a puppy, Tristan obediently sat on the toilet lid while she soaked and combed the cowlicks out of his hair.

"I can't have my boy go and make a fool out of himself in front of a pretty girl," she said. Tristan recoiled in embarrassment, at which he was reminded to stay still. He did his best to oblige despite his cheeks rapidly turning scarlet.

"It's not like that," he said. "We're just going out for a bite to eat. I'm trying to be a good friend."

"Sure," she said unconvinced. She violently tugged the comb through his hair. Having broken the teeth on the comb, she tossed it into the trash and pulled out her brush from the cabinet.

"You have hair like your father. So damned thick," she complained, battling a cowlick on the side of his head the size of Jupiter.

"And what of this other girl? The Asian one," she said, smiling. "You sure this has nothing to do with her?"

Tristan's heart began to pound.

"N—no," he stammered, trying to keep a straight face. "Of course not. I'm not even sure she likes me all that much. She just tolerates me for Izzy's sake."

Clare sighed and leaned into his eye level. "You suck at lying," she said with a wink as she hit him on the chest with her brush.

"I'm not lying!" he protested.

She rinsed out her brush and returned it to the cabinet. "Whatever you say, Tristan." She shook her head with raised eyebrows. "Whatever you say."

The Roosevelt Charter Theater was eerily silent at this time of night. Rehearsal had just ended, leaving Makiko alone onstage. The ghost light ominously illuminated her surroundings as she swept away the debris she and David had created with the power saw earlier that day. The push broom gave an unmistakable shudder. Maki lifted it in front of her, checking the damage. A screw had come out, disconnecting the broom's head to its shaft.

"Ah, crap." She sighed. Makiko pulled out her earbuds and shut them off. Poets of the Fall had abandoned her to the silence of the auditorium. The reticence was deafening.

Makiko pocketed the screw. Lifting the head of the broom, she glanced back and forth. Assuring herself that she was alone, she chucked the head aside and gave the handle a few test swings and spins. She smiled to herself. A moment later, she stuffed her gloves into her pockets and positioned herself center stage. She drew the handle behind her back, gripping it a third away from the bottom in her right hand.

"Bo Kihon!" she shouted before bowing to the pitch-dark auditorium. She drew the makeshift staff from behind and began an intricate series of movements and spins. Each move was fluid and precise, clearly honed by many years of repetitive practice. At the edge of the stage, Makiko turned her back to the seats and guarded her body with one leg raised in the air. Rapidly, she countered the invisible enemies the kata was training her against.

A loud bang caused her to jump.

She gasped in terror, pointing the jagged edge of the staff at the audience.

"Gah!" Tristan cried. He dropped his bag on the floor and covered his head with his hands. Makiko dropped her guard with a scoff. She turned and picked up the head of the broom.

"What are you doing here?" Maki said aggressively, concealing her embarrassment behind a mask of anger.

"I just stopped by to pick up Izzy," Tristan replied, cautiously.

"Wednesday. Right." Maki nodded in exasperation.

"I didn't know you did crew."

"You just missed her," Maki said, ignoring the observation. "She's getting changed in the back. She'll be out in a few minutes." Makiko pulled her gloves out of her pocket and started to pull them on. Tristan's eyes widened in horror when he saw the bloated, cracked, and peeling white skin.

"Maki, your hands! Are you—?"

Maki pulled on her second glove.

"It's nothing," she said firmly. Makiko finished screwing the head of the broom back onto the handle and resumed sweeping.

"So…" Tristan began, cocking his head to the side, "what was it you were just doing?"

Maki shook her head. "Sweeping the stage, what does it look like?"

"No, I meant when I came in just now… I was going to say it looked pretty cool."

Maki stopped brooming for a moment.

"Bo Kihon," she said quietly.

"Bo… what?"

Maki sighed.

"It's a basic bo kata. It's not really that special." She shook her head. "Now, are you going to let me do my job or are you going to keep testing my patience with these stupid questions?"

Tristan looked at the floor.

"...Sorry. I didn't mean to bother you," he responded sadly.

Izzy walked on the stage.

"Hi, Tristan!" She waved jovially. "You're early!"

Tristan met her on the stage and greeted his friend with a hug. In the glow of the ghost light, Maki saw his outfit for the first time. She furrowed her brows and got back to sweeping.

"You ready to go?" Tristan asked.

"Uh huh!" Izzy nodded. She turned to Maki and waved. "See you later!"

Maki forced a smile and returned the gesture.

"See you in class tomorrow," Tristan added awkwardly with a nod.

Izzy led Tristan through the black auditorium and out of the theater. Makiko glanced up at the sound of the slamming door. Izzy had never dated anyone before. She should have been happy for her. She shook the thought from her head as she put her earbuds back in. Surely the Christian rock group would be enough to distract her from these nonsensical anxieties. She removed the crocheted gloves from her pockets but found she couldn't put them on.

Why couldn't she keep her hands from shaking?

THE DATE

THE PAIR WALKED OUT into the city. Considering her size, Izzy was swift. Her long legs carried her rapidly across the sidewalks at a rate that left Tristan breathless.

"You okay?" she asked, casting a glance down in his direction.

"Yeah." He panted. "You just—you're fast. How are you not tired?"

"Oh! Sorry! I'll slow down." Izzy reduced her pace.

"Thanks." Tristan sighed. "Really, how are you not out of breath?"

Izzy shrugged. "Strong diaphragm." She laughed. "Comes with the craft."

A few minutes later, they were at the pizzeria. The small restaurant was located halfway down the block and up a brief flight of concrete steps. Tristan pulled open the glass door and held it open for his date. As she passed by, they both smiled at each other with ruddy faces. Clearly, this was a first for them both.

"Alright." Izzy nodded as they stepped on the line. "It might not look like much, but this is one of the best pizzerias on the south side."

Tristan inhaled the decadent aromas that wafted in from the tiled inner room behind the counter.

"Are you kidding?" Tristan said. "It smells awesome!"

"Good." Izzy smiled. She placed her hands in her pockets of her beige cardigan, shook a bang out of her eyes, and nodded at the signboard. "What are you gonna get?"

Tristan squinted at the menu.

"Hm, lots of good options. Might go with the buffalo chicken."

"Ooh, good choice!" Izzy nodded. "Too much food for me."

"What do you mean?" Tristan asked, eyeing her for a moment. "You look great."

"Oh, I don't mean like that," Izzy explained. "The slices here are huge. See?" As the line moved up, the glass display cases became visible. Each slice of pizza was the size of an iPad. A single slice of buffalo chicken was topped by at least thirty nuggets drenched in blue cheese.

"Wow," Tristan said.

"I know, right?" Izzy pulled her cardigan over her torso. "Thanks, though," she said sheepishly.

"No need to thank me. It's the truth." Tristan smiled.

"I used to be pretty self-conscious," Izzy admitted, "but the extra weight may have had a few perks in my work. Some vocal coaches suggest that increased abdominal pressure helps with exhalation for a more powerful sound. Plus, the increased testosterone helps with creating a darker sound. Not a requirement for being a good singer of course—there are plenty of skinny opera singers with huge sounds." She sighed. "I guess knowing that just helped me to come to terms with myself."

"Hey," Tristan said quietly, placing a gentle hand on her shoulder, breaking the touch barrier. She didn't seem to mind. "You don't have to justify yourself, Izzy. You look great. Really." He smiled. Izzy lifted her hand to his.

"Thanks," she said, giving his palm a gentle squeeze.

Once again, the pair stood in silence—each face blushing harder than the other. Faster than either of them realized, they each pulled their hands away and tucked them into their pockets.

"So," Tristan began, breaking the silence, "what are you getting?"

Izzy pointed at the case.

"Vegan Margherita."

"Oh." Tristan nodded. "So, you're uh… you're vegan?"

"Red flag?" Izzy asked, tilting her head and squinting one eye.

Tristan waved his head back and forth as he struggled to find the right response.

"…*No*…?" he lied. He was relieved when Izzy burst into laughter.

"I'm not vegan, don't worry!" she reassured him.

"Oh, thank goodness." Tristan laughed with his hand on his heart.

"Gosh, I'd rather starve!" Izzy cried. Her smile faded. "No, I uh, I can't have dairy."

"Lactose intolerant?"

"Nope. Allergic."

"Whoa," Tristan said.

"Yeah, I'd be dead," Izzy admitted. An awkward silence passed as the young couple shuffled forward in line. Humor had always been Tristan's go-to method for handling uncomfortable situations. He figured breaking the tension with a jest would be worth a shot.

"Well," he said with a smirk, "I suppose ice cream dates are out of the question, then."

"Not necessarily," Izzy pointed out. "Mama Yoko's has got a couple of good vegan options. I've been going there for years!"

"Mama Yoko's?" Tristan asked.

"Didn't you know?" said Izzy in surprise. "Maki's aunt owns an ice cream parlor."

"No, I had no idea," Tristan said somewhat disappointedly. "She never told me anything."

Izzy shrugged in indifference.

Within a few minutes, the duo placed their orders and were seated. Underground pizzerias in Roosevelt were famous for their fast turnaround. Slices were prepared in advance and tossed into a heater for warming before going out to a customer. The entire process generally took less than 90 seconds.

"How's your chicken?" Izzy asked. Tristan was mid-bite. He nodded awkwardly as he chewed his slice as fast as he could to respond. Clare, his mother, would often remind him never to speak with his mouth full—especially not in front of a pretty girl. Izzy chuckled to herself as he chewed faster and faster.

"Sorry." She blushed. Tristan shook his head and waved his hands. This kind gesture backfired, resulting in a piece of buffalo chicken sliding down the wrong pipe. He swallowed the remainder of the pizza as best he could while he coughed.

"You okay?" Izzy asked, leaning in. Finally, having coughed up and re-swallowed the last bit of chicken (there was no way he was going to spit it out in front of his date), he gave a thumbs up.

"Yeah, I'm alright," he replied in a weak, high voice. He cleared his throat, letting his voice return to normal. "How's yours?"

"Great!" She smiled. "Almost as good as the real thing."

"You remember what that real cheese tastes like?"

"Oh yeah." Izzy nodded. "My allergy didn't kick in until I was about six or seven."

"How'd you find out about it?" Tristan asked before stopping himself. "If you don't mind me asking of course."

"Not at all," Izzy said mid-bite. "When a bowl of Cheerios puts you in the hospital, there are only so many possibilities." She laughed.

"Ah." Tristan smiled. "That'd do it!"

"Speaking of the hospital," Izzy said, "how's your brother?"

"Doing better." Tristan nodded. "Thanks for asking."

"It must be pretty scary for you," she said distantly.

"We get by," Tristan replied with a shrug. "The stories definitely help."

"Yeah, I could imagine."

Izzy continued staring off into space. Tristan could tell that he was losing her interest. Did he say something wrong? Regardless, he changed tactics and reached for his phone.

"Want to see him?" he asked. The unexpected question snapped Izzy back into reality. She replied with a polite nod. Tristan was all too happy to circle the table and sidle into Izzy's side of the booth. His face grew hot as he unlocked his phone and opened the gallery.

"Wow, you all look so happy." Izzy smiled at the photograph. In it, the Collins family was beaming in front of a shrubbery cut into the shape of a horse. "Are those your parents?"

"Yep." Tristan nodded and swiped to the next photo. "And here we are on the Cavern Rush. Will love's that ride." While the copyright watermark and glare from the nearby lighting fixtures distorted some of the features (frugality kept the Collins' from purchasing the ride photo), Tristan and his brother could be seen in the vehicle of the 4D attraction.

Tristan withdrew his phone and swiped a few more times. His countenance grew a bit darker before showing the image to his friend.

"This was from a few days ago."

William was smiling with Tristan and Marc in the Wineland Room, caught up in an intense game of Jenga. The lights of the room bounced off Will's shaved scalp. Izzy frowned at the picture.

"I see," she said quickly.

"Yeah," Tristan began with a smile, "that was such a fun day."

"Oh my gosh, would you look at the time?" Izzy said in sudden surprise, glancing at her watch.

"Do you need to go?" Tristan asked.

"Yeah." Izzy lamented, slipping on her shoulder bag. "Sorry, I didn't realize how late it was." Tristan circled the table to let her out. He stacked their paper plates and trashed them in the nearby bin. "Dr. Nightengale scheduled another rehearsal for me tonight," she explained.

"That's alright, no worries." He shrugged somewhat disappointedly. "Let's get you home."

The small talk on the subway was far from substantial. Just the usual trivialities of college students: which professors are kind, which can't teach, which majors are the least viable, and so on.

An electronic jingle sounded, followed by a man's voice.

"Now arriving at Starlight Station."

"Well, that's me," Izzy said, rising from the plastic orange seat. Tristan rose with her and walked her to the door.

"I had a lovely time. Thank you, Tristan," she said bashfully with a sweet smile before turning to leave.

"Want to do this again sometime?" he asked, catching her attention. Her eyes darted about the car for a moment before she responded.

"Yes, let's!"

They briefly hugged before Izzy hopped off the train onto the station platform. Tristan waved his date goodbye through the windows of the train. He watched as she disappeared into the sea of people as the subway pulled into the tunnel that would take him to Bedford Station.

OCTOBER

A VERY SMALL WISH

A COOL MOONLIGHT GLOW cast azul shadows across the interior of the diminutive apartment. Masashi strode past numerous sealed cardboard boxes to the bedroom at the end of the hall. He was exhausted. He had used his day off of work to unpack more of the boxes from the move. Strenuous work for one man to do on his own—especially one with a cane. Placing his hand on the door to his room, he froze.

In the room behind him, his daughter was talking. To whom? Had she made an imaginary friend? Masashi frowned at the thought. It was highly likely. She had always wanted a little brother.

And she was so close to having one, too.

Nevertheless, Masashi turned around and approached the door to his daughter's bedroom, located directly across from his own. Silently, he creaked open the door and poked his head in.

The bedroom was sparsely lit. The pale moonlight and yellow nightlight bathed the room in a ghostly glow. Little Makiko knelt at the foot of her bed. Clasped between her hands was a small object. It took Masashi a moment to make out what it was. He soon realized that it was the palm cross her new friend had given her the other day. She was speaking—no—*praying* in Japanese.

"My friend Izzy told me you can do all sorts of great things…" she said in wonder. "I know you could help Daddy walk again… That would make him *so* happy. Maybe he could take me on piggyback rides or spin me around like how Mr. White does!" She paused for a moment, trying to find the right words. Finally, they came to her.

"...Are you taking care of Mommy and baby Mamoru?" Maki asked. "I really miss them." She frowned and looked down at her comforter. A few moments later, she looked back up at the ceiling and continued. "Could you give them a big hug and a kiss for me? ...Could you tell them that Daddy and I miss them very, very much?"

Makiko's voice broke off once more. Was any of this really working? She had to try.

"...Do you think... you could let me see them again...?" She shut her eyes. "I'd love to see them again... I miss them..."

Still standing in the doorway, Masashi needed a moment to steel himself before entering the room. Walking inside, he saw that his daughter was shaken but not crying. He lowered himself onto the small lavender bed and rested his cane against the nearby nightstand. Silently, Maki curled up in his lap, her Neko Niki stuffed animal in her arms and the cross in her hands. She placed her head on her father's torso. Masashi gently began stroking his daughter's hair.

"Daddy..." Makiko said, distantly, "is Mommy gone?"

"Yes, sweetheart. She's gone," Masashi replied, staring straight ahead into the darkness of the bedroom.

"And Mamoru, too?"

"Yes..." He gulped. "Mamoru too."

"Are they in Heaven?"

Masashi felt a lone tear trickle down his cheek. He wiped it away onto his shoulder before his daughter had a chance to look up.

"Yes, honey… they are."

"Are they with Jesus?"

No longer able to hold back his pain, the tears burst through the dam of his eyes in a silent deluge. He stared for a moment as Maki delicately fiddled with the cross between her fingers. Masashi thought it over carefully.

"Yes Maki… I think they are," he conceded.

"Daddy, I miss them," Makiko said sadly.

"I do too, sweetheart… more than anything else in the whole world."

He was not a religious man, but it seemed that there was only one solution to the problem he now faced. Masashi wiped away his tears and spun his daughter around in his lap to face him.

"Makiwara," he said, "how would you like to start going to church with Izzy and Mr. White?"

"Church?" Maki raised her eyebrows. "What do I have to do there?"

"You have a very special job, Maki," her father said warmly. "I want you to pray for Mommy and baby Mamoru. Pray very, very hard—pray as hard as you can. Can you promise to do that for me?"

Makiko nodded happily.

"I will, Daddy. I promise!"

Masashi gave his daughter a bear hug. He held her closely and—admittedly more for himself than for her—began to rock back and forth.

"That's my beautiful, strong girl…" He smiled. "I'll give Mr. White a call in the morning."

MO STÓIRÍN

"GOOD MORNING."

"Perky!" Will cheered as the slender, balding doctor entered his hospital room. Dr. Perkins strode over to his bedside and hugged the boy.

"Good morning, Dr. Perkins," said Clare. She was in a nearby armchair. Dark circles beneath her eyes spoke to the anxiety she felt regarding the doctor's arrival.

"Mrs. Collins," he nodded cordially as he checked the boy's vitals against his clipboard, adjusting his circular spectacles with his free hand.

"Alright, sit up for me," he said. Will sat up. Dr. Perkins held the stethoscope's diaphragm in front of Will's mouth, allowing him to breathe hot air on the cold metal. He did so.

"Thank you, kindly." Dr. Perkins smiled before checking Will's heart and lungs. "So, I hear you and your brother have been doing a lot of drawing lately."

"Yeah!" Will exclaimed between deep breaths. "We come up with stories together. It's really fun!"

"Very cool," the doctor said. He draped the stethoscope around his neck. The walls were lined with rows upon rows of twine that had been pulled tight and slip-knotted between pairs of Command Hooks. Wooden clothespins suspended dozens, perhaps hundreds, of Tristan and Will's sketches along the gossamer ropes.

"These are beautiful," he said with the same genuine warmth that made him a staple of St. Luke's pediatrics department. He looked at Clare. "You're going to have to take them down very carefully."

"Sorry, I thought this was allowed," Clare said in partial protest. The doctor raised his hands and shook his head.

"Of course it is!" the doctor reassured her. He stood up from the bed and looked out the window. "It's just that..." he turned to face Clare. A sly smile had etched its way across his face.

"I figured that you'd want to take them home with you."

It took a few seconds for the impact of his words to translate into any sensible meaning in Clare's mind. When she finally registered them, her eyes widened and welled with tears. She bolted out of her lethargy and threw herself into the arms of the middle-aged doctor.

"Thank you! Thank you! Thank you!" She wept. The doctor gently returned the gesture.

"Mommy?" Will called out.

"Will!" Clare cried as she sprinted to her son, wrapping him in her arms.

"Mommy, what's wrong?"

"Nothing, *mo stóirín,*" she said, kissing his forehead. Holding his head in her hands against her chest, she rocked back and forth.

"You're going home. You're going home!"

SHATTERING APATHY

THE NEXT NIGHT, Will burst through the door to the Collins' humble apartment in Bedford. After a refreshing home-cooked meal—something Will had sorely missed—Tristan had an announcement to make.

"Will, I've got somebody I want you to meet!" Tristan cried with glee before retreating to his bedroom.

"Close your eyes, dear," Clare cooed into her younger son's ear. Will nodded and covered his eyes with his hands. Marc stood opposite the couch, pointing a video camera at the joyful scene.

Tristan returned with the gift in tow.

"Okay, you can open your eyes!" he said.

"A kitty!" Will gasped.

Tristan gently lowered the black kitten into his brother's arms. She meowed and squirmed for a moment before settling in.

"Her name's Phoenix," Tristan said. "Like the bird. But she's yours. You can name her anything you like."

"Phoenix," Will said out loud. "That's a great name." He pulled the cat up to his face and felt the warmth of the fur on his cheek. She was purring loudly "Aww!" he cooed.

That night, peace had finally returned to the small home. Phoenix slept on Will's bed, Clare curled up in her husband's arms, and Tristan laid in bed with his arms folded behind his head. He couldn't wipe the smile from his face. He closed his eyes and said a prayer of thanks.

Phoenix *was* a good name. Truly they were rising from the ashes.

Unfortunately for the Collins family, peace breeds routine which in turn breeds apathy. As the weeks went by, the excitement of Will's return had steadily dissipated. Even Will's initial excitement about his return to Bedford Elementary had disappeared under the workload of homework and projects.

It was 6 am. William had at least another hour before returning to Mr. Burt's tutelage at Bedford Elementary. His parents had thought it best to keep him at the nearby public school at least until his health was more stable. Marc had just walked out the door for his accounting job in central Roosevelt. This left Tristan and Clare alone to share a quiet breakfast.

"Hey, that looks like fun," Clare said. She had been refilling Tristan's coffee mug when she spotted what was on his laptop screen: a full-page ad for a school club showcase at Roosevelt University. Archery, Republicans, Democrats, Kayaking, Debate, Rowing, Wind Sailing, E-Sports, etcetera. The ad even touted having a rock-climbing wall and a photo-op with "Albert the Sailor Duck himself." The giant, yellow school mascot clad in a blue and white naval uniform was pictured scaling the wall—his fist raised triumphantly in the air.

Best of all was the large banner that read, "Roosevelt Charter Academy Seniors Welcome!"

"It does, doesn't it?" Tristan nodded. "Too bad it's on Thursday, though."

"Really Tristan?" Clare scolded her son. "Didn't we already have this conversation?"

"What conversation?" Tristan asked.

"About being both the smartest and dumbest person I know?" she mocked with a raised eyebrow. Her son laughed in response.

"I have school," Tristan said confusedly.

"That *is* your school," Clare said, pointing to the computer screen. "Didn't you see the email they sent out on Monday? The festival is an excused absence."

"Yes, I know I *could* just take day off," Tristan conceded. "But what would be the point of that?"

"Um, I don't know," Clare said without looking in her son's direction as she refilled the coffee maker. "You could, um, plan to join a club next year." She set the machine to brew and spun around, now counting on her fingers. "Make a friend. Buy some food. Climb a rock wall. Get a selfie with the Duck." Clare leaned in. "Go on a *date?*" She said with a wink. Tristan scoffed and dismissed her with a laugh and a wave of his hand.

"Alright, alright!" He chuckled. "You win, I get it!" He spread his hands. "Great opportunities and all that." He sipped his coffee. "I suppose I just feel sort of guilty is all." Tristan gave a solemn nod to Will's room. "Having fun while he's in there."

"Honey, listen." Clare's tone became serious. She circled the island counter and sat at the table across from her son, setting her mug before her. "You two aren't attached at the hip," she said softly. "You're allowed to be a teenager. Make mistakes. Have a life of your own."

"I know." Tristan nodded gently. "It just hurts seeing him trapped in this house all this time." Clare nodded her understanding and rose from the table.

"Well…" Clare rested her knuckle on her hip in thought. "Why don't you take Will out on a trip to UR?" she suggested.

"Wait, you'd let me do that?" Tristan replied in shock.

"Why wouldn't I?" Clare shrugged off the question. "You're his brother, not some deranged serial killer. I trust you."

"Well, yeah." Tristan rolled his eyes, "Of course. But I mean, is he well enough to do that sort of trip?"

"He's been getting stronger and stronger each day." Clare smiled. "He can't spend the rest of his life trapped here in this apartment." She lifted her mug to initiate a toast. "Just keep it a short trip, okay?" She winked. Having thus been persuaded, Tristan smiled and clinked his mug with hers.

"Wait, but tomorrow's Thursday," Will said. "I have school."

"Take a sick day!" Clare said gleefully. "I'll write you a note."

"But I feel fine. I don't want to lie."

"Will, you have cancer. Every day is a sick day." Tristan said with a smirk.

A day off is always great for a kid. Makes him feel older. Grown-up. Gives him a chance to see the outside world at an hour traditionally reserved for adults. Truth be told, Tristan had an ulterior motive for taking his brother out of school for the day. Izzy was a senior as well. Could be a good chance to prove himself a caring gentleman in front of the young lady. He failed once. Maybe he could try again.

As his mother was typing the email to Will's teacher, Tristan pulled out his cell phone and updated his friends on the situation via group text. To his surprise, Maki replied almost instantly.

"We'll be there," she wrote with a smiling emoji filled with teeth.

Thirty minutes later, Izzy responded with a simple "heart" reaction to Tristian's initial text. Tristan smiled to himself. A heart from a girl? She was probably jumping up and down with excitement.

"What did you drag me into this time?" Izzy sighed. They had met in the commuter lounge in the Academic Mall: a long skein of brutalist structures housing a majority of the class buildings at Roosevelt University. Nearly a hundred tables were being set up on either side of the thoroughfare; surrounded by several hundred faces eager to sell their wares or recruit new club members.

"His brother?" Izzy continued. *"Really?"*

"Yes!" Maki exclaimed, depressing the panic bar on the exit door. A gust of cool autumnal air gave her a shiver. "He's a sick kid. He'll need all the support he can get."

"I know." Izzy nodded solemnly, stepping outside. "I've been praying for him."

"Me too." Maki nodded as well. "Smart thinking, adding his name to the list at church."

"Thanks," Izzy said. She looked at her friend with a raised eyebrow. "You think it worked?"

"Of course it did." Maki smiled. "You know what they say: faith the size of a mustard seed and all that."

"Yeah, I hope so." Izzy sighed. Maki eyed her curiously.

"Hey, what's your problem?" she asked bluntly.

"My problem?" Izzy asked, somewhat offended.

"Nothing." She shook her head. "You just seem so doubtful and distant all the time. Everything okay?"

"Ah, it's this show." Izzy sighed. "The workload's been driving me up the wall. There're even rumors that some talent scouts from the Roosevelt Opera House will be there."

"That's great news!" Maki exclaimed.

"That's *stressful* news!" Izzy countered. "Now I'm going to have to work twice as hard!" Izzy looked down and shoved her hands into her cardigan. "And as if that wasn't enough, now it's *cold!*"

"Hey, it's not *that* bad." Maki laughed.

"I'm a *vocalist*, Maki! This cold snap's gonna freeze up my vocal folds. My voice will be at greater risk for injury when I practice if I spend too much time outside, and—"

"Izzy, I really think you're overreacting."

"I am *not* overreacting!" Izzy complained, fishing a crocheted scarf—a gift from Mama Yoko—from her navy-blue shoulder bag.

"What? Do you think all opera houses just shut down in winter?" Maki snorted sarcastically. Izzy's only answer was to blush. They continued walking in silence for a little while. Eventually, Izzy broke the tension with a sigh.

"Listen, I—I'm sorry," she said. "I just can't seem to relax no matter what I do. It's just so much pressure."

"I understand." Maki nodded. "Izzy, you're practically my sister, you can talk to me about anything."

"Well," Izzy bit her lip, unsure of how to approach the subject. "You have your problems, too." She lowered her voice to a whisper. "You know, with your IED."

Intermittent explosive disorder. Bouts of intense, uncontrollable anger disproportionate to its triggers. Maki's cross to bear. It took years to get it under control. Years of prayer and focus in front of the makiwara in her room had helped her reach an uncomfortable truce with her inner demon. Even then, she still wasn't completely safe.

The mere mention of her problem had sent a shockwave running through her body. She was experienced enough now to recognize the symptoms. Her face flushed as her heartrate began to spike. Her jaw tightened as she clenched her teeth together. Unconsciously, Maki slipped two fingers beneath one of her gloves and began rubbing at the raised portions of her calloused hand. She had to calm down. She reminded herself that Izzy was her friend. A friend who was asking an innocent question and desperately needed help. And here she was, the expert on self-control, ready to give it. Maki stopped for a moment to catch her breath, allowing the cool autumnal breeze to ice the heat from her face.

Izzy had seen this scene play out countless times before. She knew to remain silent and give her friend a moment to cool off. Maki exhaled. Opening her eyes, she turned toward Izzy.

"Sorry, I shouldn't have—" Izzy began.

"No, you're good," Maki interrupted. She gestured forward and the pair resumed their walk down the University's academic mall. "So," Maki resumed with a smirk, "you had a question about Mikasa?"

The nickname got a laugh out of Izzy. After being introduced to yet another anime at one of the many sleepover's Izzy hosted, the pair began to jokingly refer to her explosive side as Mikasa. It gave them each some comfort to know that in those moments, Maki wasn't truly herself.

"Yes, about her," Izzy said. "How do you do it?" Izzy plaintively pleaded. "I've done square breathing, but the relief never lasts long. I've even tried jogging once—*hated it,* by the way—but there's always another worry that pops up. It's like a sick game of *Whac-A-Mole."* Maki took a moment to focus on her breathing before responding.

"There's a lot more to it than just the exercises." Maki said. "A lot of it—most of it, actually—is your mindset." She tapped the side of her temple. "You've got to *know* that things are going to be alright."

"How on earth are you supposed to do that?" Izzy asked.

"I never said it was easy," Maki said with a shrug. "But it *is* possible. Maybe start with prayer."

"Good thought." Izzy nodded.

They approached the Student Activities Center. The building's cylindrical window-lined exterior glistened in the glow of the sun. This is where they would meet the boys.

FESTIVAL

"YOU ALL SET?" Tristan asked his brother, who was zipping up a small backpack. Sonic the Hedgehog's snide smile shimmered on its glossy surface. Will slung it over his shoulder.

"Yep!" he cheered. Suddenly he was overtaken by a brief flash of panic.

"Oh wait! One second!" Will darted back into his room; returning a moment later with a UR baseball cap seated atop his head. The school's azul logo paired nicely with his white t-shirt, blue jeans, and denim jacket.

"Ready!" he said with a smile.

When the doctors had restarted his chemotherapy, Clare and Marc discussed multiple options regarding Will's probable hair loss. After *The Shave,* as the event had come to be known, Will had found wigs to be too uncomfortable for his liking. He preferred being bald in the company of his family; though once he was out in public, he'd cover his scalp.

After a few coos and warnings from their mother, the brothers left the brick apartment complex and headed down to the Bedford subway station. On the train, Tristan led his brother over to an open row of plastic orange seats. They pulled off their bags and sat down. Something lovely stirred inside Tristan as he watched his brother. Will was overjoyed to take in the sights and sounds of the commute that had long since become mundane for his big brother.

"So," Tristan began, "what do you want to do first?"

Will thought for a moment before he replied with an enthusiastic shake of the head.

"I have no idea!" he cried. "Everything looked like so much fun!"

"I agree." Tristan laughed. He put his arm around his brother's shoulder. "Let's start by meeting up with my friends. We can figure out the rest from there."

"Sounds like a plan!" Will smiled.

"There they are." Makiko nodded toward one of the entrance halls that abutted the rear end of the SAC's cafeteria. Despite his somewhat short stature, it was difficult to miss the shock of bright orange hair that bounced atop the boy's squarish face. The figure standing next to him drew even more of Makiko's attention. The little kid was half his brother's size, yet his eyes were huge. His bright blue irises were enveloped by his dilated pupils as he strained to take in each and every detail of his environment. If it wasn't for the cap, you'd hardly be able to tell he was bald.

Makiko stood up from the table. She quickly turned back to Izzy, who was pouring over a Wagner piece on the table and beckoned her to rise with a wave of her hand. Izzy took the hint and got up.

"Good morning, ladies," Tristan greeted his friends with a smile as he approached. "There's someone here I'd like you to meet." He gestured to his little brother. Will bounced up and down in excitement.

"Izzy! Maki!" he cheered. "It's so nice to finally meet you! I feel like I've been hearing about you both for forever! I'm Will!"

Maki stooped down to his level.

"It's wonderful getting to meet you, too, Will!" she said, shaking his hand. "Tristan's told us loads about you. You seem like a pretty cool guy."

Realizing Izzy had contributed nothing toward the conversation, Maki hit her arm with the back of her gloved hand.

"Oh, yes! Lovely to meet you, Will," she said, kneeling to shake the boy's hand.

"Wow, you're tall!" Will exclaimed. Izzy blushed. Tristan placed a hand on his brother's shoulder.

"Will, it's not nice to make comments like that," he remonstrated.

"Really?" Will asked.

"Oh, it's fine," Izzy said with a sigh. She placed a self-conscious hand on her arm, rolling up the sleeve of her cardigan as she went.

"You *are* tall, Izzy," Maki said forthrightly. She smirked and pointed at her. "You're tall," she pointed at herself, "I'm short," she pointed at Tristan, "you're an idiot," she pointed to Will with a smile "and you're—"

"Bald!" Will laughed, removing his cap. Tristan was shell-shocked. He was about to say something, but his train of thought was quickly derailed by the cacophony of laughter from Will and Maki. Izzy looked just as befuddled as Tristan. Nevertheless, their mutual confusion melted into a symphony of smiles.

"I was going to say, 'the fun one,' but that'll do, I guess," Maki said with a wink.

After planning out their day, the group departed the Student Activities Center. They had decided to do a full lap around the Academic Mall before returning to any of the booths that had caught their eye. This would save Will time and energy.

"Who said you can't run away from your problems?" shouted a woman in track shorts from the running club.

"Wanna learn how to be that one guy everyone hates?" said a unicyclist from Circus Arts. The small troupe had set up a tightrope between a pair of trees. A few brave volunteers were lined up and ready to cross the elastic band hovering three feet off the ground.

"*Call of Duty! Overwatch! League of Legends!* Play games and win cash prizes!" cried members of the eSports table.

"Face painting! Get your face painted!"

Will started jumping excitedly. He grabbed his big brother by the arm.

"Ooh, can I get my face painted?" he asked. "Please?"

"Absolutely." Tristan nodded with a smile. "We'll do it on the way back."

"Yay!"

"Come ride the waves! Join this year's parasailing team!" shouted a man in a wetsuit. The parasailing team had pulled out all the stops for this year's club showcase. Their booth displayed multiple photographs of sailors practicing and competing on the Sound. Their accompanying awards decorated the table. On top of that, the club had laid out several boats on a grassy portion of the Academic Mall.

"That looks pretty cool," Tristan commented. He glanced over at Maki. She didn't reply. Her eyes were locked onto one of the photographs.

"Hey, are you alright?" Tristan asked. Izzy was looking at the boats herself when she finally realized what was going on. She jogged over to her friend and shook her back to reality.

"Maki! You with me?" she asked. Maki shook the cobwebs out and nodded, solemnly.

"What's wrong, Mackie?" Will asked—mispronouncing the name of his new acquaintance.

"N—nothing," she said. "Sorry kid. I just, uh..." She struggled to pull together the right words. "Water and I don't really get along."

"You're like a cat!" Will giggled.

"You're afraid of the ocean?" Tristan asked with genuine curiosity. Expecting a snarky retort, Tristan was surprised when she replied with a solemn—not to mention fearful—nod. All at once, the image of the cursed cat girl popped back into his mind. He found himself unable to stifle a laugh.

"What's so funny?" Maki snapped at him.

"Maybe we should call you 'Meowki!'" he cried.

Will was in hysterics as well. A moment later, Izzy joined in. Makiko, however, remained stone-faced. The laughter became awkward when they noticed her unchanged expression. Without uttering a word, Makiko bent her elbows and raised her forearms, leaving her hands to dangle from limp wrists. She made eye contact with Will before she rolled her head 180 degrees.

"Meeeeooooooowwwwww!" she squeaked. Will was laughing so hard that his sides began to hurt. Meanwhile, Tristan and Izzy exchanged perplexed glances. Maki abruptly turned and threw a pointer finger in the direction of the final stretch of booths.

"Onward!" Maki cried. It took Tristan and Izzy a few seconds to recover and follow suit.

On their second loop around the mall, Will stopped to get his face painted. As the woman at the booth worked at turning Will into a lion, Izzy approached Tristan.

"You know, I bet Maki could do that," she commented. Maki shook her head.

"Maki, you know how to paint?" Tristan asked.

"Yeah," Makiko nodded. "Never done face painting though. Makeup? Yes. Just not this kind of design work."

"Makes sense," Tristan said. "You do work in a stage crew after all."

"And she's amazing at what she does," Izzy chimed in.

"Oh stop." Maki shooed away the compliment with a wave of her hand. Tristan watched as the painter began applying the various colored stripes to the orange foundation she had put on Will's face. A wild thought occurred to him.

"You know," said Tristan, "Halloween's next week. Will could certainly use a helping hand with his costume—"

"We'd love to," Maki answered without hesitation.

When Izzy didn't reply, Maki elbowed her hard in the ribs. No matter how much she tried, Izzy couldn't get her mind off the recital. This could be the big break she'd always dreamed of. Did she really have this sort of free time? Tristan was sweet, but his brother... the cancer. This relationship would come with a lot of baggage. Could she balance it all? Still, the chemotherapy had put the cancer in a manageable state. Surely things would be alright now, right? She had to try.

"Yes, we'll help," Izzy replied with a forced smile which she hoped would conceal her trepidation.

"Thanks." Tristan smiled. "You know, you two have really made his day. It's been a while since I've seen him so excited."

"Tristan! Tristan!" Will shouted as he ran toward his brother.

"Wow, look at you!" Tristan cooed.

"Roar!" his little brother screamed with curled-up fingers on his raised hands.

Makiko crouched down and shook her fists, cooing. "So scary!"

"They did a great job!" said Izzy. "Say, Will, how'd you like to go to the bounce house?"

"Oh, I'd love to, but... um..." Will broke off.

"Too physical," his big brother explained. Will nodded. "Can't risk doing too much too soon, you know?"

"Oh yeah I understand, of course," she said behind another forced smile. His brother was worse off than she realized. Daytime classes, nighttime rehearsals, working, practicing, score studies... could she really add dates, hospital trips, and extra commutes to the mix? Izzy didn't have an answer. She didn't want to lead him on, but she didn't want to lock him away into the dreaded friend zone just yet either. It was just a bad time.

Yes, that was it.

She'd step away and return once the recital was over. Go on a date or two if she could, but otherwise, keep him and his brother at arm's length.

That could work. It had to.

Izzy checked the time on her watch.

"Oh boy, is it that late already?" she said in an imitation of surprise.

"Really? What time is it?" Maki asked.

"Time for you to get a watch," Tristan smirked. Maki scowled back.

"Quarter to three," Izzy said.

"That's not late, Iz," Maki said. "Got someplace to be?"

"Oh, always more stuff to do at Brandy's," Izzy lied. Internally, she prayed to be forgiven for that indiscretion. "The sooner I help out, the sooner I can get back to rehearsing. Plus, I've got a project due tomorrow at midnight. Want to make sure I get that done early so I don't have to think about it at rehearsal."

"Makes sense." Tristan nodded.

"It was great getting to see you guys today!" she cried as she hugged Maki.

"You too, Iz," said her best friend. She turned around, intending to part with a cordial wave; however, Tristan already had his arms outstretched for a hug. She had no choice but to follow through.

"Thanks so much for coming," Tristan said as they embraced.

"Of course."

Izzy pulled away and looked down at Will.

"See you later, Izzy!" he cheered as he sprinted at her at maximum speed. He locked his arms around her waist and held her in the same sort of innocent hug a child would give a theme park mascot. Izzy blushed and returned the gesture.

"See you, Will. It was lovely meeting you today."

A few minutes later, she was absorbed by the crowd and was out of their sight.

"She was probably right," Tristan said. "Today was a pretty big day for Will. Probably best for us to head back soon."

"Aw, I'm sorry to hear that," Maki said. She looked at Will. "And we were just starting to get to know each other!"

"Do we have to go right now?" Will asked plaintively. "I'm not *that* tired yet!"

Tristan thought for a moment. "Well," he said before checking the time on his phone, "no, we could stay for a little while longer. But we probably shouldn't do any more walking around. We should find someplace to sit down."

"I know a good spot," Maki said with a grin.

HYDROPHOBIA

"WOW, YOU WEREN'T JOKING," Tristan remarked in awe.

Compared to the urban cacophony of the festival outside, the Saint Anna Wang Center was remarkably quiet. Makiko led the boys to the short, tiled wall that abutted the zodiac fountains.

"It's pretty relaxing, yeah." Maki nodded. She shut her eyes and inhaled, listening to the gurgle of the water as it splashed into the basin behind them.

"It's a little funny," Tristan said.

"Pardon?" asked Maki.

"You're terrified of the ocean, yet you find the fountains to be relaxing," he explained with a smile. "A bit ironic, no?"

Maki shrugged.

"Believe me, it wasn't always like that," she said. "I was pretty hydrophobic for a long time."

"Hydro-what?" Will asked.

"Afraid of water," Maki explained. She peered into the basin. "Lakes, pools, even bathtubs would terrify me." Feeling a peculiar look bearing down on the back of her head, she added an addendum: "I really don't want to get into why."

"That's alright, I won't pry," Tristan said in a manner that he hoped gave off a sentiment of reassurance—sensing that there was some trauma involved that she wasn't ready to disclose.

"Thanks," Maki said with a nod.

"How did you stop being so scared?" Will asked. The innocent sincerity of his tone made Maki smile.

"Exposure," she explained. "I faced it head-on. Little by little. Every time I would start feeling comfortable, I'd raise the stakes. When photos of tubs no longer made me shake, I'd put an inch of water in my own and sit next to it. The next time it was two inches. Then three. A week later, I'd dip my feet in. It took nearly a year but I was finally able to draw a bath for myself."

"That must have been tough," Tristan commented. "How old were you?"

Maki nodded at Will, "About his age."

Will peered into the fountain. He was lost in thought.

"What the matter, buddy?" Tristan asked.

"I was just thinking," Will began, "that if Mackie could get over her fear of water, do you think I could stop being scared of roller coasters?"

"Of course you can!" Tristan said with a smile.

"You can do anything if you try," Maki chimed in. "It's not easy, but it's possible." Like the waterfalls behind them, her sleek black hair cascaded toward the ground. She pulled a clump of it back and tucked it neatly behind her ear, revealing a bright smile on her lips. Hot pink lipstick. Bright green irises. The girl was glowing and Tristan couldn't help but stare. He'd never seen her so genuinely happy before.

Genuine.

Not long after first having heard her name, he ran an internet search—if nothing more than to check the spelling. Makiko: genuine child… the start of new things.

At first, the results made him laugh. They couldn't have been further from the truth given his initial impressions of the girl—but now? Seeing her light up like this had completely shifted his perspective. Tristan reached into his bag and extricated his sketchbook and pencil.

"Maki, do you want to help me tell a story?" he asked.

"A story? What are you talking about?" Maki was puzzled.

"Yes! Please! You can make it about Meowki!" Will cried. Seeing his overjoyed expression was all that was needed to offset any reservations she had about the situation in which she found herself.

"It's a sort of game we have." Tristan stammered, shifting nervously.

"Right of course," Maki said. "I remember." Admittedly, Maki knew exactly what Tristan was talking about. She simply hadn't been prepared to be a part of such an intimate act of fraternal love. She looked over at Will who was still beaming with excitement. Was this the first time someone else had been recruited into this little game? It may just be a series of cartoons in a sketchbook, but in Will's eyes, Tristan may as well have been laying out the red carpet for a guest of honor. She was being invited into his private world. Drawn into it—perhaps literally.

"I'm game." She smiled jovially at Will. "So, tell me Tristan, who is this *Meowki?*"

"Yeah!" Will cried. "What does she look like?"

"Well…" Tristan said, continuing to sketch. He was stifling his laughter. Maki was finally receiving a taste of her own medicine and she wasn't sure she liked it. "I'd say something like *this.*"

Tristan flipped the book around to reveal what was perhaps the most terrifying drawing Makiko had ever seen. It was a cartoon sketch of her head—complete with an oversized fang and cat ears—fixed atop a cat's body. It wore a cuffed crocheted sweater with a dangling nametag emblazoned with the letter, "M." A speech bubble above its head read, "Time for tuna! Tee hee!"

Makiko's look of frozen terror only exacerbated the boys' hilarity. Will had to wipe tears from his eyes from laughing so hard.

"Goodbye," Maki said curtly as she shot up from the half wall. She swiftly rounded the corner onto a nearby staircase and idled for a few moments to make believe she was leaving. She returned to even more laughter a few seconds later.

"Tristan... just... *WHY?*" she cried, slashing her palms through the air in the direction of the sketchpad.

He raised his hands defensively.

"Hey, this is a commission piece," Tristan said. "I'm just doing whatever my client asks for."

"If you insist." She shook her head as she returned to her seat. "Carry on—" she said with a sigh before leaning toward Will "—at the cost of my *sanity!*" she snarled playfully. The boy laughed.

"Roger that." Tristan nodded with a smile.

Meowki was a young little cat, loved by all the woodland critters of the Lakeside Apartments. Each day, she'd stride around the outskirts of the parking lot and find friends to play with. They'd run, jump, chase, and fly around the complex, always ending the playdate with a delicious picnic. Gary the squirrel would always serve acorns and nuts, but Meowki found these too difficult to chew. They were bitter and would get caught on her fang. Wolfie the dog would bring bits of cheeseburgers and French fries from the dumpster of the nearby restaurant. They were tasty, but the greasiness would upset Meowki's tummy. Sammie and Tammie, the pigeon twins, would end their playdates with worms and breadcrumbs, to which Meowki would politely decline.

One night, after another playdate with Wolfie, Meowki found herself wandering the complex's parking lot in search of food. She was starving. So tired was she from lack of food, she had to find a shady spot beneath a parked car to rest her head. She dreamt of a school of tuna gliding through the air! Oh, how happy she was, leaping into the sky with glee. Each jump filled her tummy with yummy fishy goodness.

She awoke with a start. The engine of the car she slept under roared to life. Engrossed by fear, she blindly darted out as quickly as she could. She knew not the direction in which she ran. All that mattered was that she escaped unseen. When her heart rate returned to its normal rhythm, she skidded to a stop with a hiss. Her panicked run had taken her all the way to the shoreline of the complex. Lakeside Apartments got its name by abutting a large lake. Fishermen loved to cast their lines from a nearby bridge, so fertile with life were these waters.

Especially with tuna.

But Meowki was afraid. She didn't know if she knew how to swim, but she dared not try. What if she slipped into the water and found herself unable to resurface? What if a kitty-cat-eating monster lay in wait below the surface, ready to drag furry felines down below to satiate its desire for fluffy nom-noms?

"'Fluffy nom-noms?'" Maki asked flatly.

"Would you just let me tell the story?" Tristan protested. Maki lifted her hands in faux surrender—eyebrows raised derisively.

Meowki knew the waters were teaming with life, but she was too scared to go anywhere near them. She hid herself from them behind a nearby tree. Her tummy growled. She was so hungry it hurt. At last, she had found her resolve.

"There's no sense in hiding behind this tree until I starve," she said to herself. "Better to go down in the belly of that beast than fade away up here." Meowki peered around the tree at the lake. "At least here, I'll have a chance to score some tuna for din-din!" She licked her lips at the thought. "Mmm, tuna for din-din! Tee hee!"

Cautiously, she approached the shoreline. A sudden bubble from the water caused her to jump and retreat behind a park bench. Meowki hesitantly peered around the wrought-iron bench to see the silvery tail of a tuna breaching the water. This put a grand smile on her face.

She spent the next half hour inching her way to the water, until eventually, she dared to dip her paw in. She shot back in fright. Shaking out the moisture from her fur, she examined her paw.

"No bite marks." She gasped in amazement. Slowly, she went back to the water and dipped in her paw once more.

"Maybe this is as far as I'll need to go," she said. "Now I just need to wait!"

And wait she did.

It took around fifteen minutes, but at last, she spotted some more bubbling near the surface.

"Careful now..."

The bubbling stopped. Meowki held her breath—unsure whether to give up or to hold on. She shook her head and stayed put.

"Hold..." she thought.

Suddenly, the fish breached through the surface.

"Now!" she shouted, swiping her paw through the air. She slashed the fish's torso, flinging it to the shore. Without hesitation, she pounced and ended its struggle with a single bite.

That night, Meowki dined on a delicious tuna all to herself. No longer was she afraid to go hunting for fishy goodness at the shoreline. Every time she'd be asked on a playdate by her friends, she'd have a fish to bring with her to the picnic. And so, Meowki had tuna for din-din all the days of her life.

"The end," Tristan said affirmatively. Will and Makiko clapped.

"So, buddy, what'd you think?" Tristan asked his little brother.

"I loved it!" Will said with a smile.

"Think you might want to give roller coasters another go?" Makiko asked. Will hesitated and scrunched up his face.

"Maybe a small one first?" he squeaked. Tristan laughed and patted him on the back.

"It's a deal!" he cried. "As soon as you're well enough!"

Tristan gathered their things and helped his brother down from the half-wall. The trio took the elevator up to the ground level and made their way to the university's primary entrance at the front of the Academic Mall.

"Thanks for tagging along," Tristan said to Maki.

"It was my pleasure," she said. "Besides," she shrugged, "Will needs someone with half a brain in his life."

"Hey!" Tristan shouted. Will laughed. At the front gate, she stooped down to his level.

"You be good, okay? No matter what anyone says, you're the real man of the house," she said with a wink. Will chuckled and nodded.

"Okay!" he replied.

"Come here," Maki said with a nod, opening her arms. Will ran in and embraced his new friend with a tight hug. She stood up. Unsure whether he should hug her as well, Tristan felt himself beginning to blush. Will solved this dilemma for him by grabbing his hand. Tristan used this as an excuse to back up out of the gate, waving goodbye with his free hand.

"See you on Halloween!" he cheered, flashing a joyful grin at his friend. Makiko returned the expression and waved back at the boys as they descended into the nearby subway station. Tristan ruminated on her bright pink lips all the way home.

THE SWITCH

PROFESSOR NIGHTINGALE PACED her office floor. The large studio was one of many in Roosevelt University's music building. The floors were lined with opulent rugs of varying sizes and colors that served to cover the laminated flooring. On the walls, decadent curtains and ornamental tapestries draped across windows and sound panels. Izzy stood near the grand piano. Her hands were clasped together, resting on her collarbone—rising and falling with each nervous breath.

"You're not doing that song," the professor remonstrated.

"But I've been rehearsing it for almost three months!" Izzy protested.

"'*Quando m'en vo'* is beautiful. I'll admit, your Musetta is wonderful."

"Thank you," said Izzy, who blushed at the compliment.

"But this is the Roosevelt Opera House. These are the best singers in the nation. They're not looking for *wonderful*. They're looking for *extraordinary*."

"I know, that's why I've been working so hard," Izzy said with a frown.

"Hard work is only going to get you so far." Professor Nightingale strode over to her piano and pulled a paper booklet out of her leather-bound folder. "You need the right material." Izzy took the pages. It was sheet music. Old sheet music covered in writing and stage directions. Clearly from the professor's performing days. Izzy nearly fainted when she read the title.

"Are you serious?" Izzy asked quietly in wide-eyed bewilderment. The professor's gaze never wavered from her own.

"Deadly," she replied. "I've taught a lot of singers during my tenure at UR, Izzy. Sopranos, basses, altos, tenors, mezzos, you name it. Some were good, some were bad, some were great, some were okay, but you…" She paused. Swallowing, she continued. "In my thirty years teaching at this school, Isolde White, you have the greatest potential of any vocal student I've ever taught. I don't just *want* you to attend UR next year. I *need* you to." Izzy was flabbergasted by the sincerity in her teacher's eyes. She thought she might cry at the flattery.

"I—I don't know what to say," she stammered. Professor Nightingale circled the piano to her student.

"If anyone can sing this piece, it's you," she said. Izzy felt her lips begin to quiver. A moment later, the tears came. She embraced the professor in a tight hug.

"I'll try," Izzy said. "If you think I can do it, I'll give it everything I've got."

"You're ready, Izzy. You just need to believe in yourself."

They released the hug. Nightingale set out a photocopy of the music on her piano and seated herself on the bench. She beckoned Izzy to set herself up at the nearby music stand. She opened the booklet to the first page. That was how the rehearsal began.

"Hey, Izzy! You had voice lessons today, right?" Maki said through the phone. Izzy was heading down the long hallway of the music building to the exit on the far side—in the direction of the Academic Mall. One benefit of the building's awkward configuration was that it was easy to keep out of the cold without adding additional length to the commute.

"Yeah," Izzy began, "just heading out now, actually."

"Cool. How's the waltz coming? Puccini, right?"

"Uh, it's not."

"Huh? What do you mean?"

"Well, Professor Nightingale didn't think the song was a good fit for me," Izzy explained. She reached the black exit door and opened it. The sudden blast of freezing, autumnal air caused her to flinch. She shivered, letting out a "brr."

"Tell me about it." Maki sighed. "It's not even November and we're already in the thirties."

"Th—thirties?!" Izzy exclaimed. "You're ki-ki-kidding." she shivered. She wrapped her sweater around herself as tightly as she could, now jogging to the main gate at the edge of the Academic Mall. University Station was just outside. Unfortunately, the grid-like layout of the buildings served only to increase the windchill, providing a convenient wind tunnel for the icy breeze to travel through. An adept commuter, Izzy darted in and out of the buildings lining the mall for warmth as she went.

"Yeah! You should have packed a coat!" Maki laughed.

"Thanks, Captain Hindsight." Izzy mocked.

"You're welcome." Through the receiver, Izzy could hear her friend sipping on something.

"Ah... delicious," Maki said.

"Excuse me?"

"Sorry, don't mind me. Just sipping on some hot chocolate," Maki cooed.

"Don't do this to me." Izzy sighed.

"Oh, it's *great!* Dad has the heat jacked up. I'm in my pj's. Got a blanket and slippers. Watching *Alien.*"

"I hate you *so* much," Izzy muttered through the phone as she entered the last building before the main gate.

"Noted," said Maki who proceeded to sip as obnoxiously as she could. The hot cocoa filled her mouth with a soothing mixture of sweet chocolate and protection from the bitter cold. She smiled satisfactorily when she swallowed; the warm liquid slipped down her esophagus like a burning star. One loud *'ah'* later, she smacked her lips and continued. "But what about the song?"

"The professor didn't think the song would impress the talent scouts. She more or less said it was too easy for me."

"Wow, that's some high praise," Maki commented.

"Thanks," said Izzy. "It sucks though, because I spent so much time working on a song that I suddenly have to ditch—leaving me with even less time to learn a significantly harder one."

"Yeah, that is tough," Maki agreed. "You're pretty strapped for time as it is."

A moment later, Makiko was shocked to hear her friend scream.

"Izzy! Are you okay?" she asked seriously, sitting up on her couch.

"No," Izzy whined. "It's starting to *snow*." Makiko's uproarious laughter through the phone was more painful to her than the icy night air.

"I'm glad my pain amuses you."

"Oh, it definitely does," Maki said again before taking another sip of her delicious hot chocolate. "Oh no!"

"'Oh no' what?"

"I forgot to bring the marshmallows in with me."

"Seriously?"

"Now I have to get up."

Izzy was finally approaching the main gate of the school. She could see the descending staircase that would take her to the subway through the fence to her left.

"Then do it." Izzy laughed.

"No, that requires effort," Makiko complained, falling flat on her back across the cushions. She stretched her legs and feet under the blanket with a grunt. "I'm too comfy."

A patch of black ice caused Izzy to lose her footing. Panic rushed across her body as she struggled to remain upright. Luckily, she managed to catch herself on a nearby trash bin.

"Whoa! Almost fell. Slippery out here."

"You should have brought your boots."

"Anything else I should have brought, Makiko?" Izzy seethed.

"Nothing comes to mind," said Maki.

"Alright, alright," Izzy said. "All jokes aside, to make up for the lost time, she's going to need for me to come in twice a week now. She's offered to stay after on Mondays for me."

"Monday's Halloween," Maki interrupted, now sitting up—suddenly alert.

"Yeah, I know," Izzy said, sadly. She sighed. "Listen, I—I really wanted to be there but this… this is big."

"I know," Maki said with a disappointed frown.

"Professor Nightingale said that If I get picked up, this could be the start of a career! That's how these things happen."

"I get it." Maki nodded. She bit her lip and twisted her feet inward, trying to keep her emotions in check. "Well, you should definitely call Tristan about this."

"I will once I'm home," said Izzy. "I'm about to go underground."

"Gotcha. Well, Iz, I'm proud of you. You're about to hit the big time." She forced a smile, hoping to sound cheery through the phone.

"Thanks, Maki. I'll text you later. Enjoy the hot cocoa."

"Oh, you know it!" Maki said, forcing a chuckle. "Later gator."

"Later."

Izzy put away her phone and went underground. Makiko decided to forego the extra marshmallows in favor of reclining further into her ocean of blankets and pillows. On their modest living room television, Sigourney Weaver was singing "Lucky Star" as she searched for the xenomorph hiding among the cables. Maki frowned and took another sip of her drink.

On the train, Izzy pulled out her sheet music once more and scanned through its contents. How on earth was she, a high school senior, going to learn Wagner's *"Liebestod"* in just two months?

MAMA YOKO'S

TO THE NORTHEAST OF LENOX sits a prominent docking area for shipping companies. The necessity for low-skill laborers was quickly abated by the influx of Asian immigrants gracing its ports back in the 1800s. It didn't take long for real estate developers to capitalize on the situation with an uptick of low-density housing for the impoverished locals.

Lo and behold, Yellow Harbor was born.

While Makiko was well acquainted with the derision the name faced in the modern world, she had always viewed it with a touch of cultural pride. For her and many other Asians on Copperfield Isle, this was their home.

Makiko's aunt ran a humble ice cream parlor on the border of Copperfield and the Harbor. On days when she wasn't so overwhelmed with schoolwork, she liked to visit and assist however she could. On one of these days, a certain blonde and red-haired couple paid them a visit. Business was unusually slow that Saturday, so Maki was able to sit with them and chat for a while. Little did she know, her plump aunt was lingering nearby—hanging on every word. After a few minutes of eavesdropping, she approached the table.

"Hi, Mama Yoko!" Izzy cheered with a wave.

"Hello Izzy!" said Mama Yoko, before turning to the red-headed stranger. "And who do we have here?" she said in her heavily accented English. Her mid-length black hair framed the soft face that bore the same bright smile she used to cheer up her niece throughout her childhood.

"Mama Yoko, this is Tristan," Makiko said. "He's a friend from school."

"Hello," the boy said, awkwardly extending a hand. Mama Yoko gladly accepted it and shook.

"Ah, so nice to meet you!" She smiled. "Any friend of *Makiwara* is friend of mine."

"Aunt Yoko..." Maki's neck bristled at the pet name. Izzy snickered.

"Maki...*wara?*" Tristan asked.

"It's a rice board that you use to train your punches in karate," Izzy explained, slowly punching the air in a demonstration. Maki was fuming.

"Oh right." Tristan chuckled. He looked at Maki. "Gotcha, Maki—" she glared back at him. He gulped. "Ma— ...Maki." Mama Yoko shook her head and let out a burst of uproarious laughter that rivaled Santa Claus. Izzy once referred to her as a "big Japanese teddy bear." Sometimes, Makiko could see the resemblance.

"Anyway, you go to see show?" Mama Yoko continued, looking at Tristan. "Izzy is singing."

"Absolutely! I'd love to see it." He smiled. "When is it?" Izzy gave him the date.

"Maki is going, too," Mama Yoko interjected. "You two meet there. Go together and support," she said, interlacing her fingers to match her words. Tristan nodded, nervously.

"Yeah," he said, looking at Maki. "Sounds like a good idea." Suppressing her building her rage, Makiko agreed.

The pair stayed for a few minutes more before departing. On the subway ride back to Copperfield, Izzy tapped her friend on the shoulder.

"Thanks for coming out with me tonight," she said.

"A night out on the town with a pretty girl? What's not to like?" He smiled at her. "Thanks for inviting me."

"Oh, thanks." She blushed. "Listen," Izzy began, "about the show, I've been meaning to tell you, my rehearsal schedule's been changed. Professor Nightingale, my voice teacher, just gave me a different aria to learn. This one's crazy hard and it's going to take a ton of practice, so um, I can't…" Her voice broke off. She gulped before continuing. "I have practice on Mondays now too, so I'll be booked on Halloween."

"Oh," Tristan said disappointedly. His eyes flittered out the window. Perhaps he hoped the strobing of the tunnel's fluorescent lighting would hypnotize him into feeling a false sense of security. Anything to assuage his internal turmoil. "I'm sorry to hear that."

"Me too," Izzy said with a hint of dishonesty. Her Catholic guilt shot a pang of discomfort through her gut. "That's part of why

I wanted to invite you out tonight. So at least we could do something together now."

"That was nice of you, thanks." Tristan nodded. Despite his politeness, he wasn't completely obsequious. While he had a right to be disappointed, Izzy could tell that there was something that she was missing. Thankfully, it didn't take long for Tristan to spell it out for her.

"You know, my brother really likes you," he said. "He keeps talking about you and Maki nonstop. He had a great time at that fair."

"It would be nice to see him again, for sure, but I just don't know when I can," Izzy admitted. She was so confused. Felt awful. Couldn't think straight. Was she really about to leave him brokenhearted? Her hand made its way to the long clump of hair that dangled down over her left ear, tugging away. When was the last time she'd been to confession? Surely distorting the truth a few times was only venial, right? What did the catechism say about that? She couldn't remember. A mortal sin needed three things: willful disobedience, full knowledge, and grave matter. She wasn't trying to hurt anyone. But what if it counted? What if she was going to be sent to—

No.

She was caught in a loop again. Just like when she had to check the lock on the front door eight times before she left the house that morning. Twice, she had made it halfway down the block before jogging back up the porch to check the door. This all started back in January when she found out she was colorblind. What if it was divine punishment?

And now there's this show. What if she couldn't learn the music in time and Dr. Nightengale rescinded her letter of recommendation? What if she humiliated herself onstage and got blacklisted from the opera for life? What if she went to the hospital with Tristan and picked up a virus from one of the patients leaving her unable to perform? What if...

What if what if what if what if what if?

Izzy nearly jumped when subway announced its arrival at Lenox Station.

"My stop," Izzy said, rising abruptly from her seat. Tristan nodded and rose as well. "I'll text you when I get home. Have a great night, Tristan. Get home safe."

"Of course, Iz. You too," he said with a smile. He opened his arms for another hug.

All this lying. Leading him on. She was a terrible person. She'd have to act. Do something. *Anything.*

They hugged. Just before they were about to release, Izzy surprised him with a kiss on the cheek. Before he could say anything more, she had already bolted off the train. He sat down on the hard orange plastic seats. The bright red lipstick stain on his cheek stood as a testament to the sea of conflicting emotions he now felt himself drowning in.

Tristan zoned out as the train returned to the blackened tunnel. In his imagination, his Other took over his reflection in the window.

"Did you want to talk?" Kieran asked him through the glass. Tristan smiled despite himself.

"I think I'm alright, thanks," he replied.

"Don't get cocky," Kieran said. He pointed at the duplicated lipstick stain on his cheek. "This washes quickly."

Tristan shook his head, letting his imaginary friend disappear into the black. Rather than give in, he chose to play his optimism game.

"Ah well," he thought, "might make for a funny story one day."

The small room now quiet and empty, her aunt's voice caught Makiko off guard.

"So, I guess it runs in the family," she said in Japanese. Maki felt the hair on the back of her neck shoot up.

"What are you talking about?" she responded in her first language. Mama Yoko walked around the glass-covered ice cream vats, strafing around her niece with folded arms.

"Come on, I've known you since you were this tall." She put out a facedown palm to measure. "You can't keep secrets from me."

"I really have no idea what you're talking about," Maki said, stupidly. Mama Yoko leaned in from her waist.

"Your *friend?*" she said.

"Izzy? What about her?" Maki asked, circling the counter to get towels to wipe down the table and leave this conversation as quickly as possible. Her aunt raised an eyebrow.

"Try again," she said, pithily. Wincing, Maki cracked under the pressure.

"No! It's... it's not like that!" she stammered, spraying cleaning fluid onto the table. "He's just some idiot from school!"

"That's not what your eyes are telling me."

Makiko felt her face grow hot which enraged her all the more. She sighed and slumped into the booth. Mama Yoko sat across from her. She placed a hand on her niece's and began tracing a finger across the rough texture of her glove.

"It's alright... I won't say a word to your dad," she said. "I know how he is about keeping things 'in the *gene pool*,' so to speak." She let go and looked out the window. "You were probably too little to remember what it was like when I first got married. Masashi has a heart of gold, but he can be stubborn."

Makiko dropped her facade and stared at the now-shining table.

"You know me too well."

Mama Yoko held her hand.

"You're my niece, Maki. It's my job," she lovingly reassured. Despite her aunt's compassion, Makiko had a difficult time finding words.

"Well… even if I did… *you know…*" she said, making a spiraling gesture with her fingers in the air before letting her hands collapse back onto the table. "Izzy likes him." She shrugged. "I couldn't get in the way of that."

Mama Yoko paused for a while before responding.

"Well, if that's the way you feel, then why don't you let *him* decide?" she said. Maki just shook her head.

"I wouldn't stand a chance," Maki muttered—gazing into her reflection on the table with a frown. Her aunt put a gentle hand on her chin. She lifted her face to meet her eyes.

"You might if you put in a little more effort," Mama Yoko said, coupling a winning smile with a wink.

This time, her niece smiled back.

HALLOWEEN

"SO, IZZY'S NOT COMING TONIGHT."

"No. She's got rehearsal. Too busy, unfortunately."

"That's a shame."

It was 4 pm. Clare was returning from Bedford Elementary to bring Will home to change for the night. Tristan was riding in the passenger's seat. Will had been excited to cut out of classes a few minutes early. Any kid would be. An announcement made on the loudspeaker coupled with a big farewell from your teachers and peers made you feel like a king. They were just entering their apartment lobby when Tristan's phone began to ring.

"Hey!" he answered. "Yes, we just got back now." He paused. "Uh-huh. Okay. Great. See you soon." He hung up the phone and returned it to his pocket.

"Was that your friend?" Clare asked.

"Yep." Tristan nodded as they stepped into the elevator. "She'll be here in a few minutes."

"Good." Clare smiled. She looked down at Will. "You're so fancy. You're getting your very own personal makeup artist to help you with your costume!"

Will laughed. "Yeah! I'm so excited!"

Marc entered through the front door, briefcase in hand. "Happy Halloween!" he beamed. He greeted his sons with hugs and his wife with a long smooch. His boss had allowed him to work early so he could have the evening off. With his boys heading out to the local high school's Safe Halloween, he was looking forward to a private date night with his wife. His elation was obvious.

"Happy Halloween!" Will cheered.

"Hey Dad, Happy Halloween," Tristan said. "Makiko will be here in a few minutes."

"Good, good." Marc smiled.

"Can't wait to see what she comes up with for Will," Clare said.

A few minutes later, the buzzer went off. Tristan ran to answer it. A familiar voice sounded from the other end. Clare did her best not to look as eager as she felt to analyze its sound. Subtly, she stopped rustling the bowl of candy she had been prepping on the off chance there was a trick-or-treater and cocked her head to the side. Tristan departed and returned a few minutes later with a guest.

"Mom, Dad, this is my friend, Makiko."

Makiko was casually dressed in black yoga pants, chestnut brown UGGs, and a knit purple sweater. She confidently strode forward into the room and extended a hand toward Tristan's parents.

"Mr. and Mrs. Collins, It's an honor to finally meet you." she said. Her smile was dazzling. Tristan had a hard time not staring. She had taken off her overcoat in the elevator. Seeing her from the back, he noticed how her hair had slowly but surely begun to grow out. Where it used to hang in a bob, it now fell well past the nape of her neck and somehow appeared even thicker than before.

"Likewise," said Clare who accepted Maki's hand with a smile. Marc followed. He clapped his hands together and rubbed.

"So, can we get you anything to eat? Drink?" Marc asked the newcomer.

"Oh, you don't have to do that," Maki said.

"Please, you're our guest," Clare said. "Want a bottle of water? You can take it with you when you go."

"Sure, that would be great." Maki nodded. "Thank you so much."

"Not a problem."

As Mrs. Collins fetched a bottle from the fridge, Will charged out of the bathroom and into Maki's arms.

"MAKI!!!" he screamed.

The force of the collision nearly sent Makiko tumbling backward to the floor.

"Looks like someone was excited to see you." Marc laughed. Clare set the water down on the living room end table right next to Maki.

"Thank you so much, Mrs. Collins."

"Of course," Clare said as she left the room. "If you need anything, we'll be right in here."

"You're going to your room?" Tristan asked.

"Wouldn't want to get in the way," Clare replied with a wink. Tristan rolled his eyes and sighed.

"Just let us know when you're all done," said Marc. "We've got to take pictures of the end result."

"Absolutely sir, we will!" Maki replied. She turned to Will and began to unpack her costume makeup kit on the couch. Tristan looked back up at his father who glanced at Maki, whose back was turned. He looked back at his son and gave him a thumbs up and a nod. Tristan grimaced and shooed him away with his hands. Marc had difficulty suppressing his laughter as he shut the door to the master bedroom.

"Wow, that's a big case," Will said. He wasn't wrong. Maki's costume makeup kit looked more like a small valise than something used for cosmetics. The interior was even more shocking. The case was stacked with vertical shelves and interior compartments that extended sideways from the inner shelves. Each was filled to the brim with foundations, eyeshadows, liners, polishes, mascaras, basic prosthetics, fake blood, spirit gum, and everything else you could possibly need for acting on a stage.

"It's like if Mary Poppins was a makeup artist," Tristan remarked in awe.

"Tools of the trade." Maki shrugged. She turned to Will. "You ready to get *spookified?*"

"Yes!" he cheered.

"To the bathroom!" Maki cried with the point of a finger.

After changing his clothes, Tristan watched as Maki transformed his little brother from a sickly child to a convincing zombie: complete with peeling skin, exposed brain matter, and realistic scarring.

"So, Will," Maki asked, "what do you think?"

"I love it!" he cheered. "It looks so cool!" He kept twisting his neck to examine the back of his head. The Shave had the unexpected benefit of providing Maki with more surface area with which she could work her magic.

"Go and show Mom and Dad!" Tristan said, pushing Will out of the bathroom.

"Mommy! Daddy! Check out my costume!" he cried as he ran down the hall to his parents' bedroom.

"Thanks, Maki. You did a great job," Tristan said. He turned to face his friend who was leaning in toward the bathroom mirror, applying some black makeup to her nose.

"Uh, what are you doing?" he asked nervously.

"You'll see," she said with a smile.

"*Ooookay* then," Tristan said with raised eyebrows as he stepped out of the room. He entered the master bedroom where his parents were drooling over Will's new costume.

"You look phenomenal, Will!" Clare said.

"You're going to scare the pants off the *teachers* at Copperfield High, let alone the students!" Marc exclaimed.

"Did you tell Makiko 'thank you?'" Clare asked.

"Not yet," Will admitted.

"Well, go and tell her!" she said.

"Okay!" He ran out of the room screaming, "Thank you!" Clare smiled and shook her head. Catching Tristan's eye, she beckoned him forward with her index finger. He obliged and leaned in.

Clare whispered into his ear, "She *really* likes you."

"What are you talking about?" Tristan asked. "She's just being a good friend."

"Tristan, you're an idiot," Marc said without hesitation.

"Seriously," Clare added.

"She's just being nice because she feels bad for Will. She's doing this for him, not me," Tristan argued.

"Sure," Clare said. "Because every high school girl wants to spend her Halloween going trick-or-treating with a child instead of spending it with a boy. *Right.*" She winked. "*Gotcha.*"

Will's loud laughter broke in through the bedroom door.

Tristan twisted around and sighed as his pale face rapidly flushed crimson. "Better go see what happened," he said.

Clare simply shook her head as her son exited the room. He headed down the hall and turned toward the bathroom.

"Alright now, what's going on—?"

His voice broke off when he saw what was waiting for him inside. Makiko had blacked out the tip of her nose and drawn on whiskers with eyeliner. She wore a black cat-ear headband on her head while a long, felt tail descended from the back of her waistband. She stood with her feet turned inward and her knees buckled. She tapped her index fingers together like an insecure anime girl and spoke with a stereotypical high-pitched "uwu" voice: replacing her "r's" with "w's."

"We need to dwess up, too! Tee hee!"

Tristan stood frozen. Having no response for the horror he had just witnessed, he chose to simply blot it from his memory. Shell-shocked, he shut the door and walked down the hall. Maki reopened the door and followed him.

"But I bwought youw costume, too. Tee hee!" she cooed, offering a plastic bag filled with something—Tristan wasn't sure he wanted to know what.

"Why are you talking like that?" Tristan laughed.

"You should know! You made me! Tee hee!" With great difficulty, he forced himself to look at her. Suddenly he realized why she had chosen to wear a purple sweater to a Halloween event.

"You're seriously cosplaying as Meowki?"

"Mm-hmm!" She nodded happily.

"Is he putting on his costume?" Will asked as he ran down the hall.

"He's about to!" Maki called back in her normal alto before snapping her head back toward Tristan with Puss in Boots eyes. Tristan took the plastic grocery store bag from her hand and peeked inside. Instantly, he snapped it shut and glared at her. Maki did her best not to burst into tears with laughter.

"Really?!" he exclaimed with a frown.

She said nothing. She simply glanced back at Will. Tristan looked back as well. Seeing the anticipation in his brother's eyes had overridden any sense of trepidation he had felt upon seeing the humiliating outfit. He sighed and nodded.

"Let me get changed." He cut past the group and approached his bedroom down the hall.

"I'll be waiting for youw makeup! Tee hee!" Maki called after him.

"Tristan! Ha ha ha! Oh my goodness! Ha ha ha!" snorted Clare.

"You look great, son!" Mark laughed. "Really, I'm very—*ha ha!*—Proud!"

Tristan stood in the living room, surrounded by onlookers. In his felt gray jumpsuit, he wanted to fall through the floor. He didn't know which was worse: the long pink tail, the giant circular ears he wore atop his head, or the surprisingly detailed makeup job Maki had applied to his face.

"Why am I a mouse?!" he cried—almost literally.

"Because," Maki gleefully replied, "we had to have some sort of cohesion! I had to be Meowki, obviously, and what's a cat without her little *cheese boy?*"

"Cheese boy!" Will snorted.

"Shut up." Tristan snapped with laughter. He turned back to Maki. "Then why is Will a zombie?" he asked. "That doesn't make any sense."

"Because I was Meowki's owner before the zombie apocalypse!" Will announced.

"Ah, so that's the story, huh?" Marc said between bursts of laughter.

"Did you guys invent Meowki lore in the bathroom?!" Tristan seethed between gritted teeth.

"Mm-hmm!" Makiko nodded. Tristan sighed and slapped his palm to his face.

"Hey, watch the makeup!" Clare warned. "She worked hard on that!" Catching sight of her son's face once more caused her to lose control of her laughter again. "It—*haha!*—Looks very—*Ha ha ha!*—Good!—*Ha ha ha!*"

"Thank you, Mrs. Collins," Maki replied with a curtsey.

"Alright," said Marc, rising from the sofa. "Picture time!"

"Where should we take it?" Maki asked. Will grabbed her by the hand and pointed to the living room window. Handmade paper pumpkins and cobweb decorations were taped to the glass.

"Over here! By my decorations!" Will cheered.

"You made those?" Maki said in exaggerated excitement.

"Yeah, at school!"

"Wow! Sure, let's take them here!"

And so, three costumed characters posed in front of the living room window; although, two of them were noticeably happier to take the photo than the third. After thank-yous, warnings, and goodbyes were said, the three travelers began their walk down Bedford Street to the nearby high school.

Bedford High was your average urban public high school. A menacing, brutalist exterior was offset by a more mundane, white-tiled interior that felt more like an overpopulated hospital than anything else. The administration had challenged their staff with classroom decorating competitions for the event. $10 Amazon gift cards inspired teachers and their students to convert each room into spooky treasure troves of Halloween spirit. An English teacher's Harry Potter classroom stood beside a math teacher's pumpkin-filled room. Physical education teachers dressed as werewolves and nurses as mummies. Even the school's resource officers got in on the fun—topping off their armed uniforms with black witch hats and elf ears.

Will was all smiles from the moment they entered to the moment they left. The teachers were blown away by the dedication on display in his costume. Upon seeing his chaperones, some nearly cried with laughter—much to Makiko's pleasure and Tristan's chagrin.

Nearly two hours later, they were back on the sidewalk, heading back to the Collins' apartment. Will had grown sleepy, so Tristan offered to carry him in his arms. While he protested at first, he was asleep within minutes. Slung over Makiko's shoulder was a two-pound pillowcase filled to the brim with candy.

"Well, we certainly made out like bandits, huh?" she said to her friend. He smiled and nodded his head.

"You could say that again," Tristan agreed. "Hey, thanks again for making these costumes. They turned out to be a pretty big hit after all."

"And *you* didn't want to be a mouse!" Maki mocked with a hit of her elbow.

"No, I definitely did not." Tristan chuckled.

They rounded the corner from Starlight Avenue to Bedford Street. The apartment was visible in the distant light of the street lamps. Just one hundred feet ahead rested the subway station. They were each silent for a moment, listening to Will's soft breathing. Suddenly, they each opened their mouths to speak at the same time.

"Sorry," Maki said, "You go first."

"Thanks," said Tristan. "I just wanted to thank you for coming out tonight. You've really made my brother happy."

"He's a great kid." Maki smiled. "He deserves it."

"Thanks," Tristan said. They were very close to the subway station now. If there was ever a time to say what she had to say, it was now. Maki stuffed her free hand into her pocket and gulped.

"So, you and Izzy seem to getting pretty close," she said.

"Yeah." Tristan nodded. "She's very sweet. I wish she could have come tonight."

"She's certainly been busy." Maki nodded. "I'm not sure what's going on with her."

"What do you mean?" Tristan asked.

Maki shrugged shoulders and shook her head. "Well, she's just been acting so strange lately."

"Strange how?"

Makiko hesitated before answering.

"Like she's just so hyper-focused on this recital. She doesn't seem to care about anything else."

"Well, maybe this could be her big break." Tristan offered. "If it goes well, she could be performing for a professional opera company. Iz told me they recruit young musicians all the time."

"I know that," Maki said, growing flustered. "But she's getting her priorities mixed up. Chasing after your goals doesn't give you the right to treat people like garbage."

"Like garbage?" Tristan repeated. "Izzy's a sweetheart. She'd never do that."

Maki wanted to hit him.

"You're such a moron, Tristan!" she shouted. Will stirred in his arms but didn't wake.

"Quiet!" Tristan hushed. She lowered her voice for Will's sake.

"I'm just so sick and tired of you letting people treat you like crap! *Everyone* is, yet you refuse to see it!"

"Maki, I don't know what you think is going on between me and Izzy, but she certainly isn't treating me like crap." He thought back to the kiss on the train the other day. Maki threw up her hands.

"I can't do this now," she hissed. Exasperated, she forced the pillowcase into Tristan's hand and proceeded to the steps of the subway station.

"Maki!" Tristan called after her.

"Call me when you finally *wake up!*" she cried over her shoulder. A moment later, she was gone. Will gently stirred awake in his big brother's arms.

"Tristan? Are we home?" he asked wearily.

"Yeah." He sighed. "Just one more block."

Tristan readjusted his little brother in his arms and continued his journey down the sidewalk.

NOVEMBER

RETURN

IT WAS A QUIET MORNING in the Collins family apartment. Clare busied herself in the kitchen preparing breakfast for the family while her husband dressed in the master bedroom. Her eldest son entered the kitchen and greeted her, taking a mug out of the cabinet as he went.

"Morning." She nodded. Bacon sizzled on the skillet in front of her.

"Smells amazing," Tristan remarked, pouring himself a steaming mug of coffee.

"Thanks." Clare nodded. She set down the tongs and joined her son at the island countertop. He had briefly told her about the conversation with Makiko after tucking Will into bed last night. He still wasn't in a good mood.

"She's right, you know," Clare said.

"Who?"

"Your friend." Clare took a sip from her mug. "Izzy hasn't been treating you very well."

Tristan shook his head.

"You haven't even met her."

"Yet I've met Makiko," Clare interrupted. "Shouldn't that be a sign of anything?"

"She's pushy."

"She's *helpful*." Clare stood up. "And how dare you say that about someone like that. She went out of her way to come here and give Will a nice holiday." After checking to see that the food was prepared, Clare shut off the burner and began plating.

"I thought you said this wasn't about Will," Tristan countered.

"It's not. But she cares about Will *for* you."

"What does that mean?"

Frustrated, Clare raised her voice. "It means that she knows how much you love your brother, while Izzy doesn't seem to give a damn!"

"That's not true!" Tristan protested. He rose from the table, feeling his face grow hot. "She went out of her way to spend time with him during the campus festival."

"And who else was there?" Clare countered. "Whose idea do you think that was?" She leaned past her son and shouted, "Guys! Breakfast!"

"Be right there!" Marc called.

Tristan thought back to the way the girls had responded to his offer. Izzy left a heart, but Maki… He shook out the thought. He refused to believe it.

"She's not a bad person, Mom," he said. "She's just overwhelmed with this recital."

"I never said she was," Clare said comfortingly. "I'm just trying to tell you that I don't think she feels as strongly about you as you do about her." Clare finished setting up the food in their ceramic serving trays. She beckoned her son over to help her carry them over to the dining room table.

"Boys! It's on the table! Hurry up!" she shouted. She turned back to Tristan. "You're such a handsome young man."

"Stop. No, I'm not." Tristan shrugged off the compliment in genuine disbelief.

"Yes, you are," his mother protested. "I know what you're thinking: 'Oh, you're just saying that 'cause you're my mother,'" she mocked in a deep voice. "But it's the truth. If you looked like a dog, I'd tell you."

"Um… thank you?" Tristan said.

"It's my job," replied Clare with a smile.

Marc was futzing with his tie as he entered the room.

"Sorry hon, I just can't get this the right length today."

"Ah, *mo mhuirnín*." Clare sighed and shook her head. "Come here." Marc approached to let his wife fix his tie.

"Tristan, honey, why don't you go check on Will and see what's taking him so long? Tell him the food's out," Clare suggested. Tristan nodded. Taking one last sip of coffee, he set down his mug and headed down the hall to Will's room. Though the door was partially opened, he knocked anyway.

"Hey, Will? Breakfast's ready."

There was no reply.

"Probably still sleeping," he thought. Tristan pushed the door open and stepped inside. Will was in his bed on the far side of the room, facing the wall. Tristan walked to his bedside.

"Time to get up, sleepyhead," he said cheerfully. He reached out his hand to shake his brother awake but froze in place. Up close, he could see his brother's rapid, shallow panting. Desperately gasping for air.

"No," Tristan spat out. "No, no, Will!" He rolled Will onto his back and looked into his eyes. He was conscious, staring back up at his brother with a look of pain.

"MOM! DAD! GET IN HERE, NOW!"

That evening, the Collins family sat in shock in the pediatric ward of St. Luke's Medical Center. Will was laid in the same bed he had been in just a month prior. By chance, the same room on floor thirteen was still available. Reserved for them out of kindness for its familiarity, or some sick joke—the Collins couldn't discern which. Will was asleep. Dr. Perkins had placed him on a respirator for the next few days to help stabilize his breathing. It was almost nine pm when Marc tapped his oldest son on the shoulder.

"Come on, Tristan. You've got school tomorrow," he said. Tristan nodded solemnly. He was in shock. He thought Will was in the clear, and now there they were, back at square one. He tried to stay optimistic. Perhaps it was a little slip-up, like an addict might have. It didn't set you back to the beginning. It was just a bump in the road. You always came back stronger, didn't you?

REFUSAL

"TRISTAN I—I'M SO SORRY to hear about Will," Izzy said. Tristan and his friend were seated opposite each other at the Turquoise Fox. He had withheld the news about Will's hospital stay from the girls last night, deciding that something like this was better said in person. Besides, he wasn't exactly on good terms with Makiko just then, anyway. She'd just berate him again like she always did. But Izzy? His mother had misjudged her. She would listen. He'd prove it.

"Thanks," Tristan said. "Mom's up at St. Luke's now."

Izzy nodded and took another sip of her drink—hot green tea with honey, a singer's refreshment of choice.

"What do they think happened?" Izzy asked. "Is it a relapse?"

"Not exactly." Tristan shook his head. "You can't really relapse if you haven't gone back into remission. Maybe all the walking around on Halloween was too much. Maybe it was random. Anything's possible. We'll know more later today."

"Let's pray you find out soon," Izzy said, placing a comforting hand on Tristan's. He squeezed it, wearing a sad smile.

"Thanks," he said.

"Of course." She smiled back. She looked down at their hands. It was a nice feeling, she thought, but not a realistic one. She withdrew her palm and grabbed her drink for another sip.

"You don't have rehearsal tomorrow, right?"

Izzy nodded. "Yeah. Thursdays are my free days."

"Listen, would you like to come with me?"

"Go with you?" Izzy asked, raising an eyebrow.

"Yeah."

"What do you mean? Where?"

"To see my brother," Tristan clarified conspicuously. Hadn't that been obvious from the start? Was she avoiding the topic altogether? Izzy gulped down another sip of tea. She cleared her throat as she glanced about the room. Stalling for time? Searching for the right words?

"You mean in the hospital?" she asked. Tristan raised an eyebrow and glanced away with a shrug of his shoulders.

"Well yeah. Of course. Why not?" he said, his tone becoming shaky from nerves. "No reason you can't come with me. He'd definitely love to see you."

"That's kind of you to say," Izzy said softly, not taking her eyes off the blue table. She didn't speak for a while.

"Everything okay?" Tristan asked. Finally, Izzy sighed and looked up.

"Listen, I—" She broke off again. A moment later, Izzy was rising from the table. She tossed her bag over her shoulder and left the building, leaving her drink behind. Tristan chased out after her.

"Izzy, wait! What's going on?"

"I'm sorry, Tristan," she said sadly. "I can't do this anymore."

"Can't do what?"

"This!" Izzy thrust her palms out to her sides, still facing away from him. "Seeing you all the time, knowing full well I don't have the time to commit to any sort of relationship right now."

They both stopped dead in their tracks. Tristan circled to her front.

"Are you breaking up with me?" he whispered.

"Breaking up?" Izzy shook her head in disbelief. "Tristan, we were never *together!*"

"But all those times where we—"

"I liked you, sure! But we were never a couple!" At this, Tristan felt a rage starting to burn within his breast.

"Then why waste all that time?" he demanded, raising his voice. "Why go on all those dates with me? Why hold my hand? All that sending me hearts, kissing me on the cheek—what was the point of all that?!" Izzy's eyes started to water. Watching her red lips start to quiver in the chilly Academic Mall broke his heart, but he had to have an answer.

"I guess I thought I could make it work…" she said with a stammer. "I never meant to hurt you, Tristan. But you and your brother…" She sniffled as tears began to fall. "It's just too much." She wiped her eyes and looked back at Tristan. "I've got to be ready for this show. You have your needs and I have mine. Can't you see? Now just isn't the time for us, okay?"

Tristan didn't know whether to cry or scream. He bit his lip. At a loss for words, he found himself pacing into a nearby snowbank; feeling the chill of the frozen water congealing around his boots with each stomp of his foot.

"If that's how you feel," he began calmly, before quickly falling back into a rage. "If my brother is *too much* for you, then just go!"

"Tristan, I'm sorry."

"Don't be!" he scoffed with a delirious smile. "Have your stupid show! You could get picked up. Be famous. That's what life's all about anyway, right? Agh, how could I be so *stupid?!*"

"Tristan, I—"

"Leave me alone!" Tristan snapped. Izzy shut her eyes and pouted. She nodded solemnly.

"Alright," she said, quietly. "I won't be bothering you again." Tristan didn't turn to watch as she left, keeping his eyes fixed on the snow prints beneath him. When his temper had finally cooled a few seconds later, he turned to speak.

Unfortunately, his friend was already gone.

HONESTY

TRISTAN ENTERED THE HOSPITAL ROOM with his head hung down. Clare rushed over to the door to greet him with a compassionate hug.

"Honey, I'm so sorry," she said softly.

"It's alright," said Tristan as they released. "What can I say? You were right. I should have listened to you." He stepped into the room and found Will asleep. The plastic respirator was still attached to his face by Velcro straps that wrapped around his head. Oxygen was being fed in via a tank adhered to his IV stand.

"How is he?" Tristan asked.

"Doing better." Clare smiled. "Dr. Perkins said the mask can come off tomorrow."

"Good." Tristan nodded. "Any idea what might've caused it?"

"They're not sure, but overexertion is the most likely candidate." Tristan grimaced at this answer. He fell into a guest chair and buried his head in his hands.

"Hey," his mother said. She sat adjacent to him and wrapped her arm around his shoulders. "This has nothing to do with you."

"I was the one who took him out. He should have never left the house."

"You did a good thing," Clare reassured. "There was no way you could have known this was going to happen. Besides, they can't even prove that was what caused it. They're still running tests."

Tristan nodded solemnly.

"Lately, it's been feeling like I've been upsetting everybody," he lamented.

Clare shook her head.

"Izzy was a lost cause. I knew it from the moment you showed me her picture. Forget her."

"I will," Tristan agreed. "To be honest, I never really…"

"I know," Clare completed his thought. "It was obvious. To everyone." They sat in silence for a moment while Tristan struggled to piece together the words.

Makiko.

All it took was one look from her almond-shaped green eyes to turn his life upside down. Her made up pink lips. Her hearty laugh. Her short, thick blue-black hair that danced every time she moved her head. But surely, she hated him. All those insults. The scoffs, the jests at his expense. She was there for Izzy and Will, not him.

That feeling he had in his chest the moment her eyes locked with his was the LSM launch for a coaster layout his heart wasn't familiar with. He was riding blind, with each twist and turn filling him with either excitement or dread.

A certain coaster to the south was renowned for its ferocious heartline roll: a corkscrew where the central axis of rotation was located directly at chest-height. Riders were propelled through this element at over 53 miles per hour, creating a whipping motion that threatened to careen them into the lagoon just fifteen feet below. This fear was especially poignant as riders were secured by a simple lap bar hydraulic restraint. The intense lateral-Gs would pull riders to the left, creating a feeling of equal parts excitement and terror as they were literally lifted out of their seats without the psychological comfort of a shoulder restraint.

Tristan's internal coaster was now in a heartline roll of its own. One far more vicious than Intamin could ever imagine.

"How can I fix this?" he asked. "She can't stand me."

"No, she can't stand what you've been putting yourself through." Clare corrected her son. He nodded.

"Even if that was true, is there anything I could do?"

Clare smiled at him. "I suppose you could start with a phone call."

Makiko was shocked to hear Izzy crying over the phone. After explaining the situation to her father, he was happy to let her borrow the car to head over to her home in Lenox. Thankfully, the drive from Yellow Harbor only took around ten minutes. She pulled into the driveway of the two-story colonial home. Gilbert White was already on the porch, awaiting her arrival.

"Hello Mr. White," she greeted as she jogged up the steps.

"Maki," he said, hugging her. "Come on in."

Dressed in a white and pink apron, Brandy White pulled a tray of brownies out of the oven. After setting them on the counter, she dashed over to her guest, greeting her with a hug. Save for a few extra wrinkles, Brandy was the spitting image of her daughter and just as large—towering over Makiko.

"Brownies just need a little while longer to cool. Can I get you anything to drink in the meantime?" she asked.

"I'm alright, thanks," Maki said politely. "I just wanted to check in on Izzy. She sounded very upset over the phone."

"She is." Gilbert nodded. "Something to do with Tristan, but she wouldn't explain what." He glared over at his wife. "I'm telling you if that boy tried anything—"

"Honey, I already asked her that and she said no!" Brandy countered.

"Oh. Okay, good." Gil nodded. He looked back at Maki and shrugged. "Then your guess is as good as mine—at least until she calms down."

Makiko headed up the wooden steps to the second-floor bedrooms of the home. She and her friend had fond memories of sliding down these same steps on pillows and blankets as children. Now, that same childhood companion was upstairs and in distress. Worst of all, she wouldn't tell anyone why. What happened?

The top of the steps funneled out to a blue hallway that extended to the right and left. Makiko turned right and stopped at the white paneled window at the hall's end—adjacent to Izzy's room on the left. She knocked on the door.

"Izzy? It's me, Maki."

A few seconds later, she could faintly distinguish the creaking of mattress springs and the hollow stomping of feet across the wooden floor. Izzy unlocked the door and opened it. She looked terrible. Her face wasn't made up, revealing zits along her jaw and the splotches of a rash. She had dark rings under her eyes. Her golden hair was tattered and frizzy. She didn't stay at the door long before retreating into the darkness of her unlit bedroom.

Makiko stepped in and flicked the light switch. The walls were covered with framed choir awards and video game posters. Brightly colored bookshelves were filled with science fiction and fantasy epics by Crichton and Tolkien. On top of each cabinet was what totaled to be at least a dozen trophies. Most were for singing, but a few were from her brief stint in the high school drama club.

Izzy sat on her bed at the far side of the room. A somber blue glow periodically engulfed the darkness of the chamber with its gentle heartbeat. Its source was an expensive gaming rig resting on a desk, juxtaposing the cheap rolling chair pushed beneath. Makiko dragged the chair over to the bedside and sat down.

"Izzy, what's going on?" she asked plaintively. "What happened with Tristan?"

"I told him I didn't want to see him anymore," Izzy said softly.

"Why did you tell him that?"

"I just can't." Izzy shook her head. "I have so much on my plate right now. Between work, school, and the recital, I just don't have time for this."

"But why wait till now?" Maki asked.

Izzy shrugged. "I guess I thought he was worth the effort." Izzy twitched the corner of her lips into a brief smile before returning them to a frown. "And he is. Just, not for me, you know?"

Maki nodded solemnly. "But you still haven't explained—why the sudden change? Things seemed to be going so well."

Izzy shook her head. "On the surface, yeah, things looked great. We were holding hands, going on dates… but everything was so few and far between. And now that his brother is back in the hospital…" She raised her eyebrows and spoke deliberately. "I can't be there for him. I don't have that kind of time!"

Maki gasped. "Will's in the hospital?"

"Yeah, he didn't tell you?" Izzy asked.

"No," Maki said in shock. "We haven't spoken since Halloween. How is Will?"

"I don't know." Izzy shook her head. "He just asked me to go with him and I said no."

Maki stood up from the chair and walked toward the wall, bracing herself against it with one hand and gesticulating with the other.

"So let me get this straight," she spat. "You're telling me that William, his brother, is in the hospital—*COULD BE DYING*—and you said you were *too busy* to go with him?!"

"I thought you came here to support me!" Izzy cried.

"Support you? How could I support someone so heartless?!"

"Heartless?!" Izzy shouted.

"Yes!" Maki nodded, enraged. "Heartless! You know what, Izzy? I don't even know who you are anymore."

"Excuse me?!"

Maki stepped forward from the wall. "This whole opera thing has gone to your head. You used to be fun. Bubbly. Silly. Now you're just this miserable diva who'd rather spend all day hunkered down in a practice room than take a few hours to support someone who needs it!"

Izzy shot up from the bed. "How dare you talk to me that way in my own home! Just because you're having another one of your episodes doesn't mean you can drag me down with you!"

"*You—!*"

Maki couldn't get another word out. Instead, she stormed toward Izzy at top speed, her tunnel vision narrowing in on her target. Seeing her life flash before her eyes, Izzy collapsed and took up a defensive position on the bed with her arms raised above her head. Maki grabbed her by the shoulder and raised her fist before freezing. She shut her eyes and inhaled. A moment later, she released her friend and began to pace. Izzy lowered her guard, relieved to be alive.

"You know what?" she said between deep breaths. "I hope those talent scouts *do* see you perform. And I hope you blow them away. Because they're going to be the only people in the audience who want to hear you sing!"

"Fine! I don't need you there anyway!" Izzy shouted back.

"Good, because I don't plan on coming!"

Makiko rushed out of the room with Izzy slamming the door shut behind her. Gilbert and Brandy waited for her at the base of the stairs.

"Maki, we're so sorry she spoke to you like that," Gilbert said, shaking his head. "I don't know what's gotten into her. That's not the little girl I raised."

"It's alright," Maki said, trying to control her fury with a series of deep breaths through her flaring nostrils. "I just... I just need to go home."

Feeling that it would be unsafe to send her away in this state, Brandy insisted she sit for a while to cool off. She guided her guest to the living room couch where she provided coffee and brownies. Makiko had planned on refusing out of anger but caved in as soon as the decadent aroma of the scratch-fudge brownies had traveled up her nostrils. There was a reason the cafe was named after her.

Meanwhile, Gilbert went upstairs to work on Izzy. A half-hour later, they came down and entered the living room. Gilbert seated himself in his favorite green armchair while his wife slid over a cushion to make room for their daughter. Izzy sat down and stared at the floor.

"I'm sorry I yelled at you, Maki," she said with a sniffle.

"It's alright," Makiko replied quietly. "You're allowed to get angry. Trust me, I know what that's like."

"But it wasn't fair—what I was mad about, I mean."

"No, it absolutely wasn't," Brandy remonstrated. Izzy winced.

"I just—I need to step away from things for a little while," Izzy explained. "I've been so worked up about this show. This new song. The scouts. I need some time to think."

"I'm cutting Izzy from the cafe," Gilbert said.

"You're firing her?" Maki gasped.

Gil held up a palm and shook his head. "No, no—just a break. At least until the start of the new year. After this mess is all over."

"Smart move." Maki nodded.

"If you see Will again," Izzy said, "could you tell him I miss him?" At this, the grief she didn't know she held poured out of her in a shower of tears. "I really do. I want to see him again but… the pressure, it's just…" Brandy put her arm around her daughter and shushed her. Maki frowned and put her hand on Izzy's shoulder.

"Of course I will," she smiled sadly.

In the car, Maki called her dad, letting her know she was on her way. While stopped at a red light, she was surprised when her phone rang once more. The name that appeared on the onboard display surprised her even more. She hit the green, "talk" icon.

"It's you," she said.

"Yeah, it's me," Tristan replied.

"Everything okay?" she asked.

"Yeah," he said. He sounded sad despite himself. "Just um, well, I wanted to apologize."

"There's no need," Maki said.

"No, I really should. You were right. About Izzy, I mean."

"Yeah, I know. I just got back from her place."

"So, you know," he said.

"I know she was overwhelmed with the show and didn't know how to break it to you. She ended up using you instead."

"What?" Tristan was surprised by her response. He had been expecting her to side with her friend.

"Yeah," Maki said. "Sorry, I kind of had it out with her tonight. Still a little sore. Her parents are, too."

"I was worried about that," Tristan said. "Mr. White's not mad?"

"Oh, he's furious," Maki replied, "Just not at you. Gil can't believe how much Izzy's let the show take over her life."

"Me neither." Tristan sighed.

"Same," Maki agreed. "He's taking action, too. He cut her shifts from the cafe."

"You're kidding."

"I wish I was. He's trying to lighten her workload by giving her some more space to breathe."

"That's awful," Tristan said.

"Yeah."

The light changed to green. Makiko depressed the gas pedal and passed through the intersection. The headlights of her Toyota illuminated a street sign demarcating the Yellow Harbor city limits.

"Listen, um, my brother—"

"Izzy told me. You should have said something. Angry or not, you know how much I love Will."

"I know, you're right," Tristan said. "He misses you. Talks about you constantly."

"Well, aren't I the popular one," Maki boasted. "He's a smart kid. If it were between seeing you or me, I'd choose me, too."

"Ha ha," Tristan said sarcastically.

"How's he holding up?" Makiko asked with sincerity.

"He's doing okay," Tristan replied. He comes off the respirator tomorrow. The results from his biopsies should come back later this week. We won't know for sure until then, but his energy seems to be coming back. It can be hit or miss. He can't wait to get out of bed, though."

"I could imagine. He was a ball of energy at the Halloween event." She paused, her stomach dropped as a new thought occurred to her. "You don't think that was what did it, do you?" The silence on the other end of the line sent a shiver down Maki's spine.

"No," Tristan finally answered, "It's possible, but not likely." Makiko breathed a sigh of relief.

"Good. I'll be able to sleep tonight," she replied.

"Tell me about it. That was my first worry, too."

Makiko was turned onto Sally Street. The chain link fence that enclosed the diminutive parking lot of her apartment complex was visible.

"Hey Tristan, I'm about to park."

"Oh, so you need to go?" he asked.

"In a bit," she replied. "But I was wondering: can he have any visitors?"

"You mean outside of family?"

"Yeah."

"Do you want to visit Will?" Tristan asked, feeling a smile start to spread across his face.

"Would that be alright?" Maki asked anxiously. She squinted her eyes and lifted her shoulders in preparation for his response.

"Are you kidding? I'd—he'd love to see you!"

"Great!" Maki cheered, relaxing her shoulders. "Does tomorrow work?"

"Tomorrow? Of course!" Tristan replied gleefully. Suddenly, he remembered something. "Wait, you don't have to work on painting the sets or anything on Thursdays, do you?"

"No, I tried to coordinate my schedule with Izzy when I worked there."

"*When* you worked there. Wait, did you quit?"

"I'm going to, yes." Maki nodded. "You think I really want to be a part of something that's turned my friend into some sort of walking soprano zombie?"

"Odd choice of words, but I see your point." Tristan laughed.

Makiko parked the car and let the engine idle to keep the battery running.

"Besides, I think Izzy and I are going to take a bit of a break from one another," she lamented. The solemnity in her voice was unmistakable.

"Maki, that's... that's terrible," said Tristan.

"I know." Maki nodded. "I just don't want to see her right now. At least not till this stupid recital is over with, anyway. She's not herself."

"I just still can't believe it." Tristan sighed in shock. "You two were so close."

"We're more than that. We're practically sisters." Makiko looked at the clock on her phone. It was getting late. She already had a lot of explaining to do and she'd rather not make matters worse by lingering in the car.

"Hey, I'm at my place now. Just text me the time you'd like me to meet you there and I'll head over. St. Luke's on Starlight Hill, right?"

"That's right," Tristan said.

"I'll be there," Maki said. "I promise."

"I believe you." Tristan smiled. "Thank you."

"Anytime."

Maki hung up the call. She made the sign of the cross and prayed, asking for guidance and strength for the things she'd have to do over the next few days. A few deep breaths later, she cut the engine and exited the car.

VISITING HOURS

DESPITE HAVING SEEN THE IMAGES from the Roosevelt University Department of Medicine website, Makiko still found herself taken aback by the sheer size of the hospital facility. The clock tower, The Cube, and the parking garage all stood as a trinity of well-being for their inhabitants who so desperately needed care.

It was 4 pm when she entered the building: the time she had agreed upon with Tristan. Walking through the large, seafoam-tiled lobby, she wondered if she'd see his parents today. At least one of them would have to stay and look after Will, right? Probably Mrs. Collins. His father was an accountant, right? Funny, she couldn't remember asking them about their careers. Just never came up, she supposed.

Makiko put the thought aside and approached the reception desk. She had her picture taken in exchange for an identification sticker which she placed on the chest of her black and purple hoodie.

Just as she was applying the sticker, a familiar ginger stepped out of the elevator and strode over to greet her. She hugged him without hesitation. He had nearly forgotten how intoxicating her perfume was. They each held the hug for what they assumed was two seconds longer than the other would have liked and released. Tristan led her to the elevator doors at the base of the clock tower and hit the number thirteen.

"We got the biopsy results today," Tristan said with a sigh. Maki could tell from his expression that the results hadn't been what he was hoping for.

"His bone marrow isn't looking so good."

"Immunodeficiencies?" Maki asked. Tristan nodded.

"He'll need to stay here for longer now," he admitted. "He seems alright today." The doors opened. "I'm just praying that he'll stay that way."

They exited the elevator and strode past reception. A nearby nurse was pushing a patient in a wheelchair. The child had goggle-style glasses with a strap that wrapped around her head at an angle; offsetting a large scar that traversed the opposite way across her bald scalp. She was giggling at a series of photocopied pages in her hand. Seeing Tristan, the nurse tapped the child on the shoulder and pointed. The little girl waved and smiled. Unsure of how else to react, Tristan waved back.

"Someone you know?" Maki asked.

Tristan shrugged, "I've seen her around. Never spoken to the family though."

Makiko nodded. "Nice people," she said kindly.

"Here we are," said Tristan. He nodded at the signboard on the wall marked, "William Collins."

"You ready?" he asked her nervously.

Makiko offered a sad smile.

"Absolutely." She nodded.

Clare rose from the armchair to greet the newcomers.

"Makiko, it's lovely to see you again," she said in her lilted brogue.

"You as well, Mrs. Collins," Maki said, shaking her hand.

"Maki!" Will cheered from the bed. He tried to hop off, but Tristan gently lowered him back down with a restraining hand. He had been off the respirator since three, so he was eager to get back on his feet.

"Hey, squirt! How've ya been?" Maki cooed. She strode over to Will and scooped him up into a tight hug.

"Not too well," Will admitted. "It's getting easier to breathe, though."

"Tell her about the card," Clare prompted.

"Oh yeah!" Will smiled. "My classmates all signed this card for me. Mr. Burt brought it after school ended yesterday." He gestured to a vase of white flowers on the nightstand. Next to it was an oversized card filled with student's names and well-wishes.

"Wow!" Maki exclaimed, peering at the card and flowers. "So pretty! Is Mr. Burt your teacher?"

"Uh huh!" He nodded. "He's the best! We got to make all sorts of spooky decorations for Halloween."

"Oh, were those the ones I saw at your apartment?"

Will nodded.

"He loves art if you haven't already guessed," Clare said with a shrug. "Takes after his big brother."

"I love art, too." Maki smiled. "Did you know I'm a painter?" she asked the child. His eyes widened with excitement.

"Really?!" he exclaimed. "That's so cool! Do you think you could teach me?"

"Uh, yeah!" said Maki. "Once I get all the supplies, I'm throwing you up in front of that easel."

"Ha, cool!" Will giggled.

Maki stood up and walked around the room, ending her self-guided tour at the window adjacent to the bed. Supporting herself on her two out-turned palms, she peered through the glass from the windowsill. From this lowly tower, she commanded an excellent view of the Starlight Hill beachfront and beyond that, the Roosevelt Island skyline.

"Wow, that's quite a view," she commented.

"Makes for some great sketching," Tristan agreed. He joined her at the window. The sky was taking on an orange glow as the sun was preparing its early autumnal descent. Their shoulders touched for a brief moment. Tristan said nothing but slid to the side as he blushed. Maki smiled without moving. A moment later, he cleared his throat and pointed at the beachfront.

"See that sand down there?" he said. Maki nodded. "That's Starlight Beach. We had the best parties there growing up."

"My birthday!" Will cried.

"That's right." Clare smiled. "Will was a summer baby, so we like to celebrate on the shore."

"Born in July. Making him a Cancer both literally and figuratively," Tristan said with a laugh.

"Tristan Collins!" Clare cried in playful animadversion. She tossed an empty paper cup at him with a laugh.

"Mrs. Collins," Makiko began, "I'm trained in karate. Would you like me to punch your son for you?"

"Be my guest," Clare said with a permissive wave of the hand.

Maki smirked at Tristan and raised her fists in the air. He started shaking his head.

"No. No, you're not actually going to—"

Makiko cocked her head to the side.

"I'm just following orders." She drew her right fist back. Will was coughing from laughing so hard.

"No, please don't—*Mom!*" Tristan held his palms in front of his face defensively.

"We have to respect our elders." Makiko shrugged. "We're both Catholic. It's the fourth commandment."

"Oh, just hit him already," Clare said.

"Wait what?" Tristan lowered his hands, perplexed. The next instant, Makiko lightly tapped his cheek with her knuckle.

"Boop!" She popped her lips. Will was wiping tears away from his eyes. His older brother turned toward him.

"I'm glad my pain amuses you."

Makiko laughed again and turned back to the window.

"So, Will, what do you do for fun around here?" she asked.

"Well," he said, pushing himself upright in the bed. "Tristan hooked up our Switch to the TV, I read, and there are lots of fun board games in the playroom!"

"Cool!" replied Maki, excitedly. She held up a pair of closed fists at chest height in a cartoonish display of simulated excitement. "That sounds really, really fun!"

"How are you feeling now?" Tristan asked his brother. Feeding off Maki's energy, he put on a big grin. "Do you think you can walk over with us to play some games?" He turned back to Clare. "If that's alright with you of course."

Clare raised an eyebrow and shook her head.

"I don't care!" She chuckled. "It's what Will wants. And Maki, too. She's the guest after all!"

"I'd love to take Will down to the playroom!" Makiko beamed.

"Then it's settled." Clare smiled. "I'm going to stay here and rest my eyes for a little while if that's alright with you." She locked eyes with Maki. "I don't want to seem like a bad host."

"Are you kidding?" Maki said. "Don't be silly. You must be exhausted. Take as long as you need."

"Thanks." She smiled back.

Will grimaced as he pushed himself forward, turned, and let his legs dangle off the side of the bed. He kicked his feet in the air for a moment before looking up at Tristan with a smile.

"Ready to go!"

"Then let's do it." Tristan nodded then turned to his mom. "See you in a bit." He leaned in and hugged her. When he did, he whispered two words into her ear: "Thank you."

As Tristan helped his brother off the bed, Maki couldn't help but feel a little sad. In another life, Tristan and Will might have been holding hands down the main thoroughfare of an amusement park. Playing carnival games, riding rides, mascots hugging the little boy and rustling his hair...

In reality, Tristan guided him out the door, his brother in one hand and an IV cart in the other.

It was moments like this that reminded Makiko of how unforgivably cruel the world could be. She might have given in to these dark thoughts many years ago if it hadn't been for her strong faith. Job was a blameless man, yet God still allowed Satan to afflict him with loss. The pious man remained faithful as his whole world came tumbling down all around him. Foreigners pillaged his property. Lightning struck his shepherds. His own children were crushed to death by a collapsing roof. He himself was left destitute and covered in boils and sores that he would have to scrape off his body each day. So much undeserved pain, and yet he still believed in the goodness of the Creator. Life is a test of faith. Sometimes all you can do is pray and hang on.

Makiko followed them through the doorframe. They were greeted by the jubilant smiles of the mascots who offered Will high-fives, stickers, and lollipops. Strange how all the characters in this amusement park had decided to wear scrubs. A minute later, they found themselves in the Wineland Room. Will immediately dashed over to his favorite table with a smile. His big brother jogged after him with the IV stand.

"Whoa! Slow down!" Tristan said with a laugh. Makiko watched as Tristan helped seat his brother at the table, untangling him from his cords.

"Here, let me help you with that," she said, helping him adjust some of the tubes.

"Thanks," Tristan said.

He and Makiko seated themselves on opposite sides of his little brother. If it wasn't for his fatigue, Will might have been bouncing up and down in excitement.

"So, Will, what do you wanna play?" Maki asked.

"Hmm…" he mumbled, placing a finger on his chin. "Do you know how to play Jenga?"

"Do *I* know how to play Jenga?" Maki scoffed, laying a hand on her chest. "Young man, I'll have you know that I am the Jenga *queen*!" She leaned into Will's side. Cupping her hand to his ear, she whispered, "*Let's get it set up and kick Tristan's butt!*"

"Haha! Okay!" Will cheered.

Tristan shook his head and rose from the table. Across the room stood a cubic bookshelf filled with every board game imaginable. He scanned the densely packed shelves for a moment before eyeing his prey. With an "aha!" he fetched the rectangular box from the shelf and brought it over to the table for setup.

"Alright Will, you go first!" said Tristan.

"No, Maki should go!" Will protested. "Ladies first!"

"What a little gentleman!" cooed their guest. "Okay, fine I'll go."

Gently feeling about the tower, Maki searched for a loose block. With one finger, she easily nudged it out of the tower and placed it on top. Satisfied, she nodded at Will. He shook his head and pointed at Tristan.

"Okay, now you go next!" he ordered.

"Me?" Tristan cried. Makiko hit him with the back of her hand.

"Go, moron!" she shouted, securing another laugh from Will. "Don't say 'go,' it's not nice. 'Moron' is fine." The clarification caused Will to laugh even harder. Tristan patted him on the back to help him catch his breath.

"You good?" he asked. Will nodded.

"I'm okay!" Will said. "Take your turn!"

"Okay, okay!"

Tristan found another easy piece in the tower and placed it on top. Will followed him with ease. The boys looked at Makiko with anticipation. Ignoring Tristan's gaze, she gave Will a silent wink, causing him to giggle.

"What are you guys doing…?" Tristan asked nervously.

"Oh, nothing…" Makiko sang.

She delicately fingered the bottom right block of the tower. The structure wobbled precariously, but she managed to remove the piece with ease and place it on top. Tristan was shocked. She looked as if she was about to burst open with laughter.

"Your turn!" Maki cheered.

"You are *such* a jerk," he moaned.

After some careful searching, Tristan eventually found a block to place on top. Will instantly found a loose block sending the game back to Maki. She raised her eyebrows at Will before slowly inching her hands back to the base of the tower.

"No. You're not going to—" Tristan muttered.

She removed the other outermost block from the bottom row, leaving the entire tower to be supported by the one in the center.

"Oh, come *ON!*" Tristan cried, watching her place the block on top with ease. She turned to Tristan, flashing him with doll eyes and a Cheshire grin.

"*Your turn!*" Makiko said, beaming with glee.

"I hate you, *SO* much!" Tristan replied, resulting in another laugh from his brother. He delicately tapped about the blocks in the tower, searching for some structural weakness for him to exploit. Unfortunately, he could find none.

Each tap of the tower resulted in a pithy remark from Makiko: "Nope. Nada. Try again."

"Will you shut up?" Tristan snapped, playfully. At last, he found a block that was somewhat looser than the others. "Okay, *HERE.*"

Tristan gently began sliding out the block from the center of the structure. A moment later, the entire tower tilted forward and came crashing down on the center of the table. Maki and Will were left in hysterics. They high-fived.

"Good teamwork!" Maki cried jubilantly.

The trio spent the next few hours joking and playing games together, with Makiko dominating most of them. Jenga, UNO, Life—they even managed to build a small Lego fort. When it finally came time to end the day, they collected their things and prepared to walk Will back to his room.

"Alright, Will. You all set?" asked Tristan

"Uh-huh!" Will nodded with glee.

Tristan grabbed the IV stand and wheeled it around the chair. Exiting the Wineland Room, he extended his free hand toward William. To his surprise, his brother didn't take it. He looked down to see him clutching onto Maki's instead. He smiled to himself and pressed on.

Back in the room, Clare was sound asleep in the armchair. A paperback romance lay open on her lap. Quickly and quietly, Tristan helped his brother back to bed. As he tucked him in, Will suddenly shot up through the covers.

"Can you tell me another story?" he asked.

"Of course!" Tristan whispered. "You've just got to quiet down. Mom's sleeping."

"I'm awake," Clare said groggily, rubbing her eyes.

"Can Maki help?"

Makiko smiled. She joined Tristan at Will's bedside.

"I'd love to," she said, nodding at Mrs. Collins. She returned the joyful expression.

"Okay!" Will cheered.

Tristan reached into his backpack and pulled out his sketchbook.

MEOWKI AND THE SQUIRREL

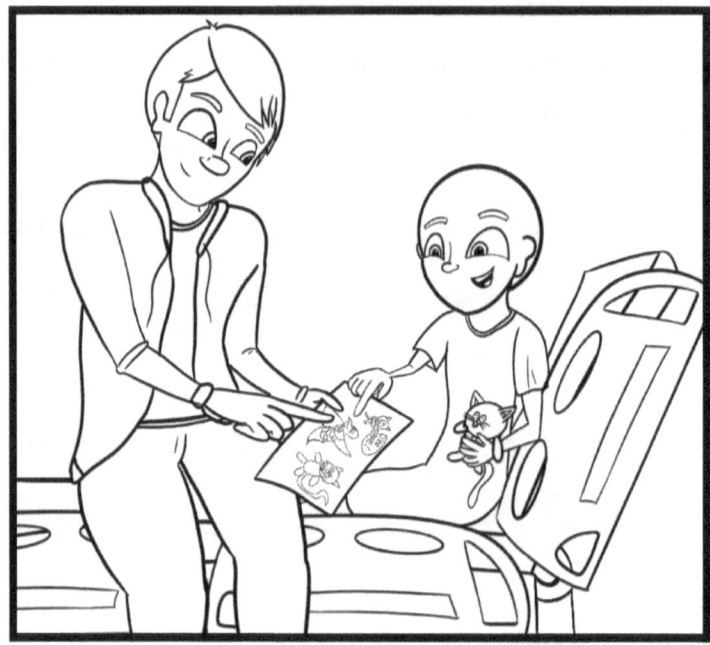

MEOWKI WAS FROLICKING AROUND near the neighborhood pond—visions of tuna dancing in her head. Still somewhat petrified of water, she had to wait for them to come close and breach through the surface. That was when she'd strike. A quick swipe of her paw would drag the fish in, allowing her to retreat with her prize on the dry land. It was difficult work, but Meowki was a seasoned hunter. She knew that a few hours of tedium would be offset by a single glorious swipe of fishy goodness.

"I'll wait as long as I have to. Tee hee!" She giggled to herself.

Just as the sun was beginning its descent over the western horizon, something disturbed the surface tension of the orange waters. Meowki leaned forward—her hind legs gently bouncing in anticipation. Finally, a fish burst from the water. The tuna's sleek blue-gray body glistened in the rays of the sun. Meowki propelled herself forward toward the shoreline with her powerful hind legs. Her paw became a black blur as it swiped across where the tuna had leapt, dragging it ashore with her razor-sharp claws. The fish flopped on the grass with helpless terror. Meowki rapidly ended its struggle with a sympathetic bite of her fangs.

At last, the prize was hers: a whole foot-long tuna all to herself!

"Tuna for din-din! Tee hee!" she cried with overwhelming gaiety.

Excitedly, she lifted her fish away from the pond and trotted over toward a shady spot to dine. She settled on a grassy patch between the nearby apartment buildings. Her tummy now full of delicious tuna, she stretched and yawned—the fatigue of the day finally catching up to her. The setting sun was dipping into the horizon.

"I should go home now before it gets too dark," said Meowki.

She rounded the corner of the building and followed the concrete sidewalk to her destination, yellow streetlamps illuminating the way. About halfway home, she was startled by a piercing cry in the night.

"Help!" a voice shouted.

"Hello?" Meowki called out. "Where are you?" She looked about but could see neither human nor animal in the encroaching darkness of the Lakeside Apartments.

"I'm up here!"

Meowki looked up. Above her, a small squirrel was resting on the pilaster of one of the apartment buildings.

"What's a pilaster?" Will asked.

"It's a decoration," Tristan explained. "It sort of looks like a support column, but it sticks out from the front of a building."

"Oh okay." Will nodded. "Keep going!"

"Little squirrel," Meowki began, "how did you get up there?"

"I was searching for acorns in that tree over there." He gestured toward a tree that was adjacent to the building. "I wanted to bring home some food for my family."

"I just came back from hunting as well." Meowki smiled triumphantly. It was a fine catch indeed. "But you still haven't explained how you ended up on the pilaster."

"Well, you see," continued the squirrel, "as I was searching for acorns, one of the humans living in this complex came walking one of their dogs. The foul beast spotted me and started barking up the tree." The squirrel bit his fingertips in fear of his recollection. "I panicked something awful and leapt to the building here. Now I'm stuck and can't get down!"

"I'm very sorry to hear that, little squirrel." Meowki frowned. "But I'm afraid there's nothing I can do to help you."

"What do you mean?" cried the squirrel. "Go get a ladder! Call the fire department! Get a trampoline! A mattress! Anything!"

Meowki glanced over at the nearby tree and back at the squirrel on the pilaster. "Little squirrel, even if I *could* do any of those things, I would not."

At this, the squirrel became cross with her. "How could you be such a heartless feline?! Have I caused you any harm? Any malice? What have I done to deserve such malevolent treatment?"

Meowki's countenance became sincere. "Little squirrel, I have been nothing of the sort. I understand that you are frightened. You are high off the ground and it is indeed growing quite dark, but it would be wrong for me to provide anything more for you than kind words and comfort." The cat smiled at the squirrel. "Though I will not help you, I would be glad to stay with you on this dark night for as long as you wish."

"No!" shouted the squirrel. "I'd rather wither away in this darkness than spend another moment in the presence of such an atrocious animal! Begone, cat! And don't come back!"

Meowki shook her head and smiled. "As you wish," she said with a bow. "Goodnight little squirrel."

"And good riddance!" the squirrel shouted at the cat who laughed all the way home.

"What a horrible story!" Will cried.

"Aw, I'm sorry buddy." Tristan frowned. "You didn't like it?"

"Why was Meowki so mean to that poor little squirrel?" he demanded to know. "He didn't do anything wrong and she laughed at him!"

Tristan looked over at Maki. During the construction of the story, she had moved to the armchair—finding it gave her more room to draw. They exchanged glances before responding.

"Because Will," Tristan said, "sometimes the best way to help someone is to teach them how to help themselves." Maki smiled brightly at Tristan.

"I don't understand," Will said.

"You see buddy," Maki began, striding over to the bed. "Sometimes, things can seem scary. You can feel like you're trapped. Like there's no way out."

"Just like the squirrel," Will said.

"That's right!" Maki cheered. "But the thing is," she sat at Will's side. "There's always a way forward."

"How do you think the squirrel could have gotten back down?" Tristan asked. Will furrowed his brows in thought.

"He could have jumped back onto the tree and climbed down!" he cried.

"That's right, buddy!" Tristan smiled. Will's smile soon dissipated as he found himself once more lost in thought.

"What's the matter?" Tristan asked.

"I still don't understand," Will said. "Why didn't the squirrel do that in the first place? He could have gone back down as soon as the dog left."

Maki smiled, "Do you remember what Meowki was doing before that?"

"Hunting for tuna!" Will laughed.

"And what was so important about that?" she asked. This question had Will stumped. He thought for a while before finally shrugging his shoulders.

"She was afraid of the water, but she did it anyway," Tristan explained, smiling at his hydrophobic friend.

"You can't be brave without being afraid," Maki said gently. Will's expression grew dark.

"I get scared sometimes," he said quietly, looking away.

Maki lifted Will's hand and squeezed it.

"That's why we're so proud of you," she said.

"You're incredibly brave." Tristan smiled, sadly as he placed a loving hand on his brother's shoulder. "The bravest guy I know."

"Is everything going to be alright?" he asked weakly.

"Of course!" Tristan whispered as he squeezed Will's shoulder. Maki rose from the bed and paced the room. It took all she had not to burst into tears. Tristan pulled up the coarse woolen covers to his brother's shoulders and took Maki's place at his side.

"The only thing you need to do is keep being you." He smiled before kissing him on the forehead.

Having regained her composure, Maki returned to Tristan's side.

"Go get some sleep. I love you," Tristan said.

"I love you, too, Tristan," said Will.

"Come here." Maki gestured, pulling Will into a tight hug. "Sweet dreams, little guy."

"Sweet dreams, Mommy," Will said sleepily.

Shocked, Maki let go. Will was so tired he hadn't even realized he had said it. Tristan said nothing, glancing at his friend with a pouted lower lip.

"I love you too, Will," she said, straightening up. "E-excuse me," she stammered, pointing toward the bathroom door behind her. Tristan nodded and sat in an armchair by Will's bedside.

Maki shut the door of the restroom, pressed herself against it, slid to the floor, and wept.

COFFEE SHOP SOUNDTRACK

IT WAS LATE AT NIGHT and the Collins household was quieter than usual. Clare was spending the night at the hospital and Marc was already in bed. Since any chance of slumber was futile, Tristan decided to get some studying done for midterms.

Lifting the glass pot, he poured the sad remains of the morning's coffee—now ice-cold—into a mug. He put the mug into the microwave, set it for one minute, and sat at the island countertop to wait. Tristan nearly jumped at the sound of his phone. Terrified that it could have been an emergency call from his mother about Will, he snatched the phone from his back pocket as quickly as he could.

"Maki?"

"Winner, winner, chicken dinner," she mocked. "What's up?"

"Uh, not much. You?"

"Just taking a break from studying for exams. Thought I'd check in." She paused. "Are you microwaving something?"

"Oh. Yeah. I'm reheating coffee." Tristan said. Seeing that the number was down to single digits, he ran over to place his hand on the handle in preparation to open the door just as it was done. He didn't want the irritating beep to wake his father.

"You studying, too?" Maki asked.

"Yes. I mean no, not really. All my work is done," he answered flatly. Tristan returned to the island and set the coffee down on a coaster.

"Tristan…" she sighed with a hint of maternal concern in her voice. "Why are you reheating coffee at 11 pm?"

"Because I can't stay awake," he replied. His voice was monotone. The response got a laugh from the girl.

"Then go to bed, doofus!" Maki scoffed.

"I can't fall asleep, either." Tristan got some milk from the refrigerator and poured it into the mug.

"Oh… I see," she said, suddenly sullen and understanding. "It's one of *those* nights, huh?"

He returned the jug of milk and picked up the mug. He took a sip. It was still terribly bitter.

"So… is it any good?" she asked.

"What?"

"The coffee," Maki said. Tristan realized that she must have heard him sipping. Gross.

He shrugged. "It could be worse."

"You know, you don't have to settle for crappy coffee, Tristan," she said.

"Excuse me?" Tristan asked, perplexed. Suddenly, her tone became playfully coy.

"Oh, I don't know. If only you knew *someone* who *literally* brews coffee for a living…"

Sipping his drink, he replied, "I haven't seen Izzy in weeks."

"Screw you," she replied without missing a beat. Her pithiness nearly made Tristan spit out his drink.

"Wait, was that a *chuckle?*" she asked. "Well, I suppose he *can* be taught after all. Wanna meet at Brandy's?"

"Maki, the cafe isn't open."

"What part of 'brews coffee for a living' did you not understand? *I have a key.*"

"How am I supposed to get there? There's no line running and it's pitch black out."

"Geez, do you have to have an issue with *everything?*" she spat, playfully. "I can borrow my dad's car. He'll let me use it if I say it's to study. Just grab your stuff and be ready in ten."

"I don't have a say in this, do I?" He listened for a reply but was met with silence. "...Hello...? ...Maki...?" Lowering his phone, he saw it had returned to the home screen. Phoenix jumped into his lap. She purred as he scratched her head.

"I guess not," he said.

Tristan shook his dad awake to let him know where he was going. Half-asleep, he had little to protest over. He text his mom for good measure, just for safety's sake. Ten minutes later, a white Toyota Corolla pulled in front of the complex. Tristan climbed into the passenger's seat. A familiar face with sharp, angular features was behind the wheel.

"Buckle up," Maki said. Tristan responded with a curious look as he hesitantly clipped his seatbelt.

"Should I be nervous?" he asked sheepishly. She rounded the corner from Tristan's street to Starlight Boulevard.

"Oh please," she said, "I'm an excellent driver."

Makiko floored it.

"Whoa, Maki!" Tristan shouted. "What do you think you're doing?!"

She hit the brakes.

"Sorry, what was that? I couldn't hear you. The tires were screeching."

"I said, 'What do you think you're—'"

Maki sped up for a split second before braking again.

"What was that?!" Tristan shouted. "Stop it!"

"Oh, come on, aren't you having fun?" she asked with a grin. He locked eyes with her and said nothing. They both broke up into quiet laughter.

"Let's just try to get there alive, okay?" he said.

"Roger Roger!" Maki saluted.

Despite the precipitous descent, the double-laned road made Starlight Boulevard reasonably navigable—particularly at night. Ordinarily, such an important road would boast higher traffic density; however, the truth of the matter was that this street was designed to funnel traffic to the bridge connecting Copperfield to Roosevelt. Thankfully for the residents of Lenox, there were much easier routes for commuters to take into the city to the north and south of the town, so this road wasn't as heavily trafficked as it should have been. Driving at close to midnight meant that there were hardly any cars in sight—allowing Makiko to drive Tristan to Lenox and the brink of insanity at the same time.

Tristan was exhausted. His eyes were shut as he rested his head against the passenger's window.

"He's going through such a tough time," Maki thought. She knew that she wasn't his mother or his therapist, but he needed someone to kick his butt back into gear for his brother's sake. Up ahead, she spotted a familiar pothole in the road. Rather than avoid it, she cut the wheel and drove straight for it.

"Oh my gosh!" she exclaimed. "Oh no, I think I hit it!" While not comfortable acting in front of a crowd, Maki could put on a good show from time to time.

"Hit what?!" Tristan said, frantically whipping his head around to stare out the rear window.

"Not sure. A—a Persian fur, or something like that!" she stammered.

"Oh no, did you hit a cat?!" he cried out, fear and melancholy mixing in his voice in a cocktail of negative emotion. Maki struggled to maintain her composure.

"Well," she said, "maybe it's not so bad."

"How could it not be so bad?" he raised his voice and his hands in confusion. "Maki, you just killed an animal! How could you be so blasé?" The angrier he got, the more she struggled to stifle her laughter.

"We're heading to a coffee shop. One that I work at," she explained.

"Yes? So what?" He stuck his head out the window and scanned the road behind them—looking for any sign of the animal in the dim light of the streetlamps.

"So, of course I'd know how to make a... *FLAT WHITE!*" A Cheshire grin overtook Maki's face. Tristan slowly retreated into the vehicle and turned toward her. His eyebrows narrowed and he wore a frown. After a few seconds, he spoke.

"Did you just give me a heart attack so you could make a pun?"

"*...Maybe,*" she said. They sat in silence for a few more seconds before she burst into tearful laughter.

"I was like, 'Oh no, a cat!' and you were all like, 'Oh no! Maki's a cat killer! Turn this car around little lady!'" which she punctuated with a wagging finger, knuckle on her hip, and deepened voice. "And then I was just like 'Hey, I work at a coffee shop so I can just whip you up a *FLAT WHITE!*"

Maki looked over at Tristan. He was still fuming.

"Get it? A flat white? Because Persians are... white?" Her voice trailed off. She cleared her throat and wiped the last of the tears away with a sigh. Tristan, meanwhile, folded his arms and glared out the side window.

"That was *not* funny," he said, fuming.

"It was a *little* funny," she muttered with a grin. In the sideview mirror, she saw him smile, too.

A few minutes later, Makiko was pulling off the road and into the business' parking lot. The students stepped out of the

Corolla, crossed the gravelly parking lot, and climbed the steps to
the porch of the cafe.

"It's so weird seeing this place at night," Tristan remarked.
He glanced about their surroundings with his hands in the front
pockets of his hoodie. He was shivering. "It's freezing."

Maki rummaged through her bag for her work keys. "Don't
worry, I'll have this door open in a sec," she said. "Just keep on
thinking about that fresh cappuccino. And I won't forget the milk
this time. Though, to be fair, I didn't exactly forget it last time,
either."

"What do you mean?" he asked. Finding her keyring, she
rose and held them up to the light—examining each in turn for the
"A19" that would unlock the front door.

"Oh, I was just trying to give Izzy more time to try and talk
to you."

"You staged that?" he asked with a chuckle.

Maki tilted her head and shrugged. "What can I say? I was
practically raised behind the curtain."

Finally finding the key, she unlocked the door and switched
on the lights. She set down her bag and instructed Tristan to have a
seat at the counter. Maki hurried back to prepare his drink.

"Won't Mr. White be a little upset that we're doing this
behind his back?" he said as he settled himself on a stool.

"Nope," she replied briskly as she switched on the necessary
machines.

"How do you know?"

"Because I asked him if we could study here tonight."

"We?" he asked, perplexed. "So, you just asked him tonight? Right before you picked me up?"

"No, I asked him this morning," she said nonchalantly, preparing the two mugs.

"So, you *knew* I was going to say yes?"

"Mm-hmm," Maki said with a nod. Dumbfounded, Tristan threw up his hands.

"*...How?!*"

"What else do you have to be doing right now?"

Tristan paused before nodding with a pout. "...Good point," he said. "But he's just okay with lending out his place of business overnight to some high school kids?" She crossed his purview to reach the minifridge to the left of the employee door. She felt his eyes on her as she bent forward to retrieve the milk from inside—she didn't mind. "Particularly a guy and a girl...?"

Shutting the fridge, Maki carried the glass jug back to the mugs. Tristan's face was red and his eyes were darting around the room, looking in any direction except hers. It took all she had not to burst into laughter. Maki sighed and started dispensing the espresso shots.

"He trusts us," she explained. "Me, I'm like some weird Japanese daughter to him and you—well..." She bit her lip as she searched the ceiling for an answer. "...he kind of feels bad for."

Tristan scoffed. "How could he feel bad for *me?* He barely even knows me."

Maki stopped pouring.

"Everyone knows about Will, Tristan."

"Well then he should feel bad for *him*, not me," he replied. Suddenly, he became sullen. "For me to accept that kind of sympathy would just be... *selfish.*"

Makiko frowned as she poured in the milk. Turning around, she placed the finished cappuccino in front of the boy.

"Self-care *isn't* selfish."

Tristan looked up and gave her a slight smile despite his somber eyes. After patiently waiting for a response and receiving none, Makiko glanced at the drink, then back at him, then back at the drink, then back at him again with raised eyebrows. Recalling the interaction with Izzy, Tristan got the hint and tried a sip.

"...Wow," he said, still smiling.

She leaned on the counter with one shoulder lifted and her head tilted slightly to the side.

"A *little* better than reheated crap?" she asked with one eye squinted.

"A *lot* better than reheated crap." He laughed. "Thanks."

Maki smiled back and finished preparing a black coffee for herself. A moment later, she joined Tristan on the patrons' side of the bar and pulled out her notes.

"So..." Tristan began, "have you heard from Izzy?"

"Not a word since that night." She sighed. "It's like she's completely cut contact."

"Have you tried reaching out to her?"

"Of course, but she ignores the texts. Tried calling but it always goes straight to voicemail."

"I'm sorry, Maki…" he said forlornly.

She shook her head. "What are you sorry about? You didn't do anything wrong."

Tristan took another sip of coffee. Maki followed suit and then went on.

"The whole thing was just so odd to me," she said. "We've been friends our whole life, Izzy and Mr. White. We're practically family! What could be so serious that he'd allow his daughter to lock herself away like this? A stupid recital?"

"I wish there was something we could do to help." Tristan said, nodding forlornly.

"Me too. But, unfortunately, it's not really our place to intervene."

For a while, neither of them spoke. There was an empty barstool to Tristan's right. They stared at it in silence, each thinking the same thing without daring to bring it to light. Surprisingly, Tristan was the first to break from this melancholy.

"Alright," he said, somewhat jubilantly as he clapped his hands together. "Are we going to sit here in silence all night or are we going to ace this calc midterm?" Makiko acquiesced to his proposition with a confident nod.

After an hour or two of running various practice problems and equations, they stumbled upon the bane of Makiko's existence: logarithms. At this point, the pair had moved from their seats at the bar to a comfy four-seater booth on the opposite side of the shop.

"I've always hated these types of questions," Maki began, "haven't you? ... *Tristan?*"

Looking up, she saw that her friend had fallen fast asleep against the window. There was something about his gentle breathing that made her smile. She watched his shoulders slowly rise and fall for a moment before she returned her gaze to the table. She hadn't noticed it before, but he had brought his sketchbook with him. He must always keep it in his bag. Maki guessed that he must have dug it out when he was searching for his calc binder.

For a moment, Makiko found herself fiddling with her thumbs as she pondered what to do next. Curiosity won out and she slowly reached across the table for the book. He had a few papers and notebooks littered about it, so she had to be careful to move them aside without waking him. With the rustle of each page, her eyes frantically traveled back and forth between her hands and the redhead at the window. At last, the sketchbook was in full view and could be slid over. The instant she put her hand on it, the boy stirred, nearly giving her a heart attack. She quickly retracted her hand before he dropped his head further into his ever-deepening slumber.

Black leather sketchbook in hand, Maki started sifting. The pages were littered with crazy cartoon concoctions: a talking seagull, a superhero in a hole-filled sock costume, a Hispanic shark riding a hoverboard—all to make a little boy smile. Many of the characters she recognized, though some were new. Aside from the drawings for Will, it looked as though he drew for himself from time to time as a stress reliever. Some pages had roller coaster vehicle designs, others had caricatures making fun of their teachers, and every now and then she'd come across a beautiful still life of Roosevelt. In equal parts laughter and amazement, she riffled through the pages until she saw nothing but the white canvas of creations yet to be. From there, she backtracked, curious as to what his most recent creation was. When she saw it, she nearly dropped the book.

It was her.

The drawing was a one-to-one copy of a photo Izzy had taken of Maki last year when she had pressured her into making a Facebook. She was posed with a hand on one hip, smiling at the camera with her usual fringe bangs. In the sketch, Tristan had paid attention to every little detail. There were heavy eraser marks around her eyes—as though he either had trouble or wanted to get them just right. Given the piece's somewhat uncanny nature, Maki believed that neither was mutually exclusive. Tristan was definitely better at cartooning than portraiture.

It was a pencil sketch, so everything was in a graphite gray, save for her irises. Judging from the test scribbles at the bottom of the page, he went out of his way to test out at least five different shades of green before he found the right color to fill them in.

Makiko snapped the book shut and returned all the papers and notebooks where she found them. Feeling her face growing hot, she brushed her hair behind her ear and returned to studying.

NO SUCH THING AS MAGIC

THROUGHOUT NOVEMBER, Will's prognosis became progressively bleaker. Something was obviously wrong. Speaking had become laborious. By the end of November, he had regressed to the point of near silence. He wasn't laughing. Wasn't smiling. He didn't want to walk down to the playroom. Couldn't. Even the transfer to the wheelchair had become too taxing. The doctors put him through an ever-growing battery of tests and procedures, all while upping the frequency of his chemotherapy sessions.

Tristan's heart sank as he watched his father at his bedside, offering whatever comfort he could. At this stage, the best of Tristan's jests could only produce a minor chuckle followed by a painful coughing fit for his brother. Clare reentered the room, her head down, looking grim.

Never taking her eyes off the floor, she shakily said, "Tristan. Marc. Step outside with me."

Tristan exchanged glances with his father; Will was too dazed to react. Marc squeezed Will's shoulder and kissed him on the forehead before setting him up with cartoons on the TV. They followed Clare outside the room and closed the door.

"He's not responding to current chemo and radiation therapies," she began. Her tone was hushed, less so for privacy and more so for the inability to process the horrors of the situation for fear of drowning in them. "In fact, they're—" she started to choke up. Grabbing her arms, she swallowed hard and forced herself to continue. "—They're killing him. They need to give him stronger doses of each to fight the cancerous cells, but his body can't take it."

"What does that mean?" Tristan interjected. "Does that mean he's going to—?"

"No!" Mom cut him off with a sharp, glassy-eyed glare. "No, he's not going to die." Of course, he wasn't. She wouldn't allow any member of her family to even so much as entertain the thought. She swallowed again to regain her composure as Marc placed a comforting arm around her shoulders. She reached up to her shoulder and squeezed his hand.

"What it means," Clare continued, "is that he'll need a BMT: a bone marrow transplant."

"That's alright," Marc said, now rubbing his wife's upper arm with his hand. "He'll get the procedure and it'll be fine."

Clare smacked his hand away and raised her voice for the first time. "No, it won't be fine, Marc! None of this will be fine!" Several nurses from their station shot the Collins trio with a mixture of sympathetic and annoyed looks. Marc frantically shushed Clare and encouraged her to relax. While it didn't work, she managed to reduce her volume—her frustrations and trepidations seethed between her teeth.

"Do you have any idea how dangerous this is, Marc?"

"I read about it in the pamphlets we got a few months ago. It didn't seem so—"

"*Normally*, it would be fine!" she interjected. "But Dr. Perkins said that since Will is so immunocompromised, there's a very serious risk of his body rejecting the treatment."

"Rejecting the treatment?" Tristan asked cautiously.

"Tristan…" Marc said, slowly, finally meeting his eyes. "It might kill him."

A silence hung in the air for what felt like hours as the news sunk in. It couldn't be possible. Treatments like this were meant to help people, right? How could it be dangerous? It's a standard procedure. The hospital worked with sick kids all the time. This was just legal nonsense, right? A requirement to disclose the risks with the family of the patient. It had to be.

"No," Tristan said firmly. "That can't be right."

His father placed a firm hand on his shoulder—his favorite means of providing paternal comfort—and said, "Tristan, there are no magic cures." Looking up at him, Tristan watched his countenance grow dim. "This is the real world. And sometimes…" he sniffled and looked away for a moment. "Sometimes, life isn't fair."

That was the first time Tristan saw his father cry.

Feeling numb, Tristan was listless as he updated his friend via text. He stared at the phone stupidly, waiting for her to write back. All the while, he was berated by forces both external and internal.

"You can't hide in there forever, Tristan. You're acting like a child."

"Please leave me alone."

"Your brother might only have tonight and you're acting like a selfish spoiled brat. Now get out of there!"

When he unlatched the door to the bathroom stall, Tristan was greeted by his father's glare.

"Mommy... what did the doctor say?"

Will's complexion was pallid. He looked like death and could hardly mumble more than a word or two before entering into another coughing fit. Clare knelt by his side.

"That everything would be just fine," she whispered, stroking the top of his head. "They're going to bring you in for a transfusion in a few hours and—" She struggled to maintain her composure, but somehow, she hung on. "—and then you'll be all better."

Hardly able to speak, Will responded with a pathetic nod.

"Close your eyes, honey," his mother instructed. She pulled up the blanket to tuck him in and began to sing:

> "*Over in Killarney, many years ago*
> *My mother sang a song to me*
> *in tones so sweet and low.*
> *Just a simple little ditty*

in her good old Irish way

And I'd give the world if she could sing

that song to me this day.

Too-ra-loo-ra-loo-ral, Too-ra-loo-ra-li

Too-ra-loo-ra-loo-ral, hush now, don't you cry

Too-ra-loo-ra-loo-ral, Too-ra-loo-ra-li

Too-ra-loo-ra-loo-ral, that's an Irish lullaby."

Marc was seated next to his wife with his arm on her shoulder. He had the air of a broken man.

Tristan couldn't take it anymore. He couldn't stay. He whispered to his father that he needed some air. Instead of disparaging him, Marc gave an understanding nod.

His eyes fixed on the floor, Tristan fast-walked to the elevator and hit the button for the ground level. He pulled out his cell phone once more, desperate to see the speech bubble icon— but no dice. Even so, he sent out one last text explaining that he was going outside. Once in the lobby, he walked out the doors and onto the main pathway that connects to Starlight Park.

WHAT A SURPRISE!

IT WAS EARLY. The sun had just barely begun its ascent over the chilly shipyards that made up Yellow Harbor. Sitting up, Makiko rubbed her eyes with one hand, cradling Niki in the other. Shivering, the seven-year-old hugged the orange cartoon cat closer for warmth. That was when she noticed the window over her bed. It had some sort of a strange, blue-white glow to it. She stood up on the mattress, attempting to balance herself upright with one hand outstretched sideways while the other held her friend closer for comfort. Now at eye-level with the windowpane, she wiped away the condensation with her pajama sleeve.

Suddenly overwhelmed with glee, Maki unclasped the latches on the window and thrust it open. Gripping the sill with both hands, she pulled herself up an inch or two—just enough to stick her head out the window and prove that she wasn't dreaming.

"Yuki!" she cried.

Maki slammed the window shut and sprinted as fast as she could to her father's room, carrying the cat with her all the way. With youthful energy, she vaulted onto the queen-sized mattress and hopped up and down.

"YUKI GA FUTTA! YUKI GA FUTTA! YUKI GA FUTTA!" She couldn't stop shouting. They had only left Okinawa several months prior, so she hardly knew any English at the time. Japanese was still the main language spoken in the home.

Groggily, Masashi woke up and switched on the lamp on his nightstand. Upon seeing his daughter's expression, he couldn't help but smile back. Heaven only knew the last time he had seen her this happy.

"IT SNOWED!" Maki cheered in her native tongue. Masashi sat up and placed his palms flat on the mattress on either side of him.

"It did?!" he asked in the enthusiastic manner you use when talking to a high-energy child.

"It's *EVERYWHERE!*" she cheered. "Come and look!" Maki hopped off the side of the bed and grabbed his wrist with her free hand—pulling with all her might. "Come on! Get up, Daddy!"

"Okay, okay!" he said, struggling to sit upright without falling off the mattress under the force of her constant tugs. "Just give me a second!"

Ignoring him, Makiko ran out of the room, shouting, *"SNOOOOOWWW!"*

Masashi chuckled before pushing himself off the bed and grabbing his cane. Makiko ran to their apartment's front door and unclasped the latch. Masashi was just pulling on a bathrobe as he exited the bedroom in his green flannel pajama pants and gray top.

"Maki wait for me!" he called, struggling to keep pace with his small child.

In a flash, she was out the door and running down the stairwell. Masashi sighed. Limping toward the elevator, he caught the eye of a curious neighbor who had poked his head out of his door.

"Kids," Masashi said in English with a shrug. The neighbor nodded with a laugh before retreating into his apartment.

Now downstairs, the little girl bolted toward the lobby's double glass doors. Upon opening them, Makiko was awestruck. The formerly grimy, urban streets of Yellow Harbor were blanketed in a thick layer of dazzling white snow. For a moment, she found herself frozen: paralyzed by conflicting emotions. Slowly, she raised her right foot and gingerly pressed it into the snow. The sudden sensation of her bare foot being encased in frost took her by surprise; so, she quickly retracted it.

"Maki!" Masashi shouted, "Not without your boots!"

She felt a smile spread across her face as her father patted her foot dry with a towel he retrieved from a nearby pantry.

"It's like really cold sand," Maki marveled.

"Mm-hmm." Her father smiled and nodded in affirmation.

Once finished, Masashi tossed the towel to the floor beside the door and stooped down with a grunt—not an easy thing for a man with a cane to do. Seated next to her, he reached forward into the frosty fondant that topped their concrete stoop and dipped his hand into it. Maki studied his movements with the wide eyes of a golden retriever waiting for a treat as he clumped some of the snow into a little sphere the size of a softball. He held it up to the light, letting the sun glisten off the droplets formed from the heat of his hand.

"When it gets really cold," he explained, "water in the clouds freezes and makes snow."

"It's... water?" Makiko blanched.

"That's right," Masashi said, still examining his creation. "Very cold water. Kind of like ice cubes."

"It's like a sea..." Makiko said, her hydrophobia drifting her away into an ocean of fears. An abyss of repressed memories. Things a five-year-old should never have to see:

A mother.

A bathtub.

A flashing light.

Water.

So much water…

"Here, listen," Masashi said, holding her by the shoulders. He gave her a little jostle to help break her stupor. "It's not really like…" he fumbled for the right words. Eventually, he found action to be a superior substitute to speech. "Here, hold out your hand."

He guided her palms up in front of her, leaving Maki posed like a hieroglyphic servant. Still a nascent karateka, her hands hadn't calloused enough to warrant the use of gloves yet. Masashi went to lower the snowball into her palms—

Makiko withdrew her hands and thrust them behind her back. Her father retracted the snowball.

"No, no, it's okay," he comforted, placing a loving hand on her shoulder. "Close your eyes." She obliged. Although temporarily blind, Maki still felt the need to turn her head away from the water-ball her father had created. Gently, he raised her hand. The sudden sensation of cold nearly made her jump. After a few seconds, she opened her eyes and dared to look at what was in her palm. She looked between the ball and her dad, unsure of how to react.

"See?" Masashi said. "It's not so scary."

Looking back at the snowball, Maki tucked her toy under her arm to free a second hand to support the snowball. Now cradling the frozen water, she raised it up to her face in awe.

"…It's beautiful…"

Masashi smiled before diving back into the snow to construct another ball.

"You know," he said, "in America, kids love to have snowball fights."

"Snowball fights...?" his daughter inquired with childish naivety. "You mean like on the tv shows?"

"Yeah, that's right!" he nodded. "They take clumps of snow and toss them at each other."

"That always looked silly!" she laughed.

Masashi smiled, "It is. It's really fun, too."

His eyes broke from hers and went to scan their snow-covered street. Dense white had blanketed every nook and cranny of the road. Rising at least a foot and a half from the ground, it was nigh impossible to tell where the sidewalk ended and the road began. Until the plowmen drove through, denizens of Sally Street would need to tread carefully or face a precipitous drop.

"Aha," Masashi said after a few minutes of surveying the area. He tapped Makiko on the shoulder before pointing at the dumpster by the curb. On a normal day, its rusted hunter-green features stood out little against the urban pallidity of Yellow Harbor. Today however, it found itself caked in snow, causing its naked features to pop against a white backdrop.

"You think you can hit that dumpster over there?" he asked with a jerk of his head. Like an extraterrestrial studying a foreign human concept, his daughter gawked at the dumpster, then at the ball in her hand, and then back again at her father.

"You mean I can throw it?"

Bending his arms at the elbows and twisting his palms up, Masashi shook his head with a laugh and cried, "Of course! That's why snow's so much fun!"

"Okay…" she stammered, looking back down at the ball in her hands. "I'll try."

Getting to her feet, she retracted her arm and threw the snowball. It plopped into a snowbank five feet to the right of the dumpster.

"I didn't hit it…" Maki sighed. To her surprise, her father chuckled.

"That's okay," he said, "just make another snowball and try again."

"Make a snowball?"

Acknowledging the trepidation in her voice, he gently held her wrists and guided her back to a seating position. "It's easy," he said reassuringly. "Here, I'll show you."

Following her father's lead, she dipped her hands into the snow and compressed a chunk of it between her palms to make a sphere.

"Now you just pat it down like this… Perfect!" Masashi nodded. "Now try again."

She threw the ball a little harder and it fell short again.

Maki shouted and stamped her foot. "Argh! Missed again!"

"That's okay!" Her father reassured her once more. "See? I've still got another and you can always make more! Try aiming higher." he raised her hand up. "Now breathe…"

Shutting her eyes, Makiko inhaled through her nose and exhaled through her mouth—just like her father had taught her to do during one of her outbursts. She opened her eyes and threw. This time, it bounced off the front of the rusted container with a satisfying *clunk*.

Masashi shot his fists into the air and shouted, *"DING DING DING DING DING!!!"* Unable to control her excitement, Makiko found herself bouncing up and down in the doorway.

"I hit it, I hit it!" she cheered. Masashi embraced her with a hug and a kiss on her forehead.

"I knew you would!" he said. When he let go, Maki looked back at the mark she had made on the side of the dumpster. There was a clear break in an otherwise undisturbed blanket of snow where her projectile had landed.

"Can we see if Mr. White will let me and Izzy have a snowball fight?" she asked—practically shaking with excitement.

"I don't see why not." Her father smiled. "I think that's a perfect idea! Let's get you dressed then I'll make the call."

"Yay!" she cried as she zoomed down the hall to the elevator.

Makiko sat at her desk. She was exhausted, resting her head on her open anatomy textbook. Her right hand unconsciously rolled a pencil up and down the faux wood of her desk. She felt lost. Where had she gone wrong with Izzy? Could she have done something differently?

Something about this separation from her friend just didn't feel right. Truth be told, nothing about the situation felt right. Had Izzy really let this show blind her?

Tonight was the big night. The ticket to her recital was pinned to a small cork board on the wall. She was already dressed to go, but she didn't feel like moving. How could she support her friend in doing something that was tearing her away from who she really was?

She glanced up at her bookshelf. An unopened set of white canvases were still asleep in their shrink wrap. A thin layer of dust wafted down from them. It had been a month since she had last touched a paint brush. In its absence, Makiko had felt the saturation drain from her surroundings, leaving her trapped in a perfidious pallid prison of black and white. She spent more time around walls of text than paint and she hated it. She slammed her book shut and tossed it to the floor.

The canvases reminded her of a promise she had made.

Will.

She held her head in her hands.

"Now there's a kid who'd been dealt a bad hand," she thought.

Making the sign of the cross, she prayed.

"Please God, there must be something I can do," she pleaded. "Please, I'm lost. Izzy's gone, Will's getting worse, and I don't know how much longer we have until Tristan starts losing it himself." She sighed, feeling tears about to come on. She sniffled and rubbed her eyes.

"I can't just sit here and do nothing," she said authoritatively. "I know I can do more. Please, show me what I can do. Please…"

That's when she heard a ping from her phone.

THE DECISION

Standing on the front porch of the colonial home, Makiko kicked the snow off her boots before ringing the bell. A woman's muffled shout was followed by some rustling. Then the latch clicked and the door opened.

"Come on in, you must be freezing," Mr. White said, gesturing with his hand. Seeing this white-haired man in a suit standing in the doorway stirred something in her. Maybe it was his aftershave. Maybe it was the Christmas tree lights and music that emanated from the living room. Maybe it was the smell of freshly baked cookies—or a shift in temperature from the cold blue outside world and this cozy, colorful little abode. Frozen, she soaked all these observations in. She couldn't hold back the tears any longer.

Mr. White grew concerned, "Maki?" he began, cautiously tilting his head. "Are you—?"

Makiko cut him off with a tight hug. Surprised, Gil hesitated a moment before returning the gesture.

"Gil?" Brandy called from the next room. "Is that Ma—?" Stepping inside, she was cut off by the solemnity of the embrace.

After around fifteen seconds or so, Makiko finally let go.

"Mrs. White," she said weakly. She outstretched her arms as she approached.

"Oh, come here," Brandy said. They hugged.

"I'd offer to grab you something to drink, but we're about to head out ourselves," Brandy said, wiping Maki's face with a tissue she retrieved from her bag.

"I know," Maki said with a nod. She looked back and forth between her hosts before shutting her eyes and lowering her head.

"I can't make it tonight," she admitted.

"Oh no," Gilbert moaned. "Is everything alright?"

"No." Maki shook her head. "It's Will."

"The Collins boy?" Brandy asked. Makiko nodded.

"He's not… —he might not make it," Maki said. "I thought Izzy would want to know sooner rather than later. Wouldn't want her to be disappointed if I wasn't there."

"Oh, sweetheart," Brandy said, wrapping her in another hug. "Of course, she'll understand."

"May I?" Maki gestured toward the stairs.

"Go, go!" Gilbert beckoned enthusiastically. He shook his head violently as she followed his command.

"This is terrible," he whispered to his wife.

Upstairs, Makiko could see a light shining from beneath the bathroom door. She knocked.

"Almost ready!" Izzy called out.

"Iz, it's me. I need to talk to you," Maki said quickly.

"Maki?" Izzy exclaimed. "I'm almost done, hang on."

"It's urgent," she said, somewhat frantically.

"Okay, okay! Hang on," Izzy said. "One second. Just need to… *there!*"

A moment later, Izzy popped open the door. A gust of steam filtered out of the room and into the hall. Standing tall in a lacey white dress, she looked the part of an opera star. Her hair dangled down the side of her face in a voluminous updo. The amount of hairspray it must have taken to hold it in place, Makiko couldn't possibly imagine.

"Wow," Maki said, awestruck. "You look gorgeous." Izzy glanced down bashfully.

"Thanks," she said, quietly. Her cheeks rapidly flashed scarlet. She really didn't know how to take a compliment. After a moment she cleared her throat and continued.

"What's going on?" Izzy asked. "Is everything alright?"

"I came to tell you that I'm not going tonight."

Izzy walked past her to the hallway window and looked out with a frown. Slowly, she nodded.

"That's alright," she said quietly, trying not to cry. "I understand."

"No, it's not like—"

"I've been a pretty awful friend to you. I get it," she said, refusing to look at her. "I deserve this."

"It has nothing to do with you—"

"Save your breath, Maki. I know what I did. I was a jerk. I sealed myself away. Cut myself off from everybody because I couldn't handle a little bit of extra stress."

"Come on, we don't have time for this!" Maki protested.

"You're right. We don't. I have to go get ready for the show. Talent scouts are going to be there. Once I sing, *then* we can talk, is that right?" She put her head in her hands. "That's what I kept telling myself. That's absolutely what I learned in church, right? Because I'm just such a good Catholic."

Maki grabbed her friend by the shoulders and shook her hard.

"*WILL COULD DIE!*" she shouted. Izzy finally looked up from her hands.

"What did you say?" she whispered.

Maki backed away and pressed herself against the wall. She nodded.

"I got a text a little while ago. It was Tristan. He's going in for a dangerous procedure tonight. They don't know how it'll turn out."

Izzy turned pale. She slunk to the floor in a heap. Suddenly the tears that she had been fighting to keep in check burst through the cracks of the dam.

"I'm a monster," she choked out, sobbing.

Makiko scooted over to her friend's side and wrapped her arm around her.

"Izzy, we've known each other for our whole lives," she said. "You're the sweetest, kindest, most trustworthy person I know. Remember in elementary school? Those kids laughed at me and poured paint in my hair, but you were the one who came to me and asked to color. You were the one who always picked me up off the floor and let me play with you during recess. You introduced me to faith, let me come with you to church—you and your dad."

Maki could feel Izzy beginning to shake. She found it difficult to maintain her composure but knew she couldn't stop now.

"And you were the one who stood by me even when I was at my worst with my... *issues*. You never gave up on me. Even when I screamed and cursed and threw things, you always came back."

Maki was trembling in tears. Her voice was shaking. She had to clench her fists to get the words out.

"Do you have any idea how much that meant to me—having a friend that I could always count on even when I could feel myself falling apart?!"

Once more, she tightly gripped both of her shoulders.

"You're my sister, Iz! I love you! I love you and I'd do anything for you!"

No longer able to cope with her emotions, Izzy broke out of her stupor to embrace her friend in a tight hug. They wept in each other's arms.

"I'm so, so, so, sorry, Maki!!!" Izzy wailed.

"I'm sorry, too..." said Makiko, beginning to feel her composure returning. "I'm sorry about what I said before. Back when we fought."

"No, you were right." She sniffled. "I was pathetic. ...A pathetic coward."

"You're not a coward."

"I was too scared to talk about what I was going through, so I hid myself away instead." They released the hug, turning to face the hallway. Izzy kept her eyes fixed on her hands. "Anyway, that's cowardice in my book," she said before sniffing and wiping away a final tear. "You were right in saying what you said."

Maki wrapped a comforting arm around her once more. When Izzy saw that Maki's face was dripping with tears, she returned the gesture with a hug.

"I love you too, Maki. You'll *always* be my sister."

They held each other for a long time—at least until their tears subsided. Once things had calmed down, they released.

"Well," Izzy sniffled. "I'm guessing I probably need to wash off this makeup, huh?" Maki saw the streaks of mascara and blush that had smeared across her face. Izzy wiped her eyes with her hand, smudging it even more. Suddenly, Makiko found herself unable to stop laughing.

"You—you look like a raccoon!" she cried.

Izzy got up, ran to the bathroom mirror, and burst into tears all over again—tears of laughter. Maki was still in the hallway, banging her fist on the ground in between snorts.

After Izzy had washed her face, she and Maki descended the staircase together. After receiving a few compliments regarding the dress, Izzy looked at her parents.

"Mom? Dad? Can we talk?"

THE OTHER PROMISE

TRISTAN FELT A PRESENCE behind him. An ever-encroaching darkness that sought to suffocate him.

"You're a coward."

He picked up his pace. He was in a light jog.

"He's not going to make it."

Faster still, he was running.

"He's going to die alone and you won't be there to help him."

Sprinting.

"This is all your fault and you know it."

At last, he had reached his destination. Without realizing it, his feet had taken him to Starlight Beach: the edge of the park that overlooked the water separating Copperfield from the Roosevelt cityscape which stretched across the horizon.

"I'll never be able to do it," Will said, plopping down into the sand with a defeated frown.

"Aw, of course you can!" Tristan said, putting a comforting hand on his shoulder. "You can't give up. Here, let me help you." He wound up the white string of his brother's kite tight to the plastic handle, giving it a meager four feet of slack.

Helping him off the ground, he explained, "Okay, here. Now take this." Tristan passed Will the handle. "And hold the slack with your other hand." He followed the directions perfectly. "Awesome, you've got it! Now, when I say 'go,' I want you to run as fast as you can."

"But running didn't work last time," Will sullenly retorted.

"That's because you didn't loosen the line. Here, I'll show you." Tristan demonstrated how to twist the line from the handle to create a longer lead for the kite. "Once you feel it nice and tight in the air above you, start twisting the extra string out. But don't stop running until the kite is firmly in the air."

After a few seconds of hesitation, Will finally nodded and agreed.

"Ready?" Tristan asked. Will looked back at the kite behind him and at the string in his hands before nodding to his big brother.

"Ready!"

"Alright." Tristan cupped his hands to his mouth and began to shout, "Runners, take your places!" Will giggled and took on a sprinter's stance complete with legitimate determination in his face. "On your mark, get set... GO!"

Will ran faster and faster down the sandy beachhead, his red hair appearing aflame in the luminosity of the afternoon sunshine. The kite started to rise.

"Untwist the line!" Tristan called, trying to keep up with him on foot. Will nodded and gave the kite more lead. The kite soared ever higher as he ran.

"That's the end of the beach, Tristan!" Will shouted as he rapidly approached a cavalcade of boulders blocking off the sand ahead.

"Turn around and sprint back!" his brother cried. "Whatever you do, don't stop moving!"

Will nodded and did an about-face, sprinting as fast as he could. The kite wavered a few times, and at once, began to nosedive. Will looked dismayed.

"Just keep moving!" Tristan shouted. At this, his little brother ran even faster, tightening the line to artificially increase the tension in the lead without Tristan needing to tell him to. Nearing the location where he started his sprint, Will had at last loosened it enough so that the kite bobbed effortlessly one hundred feet overhead. "Okay, stop!" Tristan shouted.

Will skidded to a halt and looked up in reverence at what he had just accomplished.

"We did it!" he shouted as he jumped for joy.

"No, you did it!" Tristan said, going over to give him a high-five. Will ignored his hand and instead ran in for a tight hug around his brother's slender waist.

"I never could have done it without you," Will said, gripping the line behind Tristan's back. Tristan returned the hug.

"Hey, I'm your brother," he said with a laugh. "Brothers stick together."

The sand held a bluish glow in the moonlight. Tristan found himself sitting upon the same sandy shore where his brother first learned how to fly a kite. He couldn't recall how long he had been there, nor did he even think to care. He closed his eyes. Listening to the waves, he was still trying to catch his breath.

Haven given up the chase, Kieran, joined him in the sand. For a moment, he was silent, as if he was unsure of what to do.

"May I join you?" he asked anxiously. Tristan looked up and said nothing. Returning his head to his crossed arms which rested upon his knees, he gave a solemn nod.

"It's pretty here," his Other continued. "I can see how this place used to inspire you."

Gentle waves continued to lap against the shore. In the distance, a lone gull could be heard swooping through the concrete lots beyond the park, searching for food. Kieran fell silent once more, letting them savor the soundscape for a while. Finally, he slid closer to Tristan and put his arms around him. He was startled by this gesture of kindness. The awkward side-hug was clumsy and lukewarm, as though Kieran needed it just as much as he did.

"Tristan..." he whispered, "who will we fly kites with?"

It was so sudden.

His chest grew tight—his breathing, rapid. He couldn't process his surroundings as all visible light was refracted into a myriad of blurry masses. It was then that Tristan realized that for the first time in a decade:

He was crying.

His wailing probably echoed all over the empty park, but he was too distraught to care. His brother was going to die, and he was too much of a fool to step up and face reality. Too much of a coward to stay with him—with his parents, even—for his last few minutes on Earth. He was a horrible person. He had no right to be so selfish. He prayed for God to take him instead. He fantasized about jumping into the water and not resurfacing. Anything to end this miserable suffering—

"Tristan?"

The voice broke him out of his defeatist reverie. Snapping his head up, Tristan dried his eyes on his jacket sleeve as he looked around to identify its source.

That's when he saw Makiko standing in her purple puffer coat beneath the nearby streetlamp. Was she crying? He couldn't be sure. Her eyes were fixed on the snow-covered pavement of the walking trail that abutted the beach.

After a deafening silence filled with howling wind, seagulls, and waves, Tristan finally gained the courage to speak.

"What are you doing here?" he asked.

Makiko shrugged, still looking at her boots. "I came looking for you. When you said you went outside, I figured this is where you'd be."

Nose still running, he looked away as he cleaned himself up. "I—I didn't think you'd actually come."

"Why aren't you at the hospital?" Maki began, her tone becoming firm. "Will needs you!"

At this, Tristan began to shout.

"There's nothing I can do—there's nothing anyone can do anymore!" he turned toward her. "Didn't you read what I wrote? That procedure may as well be a death sentence!"

She was quiet for a moment, still not meeting his eyes over folded arms.

"So that's just it then, huh?" Maki started quietly. She quickly moved to a frenzied shout, gesticulating violently. "After everything we've been through—after everything *you and your brother* have been through, you can't even go in to *visit him?!*"

"I CAN'T DO IT ANYMORE?! OKAY?!" Tristan screamed, jumping from his position and getting to his feet. He started crossing the sand to her location on the trail. "What did you want to hear, Maki? That I'd be alright with all of this?! Watching my brother swing back and forth from recovery to near-certain death every other month? Don't you think that kills me? You don't have any idea how many times I've watched my brother die and come back to life the next day!" Now face-to-face with his friend, he whispered, "I can hardly feel it anymore."

His back against the streetlamp, he slid down to the snowy asphalt. Suddenly, he was acutely aware of the chilly night air. Tristan had been so upset that he hadn't thought of bringing his overcoat.

"I can hardly feel anything anymore..."

The next moment was a blur. Makiko rapidly closed the distance between them and grabbed both of his wrists—yanking him up from the ground.

"GET UP!" she shouted. Fear, anger, shame, remorse—every negative emotion imaginable all seemed spread across her face at once.

"Maki, I—"

"Your brother is dying in there, and you're out here expecting me to feel *sorry* for you?!" she hissed.

"You don't understand."

"Oh, *I* don't understand?!" she spat. "Like I've never been through pain? *ARE YOU SERIOUS?!*"

"I'm sorry! That's not what I meant—"

"You think that disease is what's killing him, Tristan? No, it's *YOU!* You and your stupid immaturity! Do you have any idea—the *SLIGHTEST FREAKING IDEA* what would happen if he saw you right now?!"

Once more Tristan felt himself on the verge of tears. Maki only gripped his wrists tighter.

"THIS would kill him—and I'd put you on the stand for homicide myself."

"…I just couldn't take it anymore," he stammered. "Seeing Mom and Dad like that…"

"And how do you think they're going to feel now?" she retorted. "As if they didn't already have enough problems, now they have to send someone to fetch their son for them! If you have problems, you pray! You see a counselor! Meditate! Exercise! Talk it out! You don't do *THIS*, you… *MORON!"* She violently tossed his arms down to his sides.

"You don't think *I* was in pain when I watched my pregnant mother *DROWN?!*" she pushed him hard in the chest. Tristan stumbled back against the streetlamp.

"Maki, I—I'm so sorry I didn't kn—"

"You don't think it hurt when I was spirited away from everyone and everything I ever knew when I was seven?! Yeah, I had problems, too, but I got help for them!"

"But you *HAD* help!" he countered—a lame dog trapped in a corner. "You had a support system! You had your dad, your aunt, Izzy... —I was alone. I was trapped in my room and forced to listen to my parents argue every single night! I had no one to turn to—no one I could trust... I put on a happy face for Will's sake, but I've been dying on the inside for a long time."

A chill ran down his spine. "...I feel so alone..." He shivered.

The next thing he knew, Makiko was screaming. She stepped in with a 180-degree turn and locked her right elbow under his armpit whilst grabbing hold of his right wrist with her other hand. A moment later, the world turned upside down as Tristan was flipped over her shoulder. The snow did little to soften the fall and he hit the pavement with a searing flash of pain.

"WHAT WAS THAT FOR?!" he demanded to know as he clamored to his feet. Maki's peculiar response was to unzip her jacket, grab Tristan's hand and yank it to her heart.

"LISTEN!" she shouted.

Her heart pounded rapidly under his palm.

The next moment, Maki snapped her other hand down on his wrist and twisted her torso, hyperextending his tendons. Tristan hollered in agony as he fell to one knee—the only way to escape the position of extreme pain. Maki held the pose as tears began to stream down her face. Her heart was throbbing even faster beneath Tristan's palm.

"Don't you get it, moron?!" she cried. "The only one who's allowed to hurt you is *ME!!!*"

She released her grip and let him fall to the pavement.

In her anger (or was it fear?) she forgot what she was trying to ignore and caught a glance of the lapping waters at the shore. Petrified, her eyes grew large and her breathing became shallow. She quickly slumped into a seated position with her back pressed against the streetlamp. She was facing away from the water, trembling.

Tristan joined her side in the light snow. He did the only thing he could think to do: he raised his left arm and draped it across the girl's shoulders. He was going to let go—unsure of how to approach these sorts of things—but to his surprise, she twisted her body into his and rested her cheek against his chest. Tristan held her tighter. Her perfume was like an antivenom to his sorrows.

Tristan wasn't sure how long they sat there in each other's arms, but what he did know was that he was the one who broke the silence first.

"I just don't know what to do..." he whispered with sincerity.

"The same thing you've always done," Maki said quietly, now gently rubbing her thumb against his chest. "You have to draw."

"I can't, Maki. I can't do that anymore!"

Maki sat up. "You said you were alone, but I am *RIGHT HERE!*" she proclaimed as she patted her chest. She then became sullen and looked away. "Let me help you... please. I can't bear to watch you suffer in silence for another day..." Quietly, she slid back into their huddled position. *"...Please..."*

Tristan held her arms and pushed her away for a moment to look her in the face. Even bloodshot and sunken with tears, she still had the most stunning eyes he had ever seen. He pulled her in for a tight hug.

"You're so brave…" he thought to himself. *"Coming all the way out to the Sound… you must be terrified, yet you're still here next to me. You're trying to comfort me, but I can feel you trembling in my arms.*

"How are you doing this…? How can you be so strong…?

"You act tough and sarcastic; you belittle me every chance you get—yet you always keep me around. You always push me to be my very best even when I'm at my worst and you love my little brother like he's your own. I don't get you, but maybe that's why I choose to keep on going…

"…Was that your plan all along…?

"I may be a moron, but at least I'm YOUR moron."

"Maki, I…" he stammered. "I'm so sorry. …I'm just so scared."

"…I'm scared, too…" Maki whispered. By now, they were both shaking.

"I …I can't watch my brother die again…"

"I…" Maki broke off. *"…I can't either."*

They remained huddled in silence once more as they each contemplated the situation. They had to go back—that much was obvious—but how? What could they possibly do?

That was when the seagulls returned from their evening scavenger hunt to glide over the water…

RUNNING THROUGH WALLS

AT THE TOP OF THE TRAIL, Tristan was in for another surprise. Like something out of a dream, a woman in a white ball gown waited for him beneath the gaslit cobblestone archway.

"Izzy?" he said in shock. "What are you—? You shouldn't be here! Tonight's your show!"

"I know." She nodded, stepping out from beneath the arch.

Tristan looked back and forth between her and Maki, searching for an answer.

"I don't understand," he said. Izzy bit her lip. Her eyes darted to the ground.

"I quit the show," she said, folding her arms.

"You what?" Tristan gasped. Izzy nodded.

"When I heard about Will, I called Debbie and told her to cut the scene."

"But Izzy," Tristan began, "this is crazy! You worked the whole semester for this! There are talent scouts there. This could be your big break!"

"'What profit is there for one to gain the whole world and forfeit his life?'" she quoted. This drew a smile from Maki.

"You shouldn't have done this," Tristan said, shaking his head. Pangs of guilt began to overtake him. How many lives did he have to ruin in one night?

"Tristan," Izzy said softly. "I was wrong to push you away. I let this stupid show get to my head. It made me lose sight of what was really important." She uncrossed her arms and approached him. "Even though I'll try, I don't think I'll ever be able to fully forgive myself for that." Tears began to well in her eyes. "I'm sorry."

A lone tear slid down her heart-shaped cheek. Crystalline light refracted from its globular surface as it rolled past her plump lips, eventually falling to the ground. Watching it split Tristan's heart in two. He immediately seized her in his arms.

"Thank you," he whispered.

When no one was looking, Makiko wiped away a tear of her own. She headed back to the car and warmed up the engine, waiting for her friends to catch up. As surprised as he was to see Izzy again Tristan was grateful for the added company. There was simply no way he could have done this alone. Most people were lucky if they can find one close friend in their lives, yet there he was with two.

Once in the car, Tristan pulled out his phone with a sigh.

"Here goes nothing," he said, pressing "send" on a text to his mom. Thankfully, the drive to the hospital from the beach only took around two minutes to make. Maki pulled up to the front entrance of St. Luke's and hopped out with Tristan. Izzy got in the driver's seat and drove to the building's east side in search of parking. They both stared up at the massive clock tower: Will's home. Decorated for Christmas, it glowed in various shades of white, red, and green.

"You ready?" Maki asked.

"As I'll ever be." Tristan gulped.

Without taking their eyes off the tower, Maki's hand found his. They stepped forward into the hospital—together.

Almost immediately after entering the lobby, the elevator chimed. The iron doors slid back, revealing its occupant: Clare. Tristan released Makiko's hand. He sped toward his mother with outstretched arms—a prodigal son on the verge of tears all over again—

SMACK!

She hit him in the face so hard that the slap was heard by every single person in the lobby. A security guard ran over to see what was going on.

"No, it's alright," Tristan said, rubbing his face. "I deserved it." He briefly summed up the situation to the officer.

"She let you off lightly," he told him before looking over at Clare. "If it was my son? I would have killed him."

"Don't worry officer," she said before returning her glare to Tristan. *"We're not home yet,"* she hissed through barred teeth. The officer nodded in understanding before winking at Tristan and returning to his post. Clare was still seething with anger. Knowing he would be receiving an earful no matter what he did, Tristan had to say something. Regardless of what was about to happen, he decided it would be best to tell the truth.

"I'm sorry Mom…" he began, "I was just so scared… I didn't know what to do." All at once, hot tears began to flood down his face. "So, I ran. I didn't even know where I was going, but my feet took me back to the beach." Tristan was quivering where he stood, unable to look his mother in the eye. "We had so many fun parties there, and I just kept on thinking that Will would... he'd never be able to go there again!" He wanted to fall through the floor. He covered his face with his hands, half-expecting another blow. To his surprise, Clare embraced him with a hug.

"*Shh shh shhhhh....*" she soothed as she gently rocked him back and forth, resting her cheek on the side of his head.

Makiko, not wanting to involve herself in family matters, had ducked her head into the nearby gift shop. Following the directions she had sent, Izzy arrived a few minutes later. They met just outside the shop entrance.

"Hey," Izzy said.

"Hey," Maki smirked. "You missed the fireworks."

"Fireworks? What are you—?"

"Good evening, ladies," greeted a bespectacled white-haired old lady. She had watched them enter with kind eyes from her stool behind the counter. The gift shop contained dozens of wooden and glass shelving units carrying a host of comfort items, mostly for children. The girls said hello to the woman behind the counter. "Let me know if you need help finding anything."

"I think we're okay," said Izzy.

"Yeah," Maki began, "we should be... Wait a minute." She strode over to the counter with a curious smile on her face. "Do you have any stationery?"

"Well, we've got a big selection of cards to choose from in the back."

"No, no, no... I mean *stationery*. Paper, crayons, colored pencils?"

The woman thought for a moment then nodded. "Oh yes! We've got a few." She leaned over the counter and pointed. "Just past the candies down there and it should be on the left side."

"Thanks." Maki smiled. Izzy followed her friend down the aisle toward their goal.

"You are a *genius!*" she exclaimed, sifting through the craft supplies they discovered.

"If I'm a genius, what does that make you? Omnipotent?" Maki asked.

"I think you mean *omniscient.*"

Makiko froze and gave Izzy a neutral glare with a cocked eyebrow.

"...I see your point," Izzy conceded.

In a few minutes, they had four plastic bags filled with art supplies. Maki was going to pay for it, but Izzy beat her to the punch.

"Cash or credit?" the lady asked.

"Debit, please," Izzy said, whipping out her card.

Makiko held up a finger. "Could we have a moment?" She spun Izzy around and whispered, "Iz, are you nuts? That's crazy expensive! It was my idea, just let me take care of it."

She shrugged her hand off her shoulder and smiled.

"You've done enough for me today already."

With their baggage ready, the girls met Tristan and his mom sitting on a bench near the elevators. They rose to greet them. Clare smiled at Makiko's approach, literally welcoming her with open arms.

"Mrs. Collins, I'm so, so sorry," Maki said as she wrapped her arms around the grieving mother.

"Thank you for coming," Clare said, solemnly. Upon releasing, Clare turned her attention to Tristan's other friend. She did little to disguise the animosity behind her lime green eyes. Nobody hurts momma's little cub and gets away with it. Izzy gulped.

"You must be Izzy," Clare said forthrightly.

"Mrs. Collins, it's lovely to finally meet you," Izzy said, nervously. She extended her hand. Clare looked at it for a moment, deciding what to do. She chose to leave her hanging.

"Mom, Izzy's show was tonight," Tristan explained.

"Oh, is that why you're so dressed up?" Clare asked. Izzy nodded with a smile. Clare examined the dress. "Beautiful. Is that from Macy's?"

"Yeah, it is," Izzy said with a smile.

"Ah. Didn't know they came in that size."

Izzy frowned and zipped up her coat.

"Mom!" Tristan gasped.

"What? You expect me to *like* her after what she did to you?!"

"You don't understand!"

"Mrs. Collins," Makiko interjected, "Izzy quit the show to be here tonight."

Clare fell silent.

"What?" she whispered.

"I just... I just wanted to apologize and be here support Will," Izzy whimpered.

Clare put her hand to her head in disbelief.

"May God forgive me," she said. "Sweetheart, you didn't have to do that."

"I know," Izzy said. "But Will means a lot to everyone. It's important that he's surrounded by the people he loves."

Clare was at a loss for words. Rather than attempt to speak, she chose to act—embracing Izzy in a hug.

"He'll appreciate the support." She stepped away to look at the trio. "From all of you. Thank you." She smiled. A moment later, her attention became fixed on Makiko's hands. Clare took Maki's hand. As she looked, a peculiar expression scrawled across her face—one Maki had seen countless times before.

"I know, the gloves... I—"

"Yes, it's cold," Clare interjected. "The bags. What did you girls buy?" Looking down at her hands, Maki realized that she and Izzy divided their bags evenly between them. Clare had been so distracted by Izzy's arrival that she hadn't noticed them until now. As Izzy and Maki knelt on the floor to reveal their treasure haul, Tristan and his mom sat back down on the bench to watch with anticipation. From the bags, they revealed numerous poster boards, stickers, markers, crayons, colored pencils, rolls of tape, scissors, glitter, glue, erasers… basically a portable elementary school art studio.

"We were wondering if we could go with Tristan to write a story for Will before has the transplant," Makiko explained. "Would that be alright with you, Mrs. Collins?"

She put her hand on her heart and began to tear up. "Of course it would," she whispered.

FARRON

AN OVERWHELMING SILENCE had overtaken the 13th floor of St. Luke's Hospital. Nurses and doctors seemed to give the small group solemn nods of understanding as they passed by on their way to Will's room.

Was it really hopeless?

Clare entered the room ahead of them to explain the situation to her husband. At least, that was the only explanation Tristan could think of as to why he didn't throttle him when he and his friends entered the room.

"Tristan… you're back." Will smiled weakly.

"And not alone." Tristan smiled back.

"Surprise!" Izzy and Maki shouted with open arms as they sprinted over to the bed. The three embraced Will in a group hug.

"Oh my gosh!" cried Will, suddenly perking up in a way his parents hadn't seen in weeks. "Izzy! Maki! Hi!"

Tristan sat on the bed beside his brother while the two girls squatted down on the floor. Marc and Clare watched as the girls were hard at work organizing all the supplies they had purchased from the downstairs gift shop.

"We were wondering," said Maki, "if we could help tell you another story!" Will was flabbergasted. His eyes looked as if the doctor just came in and said he was not only cancer-free, but that

Marc had won the lottery, and the Collins were the inheritors of Disney World.

"Yes! Absolutely!" he shouted. The girls rose from the floor. Izzy took the final remaining chair while Maki athletically vaulted herself onto the windowsill, each armed with paper and a variety of art supplies. For the first time in weeks, Tristan saw a smile form on his father's face. The room was quickly running out of seats, so Clare walked over and sat on his lap. He wrapped his arm around her and kissed her cheek. She turned her head and returned the sentiment with a proper kiss on the lips.

Now that the places were set, everyone eagerly looked to Tristan to begin the main event.

"So," Tristan began, "I wanted to tell you a story about a bird."

"Lawrence?!" Will shouted.

"Yes, Lawrence! Lawrence of Australia!" he nodded, pounding his chest triumphantly as he spoke the herring gull's proper name.

"Ooh, I remember that one!" cooed Izzy from the cushioned wooden armchair. She and Maki started sketching ferociously.

"Lawrence was a seagull unlike any other—"

"He has a backpack, right?" interrupted Maki.

"Yes," Tristan answered. "And he had many important jobs throughout his life—"

"What color is he?" asked Izzy.

"Gray and white," he replied. "He was a loyal servant to many masters throughout his long career—"

"Is this orange?" Izzy asked, holding up a red crayon. "These aren't labeled."

"You know what?" Tristan interrupted, "Why don't I draw him first, then you guys can fill in the blanks as we go?"

Both his parents and Will laughed at this sudden outburst.

"Geez, and I thought I was hot-headed." Maki snickered to herself.

"Anyway," Tristan said, "One of Lawrence's first jobs EVER was as a royal messenger."

"What does that mean?" Will asked.

"It means he carried important letters from knights back to the King."

"Whoa…" Will said.

"Those are pigeons," Maki said flatly, without looking up from her paper.

"Wait, what?" Tristan asked, more surprised that he was surprised by yet another interruption than the interruption itself.

"You're thinking of carrier pigeons, honey," Clare explained. He looked back and forth between the faces of the room's occupants. Clare looked interested, Marc's eyes were fixed on his wife, Maki was smirking, and Izzy was staring at Tristan with her lips curled in a sorry attempt at suppressing laughter.

"Uh…" he stammered. "Shut up." Tristan playfully dismissed his mother with a wave of his hand. This sent both Izzy and Will into a fit of laughter.

"You talk to your mom like that?" Maki chuckled with raised eyebrows. She turned her head and tilted the eraser end of her pencil at his mother. "Can I hit him again?" This sent Clare into a fit of hysterical laughter. It even got a chuckle out of Marc.

"Can we get on with the story now, please?" Tristan pleaded with the room. After another ten seconds of hysterics, Clare finally beckoned her son to continue with a wave of her hand.

"Thank you." Tristan sighed with a smile. "As I was saying, Lawrence was raised in Australia, but his first big break was when he fell into a portal that sucked him into another world!" He sketched out a cartoon of a bird falling into a revolving void. "On the other side, he found himself in a beautiful kingdom called… It was called… uh…" He genuinely had a mind slip and had no idea where to go.

"Akita?" Makiko offered.

"No, too Asian," Tristan said. She glared at him with furrowed brows. She raised a palm and air-slapped him from across the room.

"Think European fantasy," he explained. "Irish."

"What about Farron?" Izzy suggested.

"That's a good one." Clare nodded.

"You've heard of it?" Izzy asked.

"Yes," she nodded. "It could mean handsome or adventurous."

"Oh, neat!" Izzy smiled with a nod as she sat back in her chair. Little did Clare know that she only vaguely remembered having heard it used in a *Zelda* game. But hey, brownie points were brownie points. She'd have to take them where she could get them.

"That's right," Tristan continued. "He was a royal messenger to the Kingdom of Farron."

Agent Patrick Buckley burst through the doors of the Farron Courier Services office. He apologized profusely as he nudged his way to the front of the line, holding up a medallion he wore around his neck. Catching the eye of one of the postal workers, he shouted and pointed to his coin, "Royal Post!"

The worker nodded knowingly, tipping his hat to the customer with whom he was speaking before exiting from behind the flip-up countertop. With a jerk of his head and a wave of his hand, the postal worker beckoned Buckley to meet him in the mail tower.

"Busy today, huh?" Buckley asked as they ascended the spiral sandstone stairs. "Sorry to make your job more difficult."

"Actually, I was relieved when I saw the medal." The man laughed. "I'll happily take any opportunity I can to get out of that cacophony."

Forty steps later, they alighted into a cylinder filled with hundreds of arched alcoves that circled all the way to the top. Warm light poured in from a large circular, open window near the top of the tower.

"Parcel?" the man asked. Buckley pulled the letter out of his satchel. The man went to grab it, but the knight retracted his hand.

"Sorry," he said, "Confidential." The postman lifted his hands as if in surrender.

"Just checking the size," he explained. He looked between the parchment and a variety of cylindrical leather satchels set about a wooden cubby system. "Aha!" He smiled, pulling out a black satchel. "Royal standard should do just fine." He passed it to Buckley, who tested the weight before rolling up the letter and slipping it inside.

"We've got three royal birds here," said the postman. "Sam is fast but sometimes detours. Lawrence is slower but stable, and Ridley is a good all-rounder, though he's noisy and catches the attention of predators."

"Lawrence, please," Buckley said.

"Yay!" Will cheered.

"Is this good for Buckley?" Izzy asked, holding up her paper, and revealing a childish drawing of a man dressed in a blue robe with a sword.

"Yeah... sure," Tristan said, somewhat regretting this decision.

"You could say he has a face." Clare snickered.

"Hey, I'm colorblind! I'm doing the best that I can!" Izzy laughed. She shook her head and got back to work.

"How's this?" Maki asked, flipping over her page. She displayed a gorgeous, port town filled with sandstone buildings colored in with yellow crayon.

"Perfect!" Tristan said with a smile.

"Wow, Maki. You're a wonderful artist." Clare complimented.

"Why thank you, Mrs. Collins," Maki said proudly, placing a hand on her chest. She turned her head to Izzy and stuck out her tongue.

"So, what happened next?" Will asked.

"Lawrence. Wise choice." The postman nodded as he pulled the rotating ladder over to the appropriate column of alcoves. He locked it in place, taking the satchel from Buckley before ascending the tower.

"Well, you know what they say," Buckley called after him. "Slow and steady wins the race." The postman paused.

"Do they say that?" Buckley shrugged and shook his head.

"Not a Farron expression, I suppose," Buckley said.

"No, I suppose not," said the man as he continued his ascent. "Back from the Isles I take it?" the postman said while rubbing his face, staring at the knight's sunburnt skin. Buckley opened his mouth to respond, but the worker cut him off.

"Classified, I know. I shouldn't pry," he said with a disengaging wave of his hand. Not long after, the postman reached Lawrence's cage. Opening it, he secured the black satchel to the bird's back—tying the straps around his front side like a backpack.

"That's a rather strange-looking pigeon," Buckley remarked.

"That's because he's not a pigeon," the postman said with a chuckle. "He's a seagull!"

The postman carefully pulled the bird out of the cage and slowly lifted it in his palms towards the window. As if it could read his mind, the violet-eyed bird leaped from his hands and flew out the window.

Lawrence knew the trip to the castle would be perilous. There was a dangerous monster out there. A beast in the clouds. No one knew anything about it. It just showed up one day—literally from out of the blue. It had no name. No face. No origin story. No reason for being there.

It simply existed to destroy.

And every day, it'd spread. It would multiply across the sky in search of new victims to devour. This terrified Lawrence. Scared him right to his core. But he'd face down anything—no matter how dangerous—to complete his mission. No matter how scared he was, he'd never give up.

"Why didn't he give up?" Will asked.

"What do you mean, buddy?" Tristan said.

"In all these stories, the hero always keeps going no matter what. Why?"

Tristan thought for a moment. Suddenly, he became acutely aware of all the eyes on him. He scanned the eager faces and turned his attention back to his little brother.

"Because Will, Lawrence had a secret weapon. Something so powerful, he knew there wasn't anything that could take it away from him."

"Really?" Will raised his eyebrows. "What?"

He planned his flight path carefully. You see, Farron was split up into four biomes, each with its own season. He flew out of the FCS tower, above the Port of Entry, and out over the waters of the Summerlands. Normally, they'd be peaceful, but rumors of Oilliphéists from below and the terror above had spread a sentiment of fear throughout the kingdom.

Still, Lawrence didn't give up.

In the distance, a mass of swirling black clouds appeared to take notice of his flight path. The clouds rapidly changed direction and came charging straight for the seagull. Having only about a minute before they swallowed him up, he flew down toward the water and glided his foot across its surface. He did this three times— an emergency symbol he had coordinated with his friend from the deep. He then flew up and away as fast as he could. Only a few more seconds remained before his collision with the black clouds.

They were going to swallow him whole in three, two—

SPLASH!

Out of nowhere, a supermassive tailfin shot up out of the water, whacking the clouds to the other side of the globe! Lawrence leveled off his flying and waited to see the familiar face of his longtime friend. His patience was rewarded when the enormous head of his companion breached the water. Her furry ears were each a mile tall. Her giant green eyes might have been planets. Her sharp fang was literally the size of a mountain.

"Tristan," Marc interrupted, "what the hell are you talking about?"

Tristan had been so caught up in the telling of his tale that he had failed to notice the bewildered stares of everyone around the room.

"Oh, it's Mer-Meowki," he explained.

"Wait, Meowki's a mermaid now?" Makiko asked.

"No, it's a different character. Meowki's a cat. Mer-Meowki's a giant, celestial, extradimensional, paranatural mer-cat."

The room fell silent.

"Who's Meowki?" Izzy asked.

Lawrence thanked his companion with a friendly salute as he descended back to the mainland.

"Go get 'em! Tee hee!" Mer-Meowki bellowed as she returned to the depths.

The seagull just had to pass through the Spring Hills. Through there, it would be a straight shot to Farron Castle. Hearing a distant rumble, Lawrence looked up. The black clouds had returned from their trip around the globe. He saw that the malicious entity had only recruited more of its white brethren to join its ranks, corrupting them as it went. Turning them bad. Making them swallow themselves alive.

Still, Lawrence didn't give up.

He descended to the grasslands. The hills were the home of faeries; although, it wasn't their help which he was seeking today. He whistled hard. A piercing sound that could be heard from miles around.

"Birds can't whistle," Maki said.

"They sing all the time, though," Izzy pointed out.

"Right, but do seagulls sing?" Makiko asked.

"Do I look like an ornithologist? How am I supposed to know?"

"Ahem." Tristan cleared his throat.

"Sorry. Continue," said Maki.

Following the whistle came the galloping of hooves. The silhouette of a horse crested over a distant hill, approaching at lightning speed. Within seconds, it was at Lawrence's side. The zebra slowed to match the gull's pace. It was unusually tall with a beautiful mane of thick, blonde hair.

"Izzebra!" Lawrence called.

Makiko and Will burst out laughing, pointing at their friend.

"*Izzebra?!*" Izzy exclaimed. "Why does she get to be a cute cat and yet I'm stuck being a freaking *zebra*?!"

"Sucks to suck." Maki shrugged, sketching a zebra with a blond mane.

"Can't I at least be something cool? Like a griffin or a dragon or something?" she pleaded.

"Would you rather be 'Izzy Bzzy, the Friendly Bee?'" Tristan asked. Izzy bit her lip and paused before responding.

"I've changed my mind. Izzebra is lovely, thank you."

"*Neigh!* I'm here!" Izzebra cried. Her long yellow mane valiantly trailed behind her, shining bright despite the oppressive clouds above.

"Defensive maneuvers!" shouted the bird. Izzebra nodded. She allowed Lawerence to glide beneath her torso, concealing him from the evil clouds. They descended toward the zebra at a rapid pace. From a distance, it looked like easy prey, but up close, they were confused. All those swirling black and white stripes—the bird was already being consumed! There wouldn't be enough for the clouds to eat if they scooped it up. So, the dark clouds fled to the icy Tundra to the east in search of selkies to munch on.

Lawrence flew out from beneath the zebra and thanked her for her help.

"I'll always be there for a friend in need!" cried Izzebra. "Good luck on your quest, and Godspeed!"

Lawrence crested one more hill and at long last, the beautiful Farron Castle was visible. The parapet of the princess' tower rose high above the surrounding market town. A horn sounded in the distance. He was so tired—the town was probably a dozen miles away.

Still, Lawrence didn't give up.

He knew he had been spotted by the guards. They were alerting the royal pages to notify the king of his arrival. He flew and he flew until at last, he reached his goal.

Undaunted, unafraid, he landed in the window of the princess and held his head high. The beautiful princess hastily removed the satchel from the bird's back and rewarded him with more treats than he could possibly eat.

"The end." Tristan smiled triumphantly. Grinning from ear to ear, Will applauded his brother and his friends. Marc and Clare joined in as well.

"That was my favorite one yet!" Will exclaimed.

"You really liked it?" asked his brother. Will nodded.

"I loved it!" he cheered. Unfortunately, this exclamation had him break into a coughing fit. Tristan patted him on the back. The room grew quiet, as though that one action had suddenly reminded everyone of why they were there.

A few minutes later, there was a knock on the door. Dr. Perkins entered with a nurse.

"Mr. and Mrs. Collins?" he said. "It's time."

He looked back and forth at all the guests. "My, my, Mr. Collins. You're quite the popular one!"

Will tried to smile but it was difficult.

"Alright, this will only take a few minutes, then we'll be out of your hair," said the doctor.

"Wait, you're doing it here?" Izzy asked.

"They already have the cells," Makiko explained. "They just need to attach it to his central line."

"That's right." Dr. Perkins nodded. "Somebody's been doing their homework. Premed?"

"I will be next year, yeah. How'd you know?" Maki asked.

"I can always tell." He smiled. "Alright little guy. Let's get you comfortable."

The doctor adjusted the bed to help Will sit upright as the nurse attached the stem cell bag to his IV. Once all was set up, the doctor took the tube attached to the bag into his hand.

"Just going to adjust your gown here." Dr. Perkins forced a smile as he pulled down the top of Will's gown, revealing the patch of tubing that had been adhered to his right breast. Dr. Perkins took the tube and attached it.

"Alright. Now we wait," he said.

"That's it?" Marc asked.

"That's it," the doctor said with a nod.

"How will we know if…?" Clare trailed off.

"It depends," answered Perkins, sensing her question. "It could take hours—days. If it takes longer, there will probably be a few early warning signs. But we'll find out soon enough."

Clare nodded. "Thank you, doctor."

The doctor nodded back. His nurse exited the room.

"I'll come back every half hour to check vitals. If anything happens, hit the call button. I'll see the room number and come running."

He followed his nurse out the door.

"Tristan?" Will murmured quietly.

"Yes Will?" he answered, returning to his bedside.

"I'm not scared anymore," he said with a smile. Tristan reached out and grabbed his hand.

"I know buddy. I know."

NIGHT OF FATE

DR. PERKINS HAD STOPPED BY twice to check on Will's vitals. Everything seemed stable so far, but that was to be expected. The occupants of the pediatric room were silently waiting on pins and needles. Will had fallen asleep, overcome by the excitement of the day. Clare lay by his side in the bed, holding him in her arms. The rest of them were practically falling asleep themselves.

Not long after the doctor's second visit, a young nurse knocked on the door: a bearded man who couldn't have been older than 25.

"Hi guys," he said softly. He scanned the solemn faces of the room before clearing his throat. "I'm so sorry to have to do this, but visiting hours are about to end."

"Can't we stay?" Izzy begged. The nurse shook his head.

"I'm sorry." The nurse grimaced. He always hated this part of the job. "Parents and immediate family only."

Izzy and Maki frowned.

"Alright," Maki said. She and Izzy got up from their chairs. Marc and Tristan rose to see them off.

"Thank you both so much for coming," said Marc.

"Yes, really," Clare agreed. "You have no idea how happy you made him."

The girls hugged them in turn.

"Please, it's the least we could have done," said Izzy.

"Agreed." Maki nodded. "And you know we're not leaving, right?"

"You're not?" asked Tristan, who had just mentally prepared himself to give a farewell hug to his companions. Makiko shook her head.

"Of course not, moron," she said. "You really think we'd leave you guys behind?" She jerked a thumb behind her. "We'll be in the chapel."

Clare thought she might tear up again. She readjusted Will at her side so she could stretch out both her arms.

"Girls, come here." she beckoned. They approached the bed and were swallowed in a group hug. "God bless you," she whispered. "You two are the miracle this family has been praying for."

For their part, the girls were at a loss for words. When they were at the door, Tristan hailed them before turning to his parents.

"Mom, Dad, do you mind if I—?"

His parents shook their heads and dismissed him with their hands.

"Honey, go. You'll know where we'll be," Clare said. Tristan hugged them both.

"I promise I'll come back this time," he said.

"Tristan, fall asleep in there if you have to," said Clare. "We need as many soldiers on that side of the fight as we do up here."

St. Luke's chapel was housed in a modestly sized, austere room on the clock tower's ground floor. It was deeper than it was wide, boasting bright oak walls to the left and right. These funneled down to a stained-glass window on the far wall, behind the altar. Plain wooden chairs with burgundy seat cushions were positioned in groups of three along the longer walls, forming a narrow central aisle.

Izzy, Maki, and Tristan filtered in, blessing themselves with holy water as they went. They seated themselves in a row of chairs near the altar. None of them spoke.

Izzy leaned forward, propping her elbows on her knees as she clasped her hands together.

"Jesus, please help this little boy. I know I've been talking Your ear off about him for these past few months, but this time, he really needs a miracle.

"I suppose he's not the only one.

"Listen I feel so incredibly selfish for talking about myself right now when Will needs all the help he can get, but I don't feel right asking You for anything with this hanging over my head. I'm so incredibly sorry for the way I've been acting. I let the promise of fame blind me from what was important. I cut myself off from my friends... my family... I even lashed out. I was rude—downright cruel, even! And now this adorable little kid might be on his last legs.

I could have spent more time with him. I *should have* spent more time with him.

"I know it gains me nothing to waste my energy wallowing in self-deprecation, but it's the truth. Please help me to forgive myself, God. Help me to move forward. I have to try, because the Collins family needs me right now. I can't have this defeatist mindset while trying to provide comfort to a family who needs it.

"I refuse to think that way.

"Please take care of Will… and give me the strength I need to be there for his family."

Makiko bowed her head and clasped her hands.

"Dear God. Thank you for guiding me to You. It's hard to believe that ten years ago, I hardly even knew who You were. Now here I am, sitting in a place of worship, praying for a little boy I hardly even know.

"I know I can't ask You to take away his illness. Cancer is something that stays with you forever. You can never really kill it. But you can learn to live with it. Learn to grow. To thrive.

"That's something You taught me the hard way. Years ago, when I found my mom laying there… *twitching…* No one could have guessed she was an epileptic. It was nobody's fault. Yet we spent years shifting the blame between ourselves, me and Dad. He wished he and Mom hadn't fought. He wished that he hadn't taken the keys and driven off that night.

"If I hadn't left the front door open while waiting for Dad, Mr. Shigeru wouldn't have come inside to check on us. Dad wouldn't have gotten the call from the police. He wouldn't have sped home. Wouldn't have crashed the car. His injury—his leg— was my fault. All I could do was stare at my mother—my brother— convulsing in that shallow grave.

"I wished I could have been braver. I wished I could have been smarter. Could have known what to do to help her.

"All these wishes, all these desires… they were nothing more than unnecessary pain and wasted breath. You can't change the past. You can only learn from it. It took me years to figure that out. I'm sorry for that.

"If You can't take away the illness, then please, let him live. He's just a little boy. Please. Give him the chance at life that my brother never had.

"Mom, Mamoru, I know you're listening. Please ask Him that for me. Please plead with us. He needs our help…

"Please…"

Tristan leaned forward and pressed his hands against his forehead.

"I know I haven't spoken to You as much as I should have, lately. That was a mistake, and I'm sorry.

"God… I don't know how else to say this…

"I'm terrified.

"I'm terrified of what will happen up there. I can't imagine losing him. I'm too frightened to even entertain the thought.

"Writing stories for him. That's my entire world. I can't believe I ran away. I was such a fool.

"A coward.

"Am I the reason why he's regressing? Have my trepidations rubbed off on him? Oh, please God, don't let that be true. I couldn't handle the guilt."

Tristan's anxieties had caused him to start rocking back and forth. Maki frowned and took his hand down from his forehead. He looked at her. She squeezed his hand and reassured him with a sad smile. A moment later, Izzy did the same. He shut his eyes again and continued his prayer.

"But You were always there for me. I spent years praying for a miracle. A guardian angel. You sent me two in disguise.

"Izzy and Maki are the two greatest friends I ever could have asked for. Sure, we've had our disagreements. Our ups and downs. But they'd never leave my side, or Will's. I'm convinced they love my brother as much as I do.

"No matter what happens over these next few days, I just wanted to say… thank You. Thank You for blessing me and my brother with this amazing gift.

"Even if he were to… *go*. At least I'd know that his last four months on Earth were some of the happiest days of his life."

At two am, long after the transplant had completed, Marc Collins headed downstairs to check on the kids. Entering the chapel, he found the three of them asleep in the first row, hand-in-hand. He smiled, crossed himself, and returned to the room.

NEWS

IT WAS THREE IN THE MORNING. Dr. Perkins tiptoed silently around the three sleeping figures in the room to reach the IV cart. He examined the vitals carefully. What the technician had shown him after the recent blood test had shocked him to his core. He had to verify the results for himself. His heart beat faster as he cross-referenced the onscreen data with the information on his clipboard. A bead of sweat ran down his brow. He wiped it away.

He couldn't believe it. How could he tell them?

"Dr. Perkins?"

The voice made him jump. He turned toward Clare, who had just stirred awake in the nearby chair.

"Hello Mrs. Collins." he stammered. She saw the look on his face.

"Doctor, is everything alright?"

Dr. Perkins swallowed hard. Overcome with emotion, he thought he might burst into tears. He bit his lip to fight the surge. Looking around the room, he took in the colorful cast of characters featured on the walls. Cartoons of every color, shape, size, and species. All the stories that had been told in this very room. That something so ugly as cancer could have birthed such beauty into existence was a hypocrisy that he admired. He had grown to love the Collins family like his own. Will and his stories were an extension of the pediatrics department. His world would be lost without him.

"Dr. Perkins?" Clare asked again.

The doctor faced Clare and nodded.

"Mrs. Collins," he said, "could you wake up your husband, please? There's something I need to tell you both."

"Tristan, wake up."

Tristan slowly returned to consciousness. Someone had their hands on his shoulders and was gently shaking him awake. He had heard a woman's voice. He slowly blinked his eyes open. Though the world was fuzzy, he could make out a pair of piercing green eyes.

"Maki?" he said, softly.

"Guess again," Clare replied. Tristan rubbed his eyes and realized his mistake. He sat upright. He had been lying across the trio of burgundy chairs. A coarse white blanket had been draped over him while he slept.

"Where did this come from?" he asked.

"One of the chaplains brought it in," Clare answered. "They told me when I came down."

Tristan nodded. He scanned the chapel in search of his friends. Two white masses rested across adjacent rows of chairs just behind where he sat. Still asleep. Makiko was just feet away from him. He listened to her gentle breathing as the blanket slowly rose and fell.

"They really love you," Clare said.

"No," Tristan said, turning back around to face his mom. "They really love *us*."

Clare nodded then looked down at her hands.

"Honey, I have to tell you something," she whispered. Tristan couldn't read her expression.

"What is it?" he asked anxiously.

"Dr. Perkins ran some more tests." Clare continued, never lifting her eyes from her hands. "He came in to see us at around three."

"He had news?" Tristan asked with a gulp. Clare nodded. She reached out and gripped her son's hands.

"Honey…" she whispered. Tristan watched as tears began to fall from her face. She started to shake. Looking up, Clare met his eyes with a smile.

"It's a miracle!"

The moment visiting hours began, Izzy and Makiko burst through the elevator and onto the thirteenth floor. Dashing down the hall, they nearly knocked over a pair of CNAs as they rushed into William Collins' pseudo-bedroom.

"Congratulations!" They shouted as they threw themselves onto the bed, showering Will with hugs and kisses. Izzy had purchased over a dozen balloons from the store and released them into the room.

"How do you feel?" Makiko asked.

"Woozy," Will replied weakly, "but a little better, I think."

"That'll take time," said the doctor.

"Perky!" Will cheered with a smile. The doctor stepped in from the doorway. He was grinning from ear to ear. Tristan got up from his chair and greeted the man with a hug.

"Thank you," he said.

"Please. It's my pleasure, Mr. Collins."

"What exactly happened, Dr. Perkins?" Makiko asked. Having been out of the loop, she and Izzy were a little behind on the specifics.

"A miracle," said the doctor. He walked over to examine the vitals. Whatever he saw in his cross reference with his clipboard must have been good, because he put it away with a smile.

"Normally, it takes quite a bit of time for patients to start seeing their blood cell counts begin to return to normal levels after a BMT. The American Cancer Society puts that number somewhere between two and six weeks.

"But this little guy here?" He pointed at Will. "His CBC showed a *near-instant* growth. His body took to the stem cells like a fish to water." The doctor shook his head and laughed. "And here we were worrying about his body rejecting the treatment. Don't be surprised if you have some St. Jude's researchers knocking at your door."

"What happened was rare?" Tristan asked.

"Getting struck by lightning is rare. This is completely unheard of!" the doctor replied, gleefully. "If I were you," he pointed to Marc, "I'd start playing the lottery."

Marc laughed. "I might just do that."

"How much longer will he need to stay here?" Izzy asked.

"Depends." The doctor sighed. "Definitely through Thanksgiving. But at the rate his recovery is going, I'd stake my professional reputation on him being home by Christmas."

The room became ecstatic. Clare and Marc immediately kissed. Izzy and Maki hugged. Tristan grabbed his brother's hand and shook it with joy. The doctor turned and went toward the door. Something occurred to him, causing him to freeze in place. He turned around.

"Oh, just one more thing," he said. "Tristan?"

Surprised at hearing his family's hero address him individually, Tristan raised his head and eyebrows at once.

"Yes sir?" he asked.

"Make sure you keep up with those drawings." He winked.

"Of course!" Tristan smiled. The doctor nodded and left. Tristan looked back at Clare and shrugged.

DECEMBER

FAROS

TRISTAN SLOWLY OPENED THE DOOR and poked his head inside.

"You wanted to see me, sir?"

"Come in, come in!"

The hospital director stretched out his hand toward Tristan and shook it with the pressure of a vice. Dr. Perkins was already inside, seated in a comfortable chair before the director's mahogany desk. The director gestured for Tristan to sit in the chair adjacent to the doctor as he circled toward his own giant brown leather chair on the opposite side of the desk.

Director Faros was a large man. Short and sturdy. He was well-liked by his staff for his amiability and level-headed decision-making. Earlier in the week, he had arranged a meeting with the Collins boy. The secretary had been tight-lipped on the phone. Tristan was apprehensive. He hadn't the slightest idea what he was in for. All he knew was that the director had called for him specifically. Why Dr. Perkins was in the room, he could only speculate.

The director opened a drawer in his desk and removed a manilla folder. Tristan could see it was overflowing with white sheets of paper.

"Dr. Perkins tells me your brother is on the mend," he said kindly, despite his gravelly voice. "He's had a pretty miraculous recovery."

"He did." Tristan nodded. "Thank you, sir. My family and I are incredibly indebted to St. Luke's—especially Dr. Perkins."

The doctor gave Tristan's shoulder a fraternal squeeze.

"Just doing my job, sport." Dr. Perkins said with a smile. The director nodded.

"Yes," said Faros. "We've received word that the blood sample your brother donated arrived in Memphis last night. The team at St. Jude's reminded me to thank you all personally."

So that was what this meeting was about.

"That's very kind of them," Tristan said, wondering why the director would thank him instead of his parents.

"I can tell by the look on your face that you're confused," the director said with a smirk. Dr. Perkins chuckled.

"No, no, that's not why we called you in today," Faros continued. He opened the folder and began to sift through the pages. "I saw the photos of your brother's hospital room. You're a modern Claire Wineland."

After hearing of Will's miraculous recovery, some local news outlets came in to cover the story. Clare and Will were interviewed in the hospital room. Faros must have seen one of the papers.

"Thank you, sir," Tristan said. "Though I'll admit, it's hardly a comparison. I'm not sick."

"No," said Faros, "but the drawings you did speak for themselves."

"Just trying to be a good brother is all," Tristan said, shrugging off the compliment. Dr. Perkins leaned forward.

"He's very humble," Perkins commented.

"I've noticed," replied Faros. He returned to thumbing through the pages in the folder. "Tell me Tristan, what do you make of your brother's sudden recovery?"

"Sir?"

"Well, to be frank, William Collins, a ten-year-old boy, goes from being at death's door to near-remission from stage-four cancer overnight. You don't think that's odd?"

"Of course I do," Tristan agreed. "But I can't say I know what you're driving at."

Dr. Perkins jumped in.

"Tristan," he said, "what do you think caused him to have such a sudden recovery?"

The question had him at a loss. How was he supposed to know? He was no doctor. His first guess was divine intervention, but he couldn't say that in front of a room full of medical professionals. Honestly, he was more confused as to why he was being interrogated like this in the first place.

"Well—" he stammered, "I suppose it has something to do with genetics."

Faros and Perkins nodded.

"We're certainly in agreement with you there." Faros nodded. "But I think there's something you're missing."

"You could say you're lacking some critical information," Perkins said with a sly smile. "Director?"

Faros nodded and passed the folder across the desk to Tristan.

"Do any of these look familiar to you?" he asked.

When Tristan opened the folder, he felt his jaw drop. Inside were dozens, no, *hundreds* of photocopies of his drawings. Lawrence of Australia, Holey Sockman, Nada Shark… they were all there.

Where did he get these?

"We found these circulating around pediatrics." Dr. Perkins explained.

"I—I don't understand," Tristan stammered. "How did these get copied?"

"You or your brother must have left some of them behind somewhere," the doctor suggested. "You two spent a lot of time in the playroom. Ever do any drawing in there?"

"All the time." Tristan nodded in understanding.

It made sense. In the time since his rehospitalization, Tristan must have made hundreds of drawings for his little brother. It was entirely possible that a few dozen of them got left behind in the Wineland Room. But why would anybody want to copy them?

"Who made these?" Tristan asked. "The copies, I mean."

"Patients did." Perkins smiled. "Kids."

"They love your drawings, Tristan," Faros said.

Dr. Perkins got up from his chair. He knelt beside Tristan, his tone shifting to sincerity.

"We think that's what helped your brother, Tristan: *you,*" he explained. "Your stories and drawings made him happy. Gave him hope."

"And clearly, he's not the only one you've helped," Faros interjected, pointing at the photocopies. Perkins looked back and nodded.

"It's true," he said. "I can't go anywhere in that ward without running into another patient with their nose in one of your stories."

"Kids are reading them?" Tristan repeated the obvious fact in bewilderment. Seeing the shock in his face, Perkins chose to simply respond with a nod.

"Every day, Tristan," he said.

"That's why we called you in here," the director explained. Perkins returned to his seat. "We wanted to make a deal with you."

"What kind of deal?" Tristan asked. He shifted nervously in his seat. Sensing his nerves, Faros decided to ease the tension by rising from his chair. He figured his short stature would make him less intimidating. Unfortunately, his bulging muscles had the opposite effect.

"For years now, we've been talking about disseminating an internal newspaper," he said as he peered out the window behind his desk. It offered a lovely view of the Roosevelt Isle skyline. "It'd highlight fundraising events, promotions, new facilities, prominent donors, that sort of thing. Just fluff pieces for patient morale. Unfortunately, we could never get it off the ground."

"What happened?" Tristan asked.

"Nothing." The director shrugged. "That's the problem. The ball can't roll if nobody's there to push it. You can't talk something into moving. You have to take action." Faros paced around to the side of his desk and sat on it, placing his hands in his pockets.

"That's why I like you, Tristan," Faros said. "You take action. You don't give up. And these," he reached over and riffled through the drawings with his thumb, "could really help people." He hopped off his desk and returned to his seat.

"Tristan," he continued, "how would you like to draw a weekly comic strip for Novena Health?"

Tristan did a double take.

"I—I'm sorry, what did you ask me?" he stammered. Dr. Perkins laughed. Faros repeated the question.

"You want me to make more drawings for the hospital?" Tristan asked.

"Not just the hospital." Dr. Perkins cut in. "The entire *chain*," he explained.

"Novena Health has facilities all over the world," Faros said. "I've already spoken to marketing. This would be a serial that would be stocked in the pediatric ward. *Every* pediatric ward."

"Do you think you could do it?" Perkins asked. "A comic a week?"

"You'd be earning a commission, of course," Faros clarified.

Tristan fell back into his chair. Shell-shocked, he could hardly think let alone respond.

"I, uh… I really don't know what to say." Bewildered, he looked back and forth between the men's expectant faces, unsure of how to proceed. "Could you give me a few minutes to think about it?"

"Of course." Faros nodded.

"Take all the time you need," Perkins said. "We'll wait here."

"Thanks," Tristan said, rising from his seat.

He tripped over his own feet on the way to the door. Perkins helped him up with a laugh. If you had to fall, he supposed the head office of a hospital was as good a place as any.

"So, how'd it go?" Makiko asked. She had been waiting for him in the hall. Tristan didn't respond. He simply gawked at her with a befuddled expression. She waved her hand in front of his face.

"*Helloooooooo*, Earth to Tristan?" she mocked.

"They have my drawings." He sighed.

"Your drawings?"

He nodded.

"The kids in pediatrics photocopied them. They love them. Director Faros wants to pay me to write a weekly comic strip that would be put in all Novena Health pediatric departments."

Makiko squealed. Without hesitation, she threw her arms around Tristan and squeezed him, spinning him around in the hallway.

"And you said, 'yes,' right?!" she exclaimed. When he didn't answer, she raised an eyebrow.

"You said, *'yes,'* right?" Makiko repeated more deliberately. Tristan looked at her.

"I told them I needed a moment to think about it," he said.

"What's there to think about?!" she shouted. "Your comics are going to be read by kids around the world! This is a dream come true! Just think about all the kids—*the families* you're going to help!

"Come on, this should be a no-brainer even for you, moron!" She whacked him on the chest with the back of her hand. Tristan chuckled and nodded.

"Well, to be honest Maki, I sort of fell into a rut," he admitted. "When Will started getting sick again, I just didn't know where to go. You saw it yourself, I let myself fall into a pit."

"But you pulled yourself out," Maki whispered. "That wasn't you."

"I know." Tristan nodded. "But I didn't do it alone." He grabbed her hand. "I just keep thinking that, if it wasn't for you and Izzy, Will might have—" he bowed his head—unable to complete the thought. He sighed once more. "Thank you."

"You really want to thank me? Then go in there and tell them *'yes'* you moron!" Maki scoffed, grabbing his free hand.

They were standing very close now.

"If I do, I'm not doing it alone," Tristan countered. He paused. Thoughtfully, he continued. "You know Maki?"

"Mm-hmm?" she purred.

Hand-in-hand they gently began to sway.

"I've always sucked at drawing backgrounds…"

Instantly, Makiko's hands went to the back of his head.

Tristan's to her waist.

They each pulled.

Their lips met.

ELSEWHERE

HEARTLINE ROLL

ISHAN PATEL WAS IN BED. The events of the last few days had been a whirlwind. He hadn't been feeling too well. First was the light-headedness. Nausea followed. After fainting, he found himself drifting in and out of consciousness as strange men in white coats spoke to his parents.

Why were they crying? What was happening?

His mother had tried to explain to him that he was sick. He had something called *cancer*. Apparently, this meant that the cells in his body were attacking themselves, making him very sick. He'd have to stay in the hospital for quite some time.

Ishan was heartbroken. He couldn't go back to school, see his friends, or play outside. His life had become consumed by these boring gray walls.

There was a knock at the door.

"Hi Daddy," the seven-year-old said with a smile. His father strode over to the bed and kissed him on the forehead. He had a gift bag in his hand.

"What's that?" Ishan asked.

"A present." His father smiled. "Consider it an early birthday gift." He passed the bag to his son, who gleefully accepted. Ishan tore through the tissue paper, revealing the bag's true contents. When he saw what was inside, he couldn't help but laugh.

It was a stuffed animal of a bird. A strange bird. A seagull with violet eyes and a large backpack.

"I love it!" Ishan cheered, squeezing the bird in a hug. "But who is it?"

"You mean you don't know?" His father gasped playfully. He looked over at his wife who was seated nearby. She smiled and shook her head. Mr. Patel seated himself on the side of his son's bed.

"Then I guess this ought to help you," he said, handing his son a comic book. The bird was pictured on the front cover, flying across a blue sky as black clouds chased after him in the distance. A giant cat-mermaid and a strange-looking zebra ran alongside him. The text was in Hindi. It read, "*Heartline Roll* presents: Lawrence of Australia in... The Black Clouds of Farron!"

Ishan laughed at the silliness of the cover.

"Want me to read it with you?" his father asked. Ishan nodded. Mrs. Patel smiled at her husband approvingly.

"Okay," he nodded, taking the book back. He helped Ishan sit up as best as he could before returning to the side of the bed, book in hand.

"Alright, here we go." Mr. Patel cleared his throat.

"Many of you may already know who Lawrence of Australia already is. A herring gull from Down Under with a knack for adventure! But have you ever wondered about how that adventure began?"

Ishan felt himself drawn into the zaniness of the tale. With each panel of the story, the burdens of the illness had begun to dissipate from the lives of the Patel family. They were together and that was all that mattered.

An hour later, the Patels were fast asleep. The youngest was cradling a violet-eyed seagull in his arms. A smile stretched across his face.

About the Author

Luke Jackson received his BA in Music from Stony Brook University in 2019, and his Masters in Music Education from the University of Florida in 2024. He began his career in education after relocating to Florida during the COVID-19 pandemic, where he became a choir director. He happily resides in Orlando with his two cats, Lucy and Chelsea. He hopes his writing, teaching, and illustrations will inspire the next generation to use their God-given talents to bring light to the world.

Follow me on Instagram @ljjbooks for updates, illustrations, and more!

If you like what you read, please give me a 5-star rating and share your

thoughts on Amazon! Thank you so much for reading my book!